Sarah Hall was born in Cumbria in 1974. She is the prize-winning author of five novels – *Haweswater*, *The Electric Michelangelo*, *The Carhullan Army*, *How to Paint a Dead Man* and *The Wolf Border* – as well as *The Beautiful Indifference*, a collection of short stories. The first story in the collection, 'Butcher's Perfume', was shortlisted for the BBC National Short Story Award, a prize she won in 2013 with 'Mrs Fox'.

Further praise for *The Carhullan Army*:

'*The Carhullan Army* is as gripping – and shocking – a piece of writing as any you will read this year.' *Metro*

'Whether imagining the future or the past, Hall's evocation of place and atmosphere is a joy . . . The farm and its community are a triumph of imagination: you could almost believe the author had lived among them as part of her research. This, combined with the luminosity of the prose casting its light across an emotional and intellectual landscape as bracing as the fells themselves places *The Carhullan Army* at the vanguard of the new wave of futuristic dystopian literature.' *Literary Review*

'Her work renders the darkest emotional landscapes with a sharp eye and a warm heart.' *Time Out*

'Everything is earthy, nothing idealised. Hall makes her survivalist women properly foulmouthed and uncouth. Jackie Nixon herself is a splendid creation, ablaze with the schizoid, lacerating intelligence of a guerrilla messiah, or warrior queen.' *Guardian*

by the same author

HAWESWATER
THE ELECTRIC MICHELANGELO
HOW TO PAINT A DEAD MAN
THE BEAUTIFUL INDIFFERENCE
MRS FOX
THE WOLF BORDER
SEX & DEATH: STORIES (edited by Sarah Hall and Peter Hobbs)

The Carhullan Army

SARAH HALL

FABER & FABER

First published in 2007
by Faber & Faber Limited
Bloomsbury House, 74–77 Great Russell Street
London WC1B 3DA
This paperback edition published in 2017

Typeset by Faber & Faber Limited
Printed and bound by CPI Group (UK) Ltd, Croydon, CRO 4YY

A CIP record for this book
is available from the British Library

ISBN 978–0–571–31562–8

2 4 6 8 10 9 7 5 3 1

For Jane and Mae

English Authority Penal System archive
- record no.498: Transcript recovered
from site of Lancaster holding dock

Statement of female prisoner detained
under Section 4(b) of the Insurgency
Prevention (Unrestricted Powers) Act

FILE ONE

COMPLETE RECOVERY

My name is Sister.

This is the name that was given to me three years ago. It is what the others called me. It is what I call myself. Before that, my name was unimportant. I can't remember it being used. I will not answer to it now, or hear myself say it out loud. I will not sign to acknowledge it. It is gone. You will call me Sister.

I was the last woman to go looking for Carhullan.

It was a wet rotting October when I left. In the town the leaves had begun to drop and their yellow pulp lay on the ground. The last belts of thunderstorms and downpours were passing through the Northern region. Summer was on its way out. The atmosphere felt as if it was finally breaking apart, and at night and in the mornings something cooler had set in. It was a relief not to wake up sweating under the sheet in our room in the terrace quarters, coming out of some hot nightmare with milky dampness on my chest. I have always slept better in the winter. It feels like my pulse runs slower then.

This freshness seemed to cleanse the town too. The bacterial smell of the refinery and fuel plants began to disperse at night when the clouds thinned and the heat lifted. Each year after the Civil Reorganisation summer's humidity had lasted longer, pushing the colder seasons into a smaller section of the calendar, surrounding us constantly with the smog of rape and tar-sand burning off, and all of us packed tightly together like fish in a smoking shed.

The change of temperature brought with it a feeling of excitement, an alertness that went beyond nerves or the heightened awareness of the risks I knew I was taking. It was restorative. The cool reminded me of my childhood. Back then the weather had been more distinct, separated. Some older people in the factory where I worked said of all the English traditions to have been compromised, the weather was the saddest. As if there had been a choice of some kind, a referendum for these semi-tropics.

I still recall the fresh ticking of hail on my face in March as I stood to catch the bus for school. And autumn blusters, when objects large and small were bellowed back and forth. The deep-vein chill of January; my hands and feet numb under fleece and wool. You don't fear possibility when you are young. You don't believe the world can really be broken or that anything terrible will happen during your lifetime.

Even the rain is different now; erratic, violent, not the constant grey drizzle of old postcards, jokes, and television reports. It's rain that feels wounded. There is seldom any snow on the fells, though people in the town look for it out of habit.

Where I was going the altitude was high, it was remote, and part of me hoped that if I stayed there long enough I would see those white drifts again.

I left at dawn, so I could get out of Rith without being noticed. My rucksack was packed light enough to carry a long distance, then on, up into the mountains. I was not bringing much away with me – clothes, boots, some tins of food and squares of rusk, a canister of water, a medical kit in case the regulator could be taken out of me, though I didn't know if that would be possible. And I had an old Second World War rifle, packed between the jumpers and waterproofs; its stunted barrel nuzzled against the top flap. This was what I planned to bargain with at Carhullan.

I had hidden the bag in an alleyway behind our building the previous night so I could get down the stairs without the extra weight, without bumping and scraping the walls on my descent. It was pushed into an alcove behind the main chamber of the rain tank where it was dark and dry. I'd put it there while the families in the other quarters were eating dinner, and before my husband got back from his shift, checking the void first with a stick to make sure there were no rats' nests.

6

In the early morning I left our bed without waking Andrew and dressed quietly in the communal bathroom. I'd stowed a plastic bag in the pocket of my trousers to collect the items I needed. There was a new packet of soap on the shelf belonging to the family in the next room, and I took that too, slipping it into the bag with my toothpaste, deodorant, a razor and some blades. I paused for a moment before opening the little medicine cabinet they used. There was some aspirin, a packet of sanitary towels, and a sachet of powder for treating cystitis that was long out of date. I gathered them up. Then I made my way along the hall and down the stairs.

Outside the door of the building I waited a minute or two to be sure that Andrew had not heard me leaving, trying to be calm. My heart was sending fast volleys of blood up through my chest. I could feel the contact and back-turn of pulse in my fingertips. I told myself it would be OK. In the last month I had trained myself to wake early and had practised this departure. Always I'd made it out silently and safely, then I'd walked around the dark town, careful to avoid the patches where the feral dogs roamed, before coming home again. But this was not a dry run. I breathed deeply, blew the air out, and waited. The last thing I wanted was to have Andrew following me down, calling me crazy, creating a fuss and waking the people above. He would never have let me go off with a packed bag, out of the official zones, even though we were at odds now, hateful or silent towards each other.

I was tied to this building. He knew it, and I knew it. There were no other options for us. And if he'd discovered me, he would have pulled me back upstairs, or held me down in the road as I struggled, until a monitor from the Authority arrived, perhaps making an excuse for my behaviour, saying I was high, or had had a nightmare. He would have told me to wait it out, saying no matter how bad things were now, we could get through it, and then we could part company when everything was less fraught, less dangerous.

I leant on the terrace wall and listened for his footsteps this last time. The only sound I could hear from above was the waspish hum of the energy meter on standby. I looked up. The sky was the dun colour of bitumen, like the shale turning in the vats at the refinery where Andrew worked. There was a white smear of moon, a ridged and filmy ulcer in the lining of cloud. There were no lights on yet in Rith, and none would come on until the morning power allotment at six, when people would have time to heat water and food, and could watch the early news for bulletins from one of the fronts and the lottery numbers. By then I was planning to be long gone.

After a few minutes I went to the alley and collected my bag. I knew I had to move quickly now, without over-thinking. Usually the town was dead at this hour, but it was possible to run into an Authority cruiser. The thought of it made me sick. I wouldn't stand a chance of explaining myself to them. And I didn't want to contemplate what I was doing, and falter in it, though I was sure now that I would not. Not after the last few weeks. I walked through the town, away from the combined residences, past the old shopping centre with its boarded windows, and the turbine warehouse where the metal hulls were stacked up waiting for dispatch, as they had been for years. The streets were deserted and everything was quiet. Only the glaze of the old red masonry, the slates, and the tarmac reflected any light, showing a version of the settlement that seemed ghostly and unmodern.

It was hard to imagine all the people behind the bricks, sleeping two and three to a room, or lying awake, talking softly so as not to disturb the other families. Some of them crying, being comforted or ignored. Some not caring who heard them through the walls, pushing away from a sore body as the hits of cheap ephedrine began to wear off. Each time I had ventured out in preparation, these dawns seemed to have an atmosphere of reduction, as if there had been a cull, not a condensing of the people.

On the end of each row of terraces were the silhouettes of meters, small buzzing cysts that had been designed to read the flow of energy from photovoltaic tiles. Now, they were being used to regulate consumption from the old domestic power grid. There had been few improvements made after Reorganisation. The ten-year recovery plan was becoming a hopeless myth. It was hard not to look behind me, back the way I had come, to see if there was anyone there, following, or just watching me go. I made myself not turn round. I told myself the best way for me to keep going was to give my eyes one simple option – forward.

There was a soft crackle in the sky and the drag of thunder to the west. I knew it would rain sometime soon, that I'd have to stop and put on my waterproofs. But I could not afford to pause while I was still inside the perimeter. Maybe later, when I was clear of the place and warm from the walk, I would strip down. I knew that I would dry more quickly than my clothing.

For years I had not been out of Rith. No civilian had, unless they were being transported to a detention centre. The zones did not allow for transference. The original register bound people to their areas at the time of the collapse. Only government agents and the Authority had any need to travel, or the means to do it, and then it was usually by train.

It was my hometown and I was familiar with the surroundings – the steep streets and welter of roofs, the Beacon Hill, and opposite, on a twin tor, the castle. I kept on, along the old motorway flyover. Beneath it were heaps of scrap and rubbish, and I could hear rustling animal sounds. Past the settlement border, in the lower areas, the roads had deteriorated. They were much worse than I had imagined. In their years of redundancy they had sagged and rucked. Whole sections had been pulled away by the floods. They felt loose underfoot, like scree. In places there were small craters full of rainwater; I stumbled into them, soaking my trousers up over my boots to the knee. I realised it was true what people said at the factory and in quarter meetings. Nothing was being repaired except the arterial routes used by the Authority.

To begin with I jogged where I could, concentrating hard so as not to trip or turn an ankle, and pacing myself for what would be a long hard day. After half an hour I reached the rise where the white tollhouse stood. Its windows were out and the roof had given at one of the gables. I remembered from a local history lesson that it had been burnt down twice by the Scots, then rebuilt. Now it was almost a ruin again. The owners must have long since moved into Rith, with all the other outer-lying residents.

Down the hill, a little further on, the old Yanwath traffic bridge was still intact. I had driven over it many times before the travel ban. The signal that had once controlled it was dead; the glass lights black with dirt and its post askew in its concrete bed. Where the road dipped down before rising to the bridge's abutment, water pooled and eddied. There was debris afloat in it, mostly indistinguishable, perhaps lumps of render from the houses upstream. I forded it, walked to the middle of the span and peered over the parapet. Below, the river Eden was brown and swollen and slipping past with frightening speed. In the half-dark I saw the bright movement of its edges, the backwash of white caps and whirlpools. It had broken its banks in the rains, spilling into the ditches and gardens on either side. I could hear the lower branches creaking as the trees along its sides were stripped of leaves.

The cottages next to the bridge were window-deep in the current. There was a strong odour of wet mortar, fabric and silt. It was the familiar smell of flooded homes; the riverbed slurrying up house walls, rotting curtains and carpets. It was the smell I had woken to over a decade ago, when I had come downstairs to find my house full of litter and sewage.

I knew the road on the other side of the bridge led away through a small empty village, into the green abandoned wilds of what used to be national parkland – the place my father's generation had called the Lake District.

By the time the vehicle appeared it was midday, and raining hard. At first I thought the noise was just water, moving heavily in the air or through underground channels beneath the road. Then I heard a shift of gears. I jumped up onto the verge and turned round, half-expecting to see the dark blue shape of a cruiser and ready to duck behind the wall. A white civilian van was coming towards me, making its way slowly along the derelict road. Its suspension looked loose and amplified, as if the body had been raised from the chassis somehow, and it rocked slackly over the ridges and potholes. The windows were filthy with dirt, seedpods, and leaves that had been shaken from the trees in the latest slew. Behind it was a waft of greasy brown exhaust. It passed me by, then slowed, and finally stopped. Nervous, I walked up to the driver's door; the window squeaked down.

'Where are you off to then, lass?' The man had a red face like a daub of glass taken out of a furnace. His pale eyes ran over me. I was a mess. My hair was dripping, and the old white tank top I had on was sopping and clinging to my skin. I shrugged my shoulders forward and lifted my arms over my chest to cover up. He laughed. His teeth were rotten along their edges. Each tooth had a dull yellow plateau at its tip and around his gum line was a telltale seam of silver. 'Well, a spot of hiking it looks like. Last of the Wainwrights, are you? Or maybe you want to be the first one up onto the tops again. Plant a flag. Things must be improving in town if that's the case. Come on. Best you get in.'

I hesitated. I hadn't wanted to get involved with anyone on the way, and I knew questions might mean trouble, but my shoulders and feet were aching and I did not pause for long. I walked around the back of the van to the passenger side, pulling the wet material off my chest and wringing it out. He leant over and opened the door for me, like my father always used to when he drove me to school. He'd put a dirty-looking rag on the seat to keep it dry. I lay my rucksack on the floor of the cabin and climbed in. 'Good girl,' he said. 'Good timing this, isn't it?'

He put the van into gear and pulled away. It felt strange.

I had not been in a car for years. I'd handed my keys and personal information in along with everyone else, and I'd forgotten what it was like to be in control of a vehicle, to be enclosed but free to go anywhere. Watching him dip the clutch and flick on the wiper blades felt like a dream or a lost memory. The smell in the cabin was strong, tart, like old clothes, vinegar mixed with urine, or maybe it was the unwashed smell of the man himself. But I didn't complain or make a move to wind the passenger window down. I was glad just to be out of the rain.

The soles of my feet were already tender, though I had on two thick pairs of socks. I felt the prickle of pins and needles start up in the ends of them and I curled and flexed my toes. I had not expected a ride from anyone. I'd been practising walking for months when I wasn't on my shift, aimlessly at first, as if to pass the time, and then with purpose, looping round Rith's periphery, up the hill to the Beacon and back down again. There was no crime in that, just walking, though Andrew thought it stupid to risk the dogs that scavenged around town, rooting for food in the tips. They were filthy and distempered, he said, and I was asking to get bitten. Occasionally there were attacks, but none of them fatal. I had not been able to wear my bag on any of these occasions; it would have been too suspicious, and it was a shock to my body, the weight of it.

I'd made sure to eat well all week; two portions of rice instead of one, sardines for breakfast, even though it took the box of provisions low, and Andrew would suffer for it for the rest of the month. I was as fit and as fed as I could be. But turning circuits round the citadel in the dim morning and eating extra cans of fish was one thing; hauling out to the abandoned park with my possessions on my back was altogether another. I'd come about twelve miles and I was sore. The bag on my back had been pulling down hard and my spine felt compressed. Showers had been coming and going for hours, the hems of my clothes were damp and chafing. Every step took me further away from the town and out towards my own limits. The appearance of any vehicle was unlikely, almost miraculous, and I was thankful for it.

The van pitched and swayed around bends in the road, the man taking corners wide to avoid obstacles, holes, and bales of undergrowth that had burst out of the verge. I put my palms on the seat either side of my legs to brace myself and stayed quiet. I didn't want to make conversation or have to navigate an interview that could perhaps be reported back. Every once in a while the man looked over at me and sniffed. I could tell he wanted to talk more than listen anyway. He had the air of someone cabin-fevered, cut-off. He must have a work-station out of the zone, I thought.

'So. Have they lifted the restrictions, then?' he finally asked. 'You're the first one I've seen in, God, I don't know how long. Quite a buzz it was, seeing you on the road up ahead. I thought the bloody hock had got me seeing things.' He pointed to a small silver bottle in one of the moulded wells on the dashboard, and offered me a swig. I shook my head and put my feet on top of the rucksack to keep it from rolling about as the van ploughed through the shallows of a stream. The chassis grated on the stony bottom, scraping hard, so it sounded as if we were shovelling up pebbles. The man stamped on the clutch, shifted to a low gear and revved the engine high.

There seemed to be new becks everywhere, spilling out of the walls and fields. When the tyres gained traction again he eased off. He repeated the question. 'They've been lifted for me, yes,' I said. I tried not to sound anxious or furtive. I looked over at him, thinking that, for all his talk of hiking, he had probably guessed something was wrong anyway; me alone on the road, having ranged so far out of town, and with no apparent way back. I waited for him to challenge me.

He pointed to my rucksack. 'Have you got a tent in there? Cause you'll not be getting back for a bit. I'm going to Rosgill and then on to Blackrigg. You'll be all right if you've still got people out here. I'd probably know them, I know everyone that's stayed. Only a handful left, if that. Most have been struck off, daft buggers, but not me – I work up the reservoir, at the draw-off tower. There's not much to do, just sit about and work the sluice. I've got a permit and a priority quota for the van; it's all official, like. I'm doing my bit for the recovery. No one else is much in and out these days, just me when I pick up my supplies, or come for an engineer, and I won't be off again for a good three weeks, maybe more. You were lucky I was passing when I was.'

I was lucky. I knew that. If I rode with him to Rosgill he would save me fifteen blistered miles. He rattled off a short list of local people who had been stubborn enough to stay, as if I might volunteer to some relation, and then began to complain about the ever-tightening allocation of fuel and the lack of fresh rations in his blue box. 'UHT milk, I bloody hate it,' he said. 'Tastes like cock-wash, doesn't it? Excuse my manners. It's what we get for shafting the farmers, though, all that centralisation nonsense. When we need them, they've all been put out of business.' I let him talk, trying to keep my head clear and my mind focused.

The original plan had been to leave Rith as early as possible and walk the whole way. If I kept a good pace and didn't rest too long I thought I could be close by dusk. I'd looked at an old OS map that Andrew kept in one of the boxes under the bed, and it seemed feasible in a day, or at most a day and a half, though the last bit looked steep, tightly hatched with contours as it was. It was going to hurt, getting there. But it would be worth it. When I got to the farm everything would be better. The women would see to that.

In all the weeks of planning, I hadn't contemplated the possibility that they would be gone. Or worse, that they would turn me away. I hadn't given those ideas any room for development, fearing they would throw me off course. The only thing left for me was to hope. It was hope that nourished me day after day, in a way the imported canned food never would. The reality was that I could not be sure of the reception I'd get at

Carhullan, what I would find there and who. But I was unwilling to believe the place would now be empty, that they'd have given up. I knew if I'd let those thoughts stay with me, I never would have set off.

No genuine rural reports had been broadcast for at least five years. It wasn't in the interest of the Authority to issue them. Their circulars never made mention of the other half of the landscape, the other half of Britain. Occasionally some diehard would turn up on Rith's outskirts, a rider on a pony, a customised bike, or on foot, but they only came to see what developments were being made, to stare at the New Fuel factories, the Uncon oil refinery, or to make a plea for antibiotics. Sometimes they exchanged things on the black market. Now and then they would come to report a death, a burial. But it was of little concern to those in charge. Anyone who had not participated in the census was now off record. Anyone living beyond the designated sectors was considered autonomous, alien. They were discounted. They had chosen not to help with the recovery, and they were no longer part of the recognised nation. The Authority simply called them Unofficials.

'Don't get me wrong, I couldn't stand all the tourists,' the man was saying, 'but it's been dead out here. There's no community and we used to be good at that. There's no life. There's nothing but rabbits and bloody deer. I'm not a man that does well without people.' He looked over at me again. I leant forward and unlaced the fastening of my bag, and carefully took a jumper from inside. I pulled it on over my wet vest, wishing I could strip off first. 'Oh, you should have said if you were cold. The heater works.' He opened the dashboard vent and I felt a rush of musty warmth against my face and my shins.

The man went on. 'Not that I'd want to be in town. I can't stand the town, especially now, when it's like a bloody ghetto. All the rules. And the vermin. It's a joke. Who'd have thought we'd end up like a bloody third-world country. I'm glad I got the post here. I've got some space and some clean air. I'm my own boss.' I nodded and he quickly looked over again. 'Listen, don't do anything daft when you get out there,' he said, 'otherwise I'll feel responsible for dropping you off. You better give me your section number, just in case. Write it down or something.' I nodded, but said nothing, and looked out of the window.

His conversation ran on to fill my quiet. 'Aye. It's nice to have a visitor back. Things must definitely be looking up. It's been so bloody desolate out here, especially now there's no pub. And I can't stand the news. It's all lies. They think we can't take it. They think we don't know what a mess everything is. Don't get me wrong. I'm behind our soldiers a hundred per cent, and the King – he's got balls to be out there – but come on, what is the point?' He sighed. 'You know, you forget what it's like to talk normally with folk. You forget a lot of things.'

The air inside the cab was quickly hot and stifling. I felt a trickle of sweat or rainwater run down the ridge of my back. I could smell the gamey damp underneath the man's arms as he lifted his elbows and leaned forward on the steering wheel. He opened his window a crack. 'You never said where you wanted to be dropped, did you? Look, tell you what, if you like you can wait a while with me before heading up the fell, have a bit of food, and rest up. I've just picked up some dried pork.' He put on a sarcastic American accent and said, 'It's from our Christian friends in the Yoonited States.' Then he laughed, snidely, shaking his head. I felt his gaze on my legs, moving over the wet contours of my thighs. 'Hey, listen, do you mind my asking, are they still, you know, sorting the women out, so we don't get overrun?' He laughed again, his face glowing. 'That's the one good thing about all this, I reckon, a return to the era of free love. Mmm, yes.' His fingers flexed on the steering wheel.

A flare of adrenalin went off inside me. I felt it scorch against my breastbone and light my nerve endings. Suddenly I wanted to be out from under everything, I wanted to be as unsnapped and reckless as this journey I was undertaking warranted. I had made it this far. I'd made it out and away, without hesitation or incident. I would not be taken into the back of a cruiser and humiliated again. Behind me was a husband I could no longer bear to speak to, a factory of useless water rotors where I hated punching in, and the monitor who had me lower my overalls in front of his colleague, who had come forward with a gloved hand, joking about dog leashes, and though the wire of my coil was easily seen, he had still examined it.

There were no regulations out here. There was no human mess, no chaos, poorly managed, and barely liveable. There was just me, in my own skin, with my blood speeding up. I was taking a chance on something that felt not like a gamble now but like my only option.

'I'm not going walking,' I said to the man. 'I'm going up to a place called Carhullan.'

He made an airy sound with his nose and jerked his head back, as if blowing a fly out of his nostril. 'Carhullan?' he repeated, breaking the word into two pieces as if it was too difficult to manage all in one. 'Is this a joke? You having me on?' he asked. 'No,' I said 'That's where I'm going.' He blew air down his nose again. 'Oh my God. You're serious. That bloody place! You stupid, stupid girl. What the hell are you thinking of . . .?'

He left off, scowling now, his mouth slack. I knew he had heard of it, more than heard of it; he had an opinion about the farm's residents. And I had said the name with little doubt that I knew its history also. I glanced over at him. His face had flamed redder. His eyes were shuttling about in their pink sockets, left to right.

'Well. I don't know. Whatever you're doing, or think you are, you've got the wrong idea. I don't know. You better just be careful of that lot, eh. I don't know. They're worse than ever they were, I've seen them, marching about. I don't know what they think they're on with. Or why anyone would bother with them. A nice woman like you. They never should have been allowed to stay up there, like a gang of bloody terrorists. It's sick if you ask me.'

I looked straight ahead, lowered my voice. 'I didn't ask you,' I said.

I felt another flash across my chest, but it was exhilaration this time, not anger. They were still there then. They were still at Carhullan. They had held on after all, through everything. How many would there be now, I wondered. Fifty? More? And what kind of conditions would they be living in? I wanted to ask all this of the man sitting next to me. I wanted him to say something else about them, bad, insulting, prejudiced though it may be, just to give me another positive confirmation that the place was up and running. I wanted to know what else he could tell me, even if he told it in anger and disgust. What I wanted to know most of all was whether she was still there. Jackie Nixon. I wanted to know whether she was still involved. Whether she was still in charge. But it was too late now. I knew it would be impossible to find these things out from the man. The conversation was over. After this exchange we wouldn't speak about it again, or about anything else.

The van sped up and he fought with the steering wheel to take a sharp corner. He was bright with indignation and disapproval and I heard him curse softly under his breath. When the bend was rounded he shut off the heating vent, no longer keen to make me comfortable. Like the smell in the van, the atmosphere had turned sour. We had gone to war, it seemed, over one simple word. I had declared my proclivities, as he had his. I was no longer good company for him, no longer a person he might share his food supply with or try to fuck. All these months he had no doubt been hoping to see a return of residents to his lovely wilding valley, a sign that civilisation was being reinstated, with its old arrangements, its traditional preferences, and what he'd got instead was a deviant, a deserter.

He didn't try to talk me out of it. I think he must have realised that I was serious. There was a reason he had seen only one person travelling on this road in the years since the collapse. I knew there was more he would have said, given the chance, that he was composing arguments in his head, or readying insults. There were other choice words, no doubt, perched on his tongue, sitting behind his stubby decaying teeth, and I had heard them all before. Cult. Faction. Coven. I thought maybe he would spill his vitriol; reiterate all the worst rumours about Carhullan from the time before, when there was a media to be curious and to condemn the place. The babies, the mutilation, other terrible practices. Or I thought maybe he would slam on the brakes and make me get out.

But the old van ground on, over trellises of disrepaired concrete, and through the autumn sluice. I held my nerve, waiting for whatever would happen next.

With no one to cut them the hedges had grown tall and wide. Branches reached down over the road, scratching the paintwork as the van crept underneath. There were brambles everywhere, but the fruit looked black and tiny, as if it had ripened too soon and too small and then shrivelled away. Rhododendron was slowly taking over the lower fields. And there was a plant I didn't recognise, a thick green creeper that had wound its way up the telephone poles and round the trunks of trees.

We passed through a hamlet and I saw a dozen or so cars, left to rust in gateways and cottage garths, abandoned on the roadside. Some were covered with flapping tarpaulin, or belted down under plastic sheets, their previous owners hopeful maybe that at some point they could be recovered, converted to bios, or that there would be some kind of compensation paid out. In Rith there were yards of parked vehicles where the supermarkets had once been, their keys locked away, their number plates recorded in the Authority's logs. Here people had been far less trusting, it seemed, unwilling to give up their former property, unwilling to be disqualified.

I looked at the manufacturers' badges as we passed by, imagining people choosing them in showrooms and dealerships. The loans that had been taken out to finance them. The observances of airbags and seatbelts, stereo systems. It all seemed so ridiculous now. In the gardens of the empty houses, grass had grown up around their wheels and under their hubcaps. Mildew smeared their windscreens, and their wing-mirrors hung at broken angles. Rain had eaten at the bright paint. Inside, their engines had no doubt rusted and clogged, mice and birds had probably nested among the metal frets and shafts.

It had all come about so quickly and ruthlessly, the shortages and price hikes, and soon afterwards the ban. Nothing on a large enough scale could have saved them, and now nobody believed it would. They were useless, husks of a privileged era. The New Fuel industries and Uncon combined could barely supply the power grid, let alone wide-scale transport. Ordinary people would continue to be deprived. I realised then what the strong smell in the van was. It was one of the petrol collocates burning in the exhaust.

I got out when the man next slowed down, not even waiting for him to come to a proper stop. I opened the passenger door and leapt down, landing messily with my rucksack in a rit of gravel. He braked savagely and a few feet on the van skidded to a halt. 'You stupid bitch!' he shouted after me. 'If you think it'll be any better up there, you're dead wrong. You've got no bloody idea, have you, girl? Give it a week and you'll have your tuss back down here and you'll be begging me to take you home. I guarantee it.'

I was already walking away. He reached over, slammed the door and drove off, my security details forgotten. His voice had contained an alarm that bordered on hysteria. I could almost believe he was afraid for me. For a moment I felt sorry for him. He had picked up a woman off the road and helped her, only to have her say she was signing up to a life where he was nothing, no more use than one of those redundant cars. I hadn't flirted. I hadn't been interested in him, had not even made a pretence of it for the sake of the ride. There was nothing he could take away from the meeting, to keep in his head and use later. Or maybe just a picture of a rained-on body would be enough.

I shivered. The air was cool and damp outside. But I was glad to be out of the van. Suddenly I saw an image of the man bent over me, his broad white thighs rocking, his hands holding down my arms, smothering my mouth, blind with what he craved and unstoppable. I was not frail, but I would not have been strong enough to stop such a thing. I knew that. I hadn't properly calculated the risks of accepting the lift. He had probably been alone at the reservoir for years, getting more and more frustrated, his faculties congealing with loneliness, his fluids thickening up.

But as quickly as the image of our struggle arrived another one took its place. In it I was standing over the man, heeling him in his face until it split and came apart like a marrow. And it was clearer to me, this second image; it was the stronger of two possibilities, if only in my mind. I knew that I had done the right thing by leaving Andrew, leaving the harsh orchestration of the town, the dismal salvaged thing that the administered country had become.

The van disappeared behind the tangle of waxy green bushes lining the road. I heard it stall, and its ignition turn over phlegmatically, like the congested coughing of the town's sick dogs. It caught, revved dirtily, and grumbled away out of earshot.

I hadn't asked the driver how to get to Carhullan. But I had not needed direction. Vaughsteele was written on the signpost opposite. Up ahead the road split and a church stood to one side. I'd memorised the map before I left, got the directions locked in my head. I'd need to bear right through the settlement, and at the last building take to the rocky howse, then go about four miles, moving gradually upwards on the fells, until there was a split in the track. I'd keep to the right past a property called Moora Hill and go on up, another three miles, imagining the High Street summit, following the old dry-stone walls until they finally ran me in through Carhullan's gateway.

I'd left the map in Andrew's box under the bed. I wouldn't need to use it again. I wasn't planning on going back.

For a minute or two I stood in the village. It was deserted as I'd expected it would be. The slate cottages were dark. They looked cold and hollow now, like cattle bothies. They seemed nothing more than the elements of which they had been built. I knew this village reasonably well. When I was very young it had been popular with walkers and tourists, and my father had brought me here to hike. There had been a working school and several farms that had survived the troubles at the turn of the century. People from the South had once bought retirement homes here, under the blue shadow of the fells.

After the fuel crisis it had been left to its own devices, and slowly it must have emptied like all the others, before the orders were finally given to evacuate. On the wall of one cottage someone had written the words *Rule Britannia* in red and white paint. They had tried to draw the Cross of St George but it looked distorted, bent out of shape. I couldn't tell if it was an act of vandalism or one last loyal statement from the proprietor before leaving.

It was eerie. There was no drift of chimney smoke, no voices outside the pub, no washing snapping dry on lines strung across the gardens. The strange ivy creeper ran up gables and onto roofs. TV aerials were strangled by it. No signals or electrical impulses had passed through them for years. These were non-priority venues. The plots of land next to the houses had run amok. Gooseberry bushes, vegetable patches, rhubarb and vetch had grown wild, furling over lawns and tangling up gateways and arbours. Anybody coming back to their old rural lives would have to slash their way through foliage that had grown huge and confident, swallowing the habitations back into the earth.

The rain had cleared for a spell and all around me water was trickling off walls and around stones, finding wider channels to join. The sun was out and a harsh wet light made me squint.

It lit up the long blades of grass on the verge, and turned the grey roofs flinty.

My stomach grumbled. In an effort to gain distance I had not stopped for breakfast, just eating a protein bar on the move. I looked at my watch. I'd wound it carefully before I left. It was half past twelve.

Andrew would have woken and found me gone. He wouldn't have found a note; I hadn't left him one. Nothing I could say would explain. I no longer felt it was my duty to. And I didn't want to apologise, or confess to my plan and be traced. I hadn't really imagined that one missing person would be worth a search party, but my concern was that I would somehow lead the Authority to Carhullan, that I'd cause trouble for them even before arriving, before I'd had a chance to prove myself in any other way. If anyone cared enough they could find me through the driver of the van. But more likely I would simply be written off as another missing person.

I sat on a low concrete stand and took out a tin of fish, the tin opener, and a square of rusk from my rucksack. I was almost thirty miles out, too far to have turned back that day, even if I had wanted to. Now that I wasn't moving, everything I had walked away from seemed to be stalking me. I'd left behind a husband, and a life that guaranteed basic survival, even if there were penalties, sacrifices. I had wilfully turned away from society, to become nothing and no one. It should have scared me, but it did not.

At first Andrew would assume that my number had been called up for half a day's extra work; he'd assume I had signed the early rota for extra credits. Or he might think that I was just walking, roaming about town, as was my habit recently, collecting blueberries from the Beacon Hill, or mushrooms, and looking for a sign of something down below in the town, anything that did not seem spoiled and wrong.

For all our differences, he knew me. He knew that I was restless, that something was scratching painfully in me and I couldn't make do with the way things were. I was no longer one of a pair, holding on to the other to get through this awful time among the squalor and overcrowding. It had become obvious I did not enjoy sex with him and I had long ago stopped instigating anything at night, or letting him touch me. He'd kept asking me why I couldn't, what was the matter, and why I was so inflexible that I couldn't knuckle down to help make things better, put up with the inconveniences. Perhaps he'd thought I was depressed, like so many others, and that I wasn't trying hard enough to find the spirit we were all being asked to conjure, like a replica of that war-time stoicism of which the previous century had proudly boasted. The truth was that he had accepted the way of things, and I couldn't. I'd despised the place I lived in, the work that brought no gain. And I had begun to despise Andrew.

It hadn't always been that way between us. We had been like-minded once, two feisty students, full of the sense that things could be better, that the worst could be prevented. We had been at college together in the Solway City. I remember seeing him in the Union bar, strong-featured, attractive I thought. Both our flats had been flooded when the new estuary defences failed, and we were caught up in the first of the big insurance scandals, put in temporary housing, close to each other. It had seemed symmetry enough to bring us together. My father had died shortly after and Andrew had helped me arrange the funeral. It had been a relief to have him take my hand and console me. We talked of going to Scotland, making a life there, but in the end we moved back to Rith. I had loved him then, and I leant on him in the years that followed.

As the rolling conflicts began abroad, and the recession bit at home, I'd taken comfort in venting my half-formed opinions to him, and hearing them echoed fully by his own. We seemed united by our disappointment, our anger, and our distrust of the reinvented Forward Party, who had taken office under the banner of reform, and had then signed the Coalition Oil Treaty. The failure of international policy was so clear. The war was geopolitical. It was not ours to fight. We had the technology to disengage from our allies abroad, but not the will to invest.

We had protested. We'd travelled to London and rallied at Parliament; the crowds were so large people were crushed and the gathering was broken up with tear gas. The troops continued to be dispatched. Every day along the pipelines soldiers were blown apart. More were sent. Andrew said it would probably go on for years, and if he were called up to serve he would refuse. If we had known what was coming we would have left the country then. Though I don't know where we would have gone.

As I ate fish out of the can in the abandoned village, I remembered us sitting on the Beacon Hill. The dark red of Andrew's hair had caught the final rays of sunlight. His head had blazed as he talked and his eyes were alight with frustration. It was the night the prime minister had made his final address and stepped down. Within a year of taking office the Forward Party had split, and from the ashes of its new image old doctrines had risen. But something was different, I knew, something was terribly wrong. There was a feeling of unsettlement around the town, as if the world was turning quicker on its axis, as if it was slightly out of control. Andrew's brow was furrowed. He looked like a man twice his age. 'They've signed us up for dependency and bankruptcy,' he said, tossing a stone hard into the air and watching it fall towards the bushes on the slopes. 'And now Powell's got control of the party there's no way out. The man is dangerous. He's one of the old guard. He's power hungry, and he's a bigot.'

Back then he had seemed unafraid, undaunted by the gravity of approaching disaster, even when the market crashed, businesses began to go bust, and jobs were lost, even as the country began to stagger towards collapse. I would listen to him seethe about all that was going on, and his fury was almost tactile, almost mine. I was young. I looked to him for reason, for a voice. He bristled at each new measure the government put in place, blamed them for everything: the widening of the conflict

abroad, the new fronts in China and Venezuela, the ruthlessness of the banks, blackouts, deportations, empty supermarkets, and hospital closures. He resented the extreme measures
put in place to administer the crisis. The ten-year recovery plan
was just a contrivance to keep people in check, he said, and
decoy their attention. Most of all he hated the creation of the
military police force. It was un-British. The Authority was an
affront to the rights of the public.

When the general elections were suspended, all hell broke
loose. He told me to stay home, and went out on the street
with a group of local men. He threw rocks at council windows,
surged up towards the civic offices in the castle, and took a riot
stick in his lower back. The monitors fired live rounds into the
crowd. Five people were killed. It was the same in the other
towns and cities. Nobody stood a chance.

Andrew came home and peeled off his shirt so I could see the
lesion. I remember putting my fingers gently on the soft red
welt. There were bubbles of blood trapped under the skin. It
looked as if some creature from the sea had stung him. For the
first time his eyes were despairing. 'I think this is it,' he said.
'There's no going back from this.' I could hardly believe it. The
awful truth was upon us; things were breaking down, completely, irreparably; all the freedoms we had known were being
revoked, and nothing could be done to stop it.

That night we were full of angry passion, and reckless.
Andrew winced through the sex, asking me to make him hard
again and again with my hands and my mouth. We didn't use
the issued contraceptives, though we knew what would happen
if I conceived. Maybe it was the only protest left for us. The
next morning we decided to get married, to secure ourselves as
best we could. We were a good unit. We could care for each
other. The laws were changing quickly. Our rights were slipping
away and there was no telling where it would end.

We made our quarter in the old terraced house in Rith as
comfortable as possible. There was nothing to decorate with
and no furnishing to buy. But I hung the pictures I had kept

since college and put the quilt my mother had bought for her own wedding on the bed. We were given work papers and placements, he at the refinery, me at New Fuel. We made the best of it.

When I received notification of my appointment at the hospital, Andrew was kind, as sympathetic as he could be, saying it was completely unfair and that he was sure it would only be temporary. I cancelled twice, citing ill health. The third letter came with a red stamp on the envelope. It was delivered by a monitor. I recognised him. We had been at the same school. His name was Tye and he'd been captain of the football team. He was dressed in the dark blue collarless uniform of the Authority. He held the document out to me and said nothing.

Six weeks later I walked to the hospital in Rith and went in to be fitted. In reception I was fingerprinted and handed a thick cotton gown. I waited in a room with twelve other women of varying age. The youngest was about sixteen. She looked terrified, and every few seconds she sniffed and rubbed her nose. I wondered if she had even had sex yet. Nobody spoke. A nurse came in and quickly explained what would happen to us. She held up a model of the device. It was made of copper and was about the size of a matchstick. Two threads ran from it. She pointed to these and said they were longer than those of the original coils, so that the vaginal checks we would undergo to see whether they were still in place could be made more easily, and not necessarily at the clinic. I didn't understand then what she meant. It was only later I found out the Authority was making random examinations; that women were sometimes asked to display themselves to the monitors in the backs of cruisers.

The nurse clenched her fist around the coil to signify a womb, and she smiled at us. We could all expect heavier periods after insertion, she said, and perhaps a fraction more pain. But really it was nothing to worry about. She left the room. A few moments later my name was called. A couple of the other women looked at me as I stood up, as if my face would set the

27

tone for each of their own experiences. The procedure took ten minutes. It was a male doctor that came into the surgery, fingering into his gloves, and I asked if I could have a woman doctor instead but he said there was no one else available. I lay back on the creased paper sheet, wishing I had taken a painkiller that morning as those I knew who had already been fitted had recommended.

Afterwards I came back to the quarter, nauseous and cramping. The sensation of pressure at the neck of my cervix remained for the whole afternoon. I tried not to dwell on it but I felt awful. My nails kept digging into my palms and I had to shake my hands every few minutes to relax them.

Andrew was rostered at work until the evening, so I sat in the yard in the muggy sun. There was a strong UV warning but I didn't care. All I could think about was the doctor who had rubbed cool lubricant inside me, inserting the speculum and attaching the device as efficiently as a farmer clipping the ear of one of his herd.

I looked at the plastic pots in which I had tried to grow courgettes and beans the summer before. They hadn't sprouted, and in places the soil looked interfered with, as if it had been dug out by an animal. I had seen rats from the upper windows, scurrying the length of the wall. By the end of the afternoon the yard was full of shadows. I wished again we had signed up for an allotment, or had been placed in a house with a proper garden, but the waiting list was now so long and there were so few of them available to civilians that it seemed hopeless.

When Andrew arrived back he asked me if I was OK and if he could see it. We went inside, shut the door to our section of the building and I took down my trousers. I sat on the bed and he gently opened my legs. Everything felt inflamed. I had cleaned myself up with a towel after the procedure but the water would not be hot enough to wash properly until later that night. There was still some translucent medical jelly there. It glistened and felt almost unbearably slippery as Andrew ran his thumb over me. 'How does it feel?' he asked me again. 'Is it uncomfortable?' He was kneeling in front of me. I shrugged, shook my head and looked away. 'You're still you,' he said. 'Beautiful you. They can't control that, can they?' His thumb was rubbing me gently. I wanted to ask him to stop, it had been too traumatic, and there was still some blood, but neither one of us had ever said no to the other.

I felt him slip his middle finger inside me. He meant to do it slowly and carefully but the lubricant made his movement easy, and I heard him murmur a noise of surprise and arousal. My eyes were closed. 'Is that nice?' he asked me. There was the small wet sound of him drawing out and pushing his fingers in again.

His breathing changed, became thicker. 'God. I'm sorry, I just want to be inside you,' he said. 'Can I? Will it make you forget it maybe? Come on. It'll be just us.' He leant forward to kiss me and unzipped his jeans. 'Here, you,' he said. He took my hand and put it to his groin. He was hard and as I gripped him I felt the blood straining underneath his tightened skin. He moved forward a little on his knees.

At the clinic we had been advised by the nurse to wait twenty-four hours. But after the hands of the doctor and the sharp bite of the tubing, any prohibition now seemed pointless. 'Oh, God, yeah,' he whispered as I pushed him inside, 'it's so wet.' I could see in his face, the degree by which he felt the sensation more than usual. His mouth was open and his eyes seemed unfocused, with a pleading look.

As if still afraid it would be painful for me he didn't move much, but there was a deep rawness to it all. He came quickly, and with more intensity than he ever had. As he pulled out I felt the warm fluid escaping onto my thighs. He held on to me, breathing hard, then his body jerked as if he was coming again. He put his thumb to me and began to rub, but I told him not to.

When the power came on he ran a bath for me and told the family in the room next door I would need a bit longer than usual. 'Tough day,' I heard him telling them. 'She's been at the clinic.' For the rest of the night he was attentive, treating me with kindness, and he seemed happier than he had in months. It wasn't to last.

The conditions were hard on all of us. Life changed in every way and it was difficult to adjust. There was despondency and resentment, food shortages, humiliations. Any small feeling of bliss, any cheap narcotic substance available to mask the difficulty, to make people forget what they once had, was easily sold. In the poorest quarters people took low-grade drugs, ketamine, and hits of silverflex, which rotted their jaws. They passed syphilis among themselves and the clinics cut tumours from the genitals of those who abused the animal tranquillisers for too long. There was almost no money, and what little there was seemed meaningless. People traded with their bodies, their possessions, they signed up for futurised loans.

This was not England, everyone said. This was some nightmarish version that we would wake from soon. The overdose and suicide rates climbed. Each time another occurred in Rith, and was talked about at the factories and plants, Andrew and I walked up the Beacon and held hands. It wouldn't be us, we said. We were stronger. We'd come through OK.

But over the years I saw Andrew become weary and practical, reduced to the base mechanism of getting by. Or perhaps he simply lost faith and the energy to resist, realising how close we had all come to something far worse than the critical existence left to us. As time went by he became less outspoken. He no longer seemed lit by anger when talking about the recovery's directives. Perhaps the government had done the only thing it could have to keep the country from breaking apart, he said, and I began to wonder what that early version of him had really consisted of. Meetings of opposition in the packed terraced houses concerned rather than excited him. The speakers were frauds and fantasists, he said, with no sense of financial solution, only contrary ideas and gripes. He didn't want to get sick being around all those germs. He began not to attend. Instead he visited the bar near the castle, where the off-duty monitors drank.

He went to work, slept soundly through the night and reached for me in the mornings. Sex was one of the few remaining pleasures, he said; it was nice to feel me without any barriers. He ate the cubes of meat and fruit, from the shipments of tins sent from America, without complaint. After a while he began not to take small ritualistic pleasure in burning their labels in the old cast-iron fireplace of our quarter, as we had once done together. When he was promoted to overseer at the refinery he seemed grateful, and told me it was madness to be anything other than complicit in Britain's attempts to rebuild herself. Once stability returned, so too would the freedoms we had lost. 'We can be bitter,' he said, 'or we can just get on with it.'

When he'd said this I'd bitten my lip, and then turned to face him. Out of a deep place in me I'd felt my fury rise. 'She's a female, is she, this country that's been fucked over?' The cup I had been holding left my hand and I heard it explode with brittle force against the wall. He ducked, his eyes clenched shut, as the fragments showered him. Before he could recover from the shock, or answer, I had left the room, slamming the door behind me.

For months we bickered and sulked. Our conversations began to fail on even the smallest of levels. Who had not written *tea* on the monthly provisions list. Who had eaten the last vitamin tablet, the last omega supplement. Who didn't understand the importance of this principle, or that political necessity. I knew he saw me as stubborn and naive, too upset to become empowered again. In bed he tried to negotiate, and have us agree physically, as if this would be the way we could still function together, as if I could separate my mind from my body and he could continue to communicate with one if not the other. 'We could ask for anti-depressants,' he said. 'There are some coming over from America now and I could maybe swing something at work to pay for it.'

But he must have known at heart that I was not depressed. He must have known it was more than a simple chemical response to the ongoing situation. Mine was a different kind of sickness. I didn't feel listless or oppressed. I didn't want drugs or numbness to mask my consciousness. I knew that everything around me was wrong. I could see it. I could sense it. And I had not yet found a voice with which to make my arguments. It still lay somewhere inside me, unexpressed, growing angrier.

I scraped the last flakes of tuna out of the tin with my fingernail and finished the rusk biscuit. It was a dry meal and I had swallowed half the water from my canteen. It was all right to take so much fluid on board, I thought, even though I still had a long way to go; I would just refill the container from a stream when I was higher in the hills. This was always what I'd done when I'd hiked with my father, and I had loved the cold mineral rush against my lips. It had been years since I'd walked in the district but I could remember the taste, fresh, with the faint brine of limestone and moss.

I unpicked the label from the tin and looked at it for a moment. The brand was Blessed Friends. The American and British flags flew in opposite directions from the same flagpole and there was a small prayer printed next to the ingredients. *Lord, keep us from the forces of evil, bless our sacred liberty, and let those in darkness find your light. God save the King.* I tore the paper into small pieces and let the wind take them from my open palm. There were a couple more tins in my rucksack, some sardines, and peaches in syrup. I hated these metal cargos the country depended on. Everything in them was either too sweet or too salty. After the tins in my backpack were finished I would never have to eat anything imported and reconstituted again. I would not be fed anything else that stuck in my throat.

Maybe when he woke, Andrew would guess the truth – that all the silences, all the tensions, had been leading to something like this. That it went past upset over the new rule of law, the housing conditions, the uterine regulator that had been inserted. He would remember all the arguments, just as I was thinking of them now, hearing the echo of our raised voices.

'Why the hell would you want to bring a baby into all this mess anyway, even if your number came up for it?' he would ask me, each time I scowled at the hair-thin line of wires resting between my legs and said I wished I could just pull it out and be rid of it. 'I mean where's the problem, really? You're still a young woman. This won't go on forever.' 'You just don't get it, do you?' I would tell him. 'It's not you, is it? It's never you.' 'Never me what?' he'd ask. 'Never men, you mean? Look, you know it's just a practical thing! There's no conspiracy here. Can't you focus on what really matters? You slope around town when you could be volunteering for overtime and getting us a few more perks. Fucking hell, this country is in bits and you're obsessing over your maternal rights! Where are your priorities?'

I would try to explain my side, the legitimacy of my grievances, and I would fail. I felt that if I could just have some space to think clearly I would be able to find the right words, and convince him, bring him back some way from the direction he was heading. But he could not comprehend such petty complaints in the face of greater issues. And I knew in a way that he was right. There were desperate priorities. Everything was at stake. At times I began to doubt my own mind.

Every day I'd woken and told myself to concentrate on being optimistic. But I'd felt like an animal wanting to lash out, wanting to scratch and maul. Sometimes Andrew would catch me looking his way, and then he'd ask why I hated him so much. I had no reply. In the end, past the practical exchange of timetables and supplies, we had not talked. I made no more confidences, said nothing provocative. He did not try to touch me. And we lived in a state of unhappy peace. After I was spot-checked in the cruiser, once they had finally let me go, I walked to the top of the Beacon Hill and sat through the night in the tower, holding my knees and listening to the bark and howl of the feral packs below. When I arrived home in the morning I said nothing. Andrew stood up from the chair in which he had been sitting waiting, pushed past me, and went to the refinery.

Maybe today, I thought, some kind of intuition would tell him that our end of the building was even quieter and darker than usual, as if a genuine departure had occurred. He'd ask the family in the other quarter if they'd seen me, and they would say no. At some point he'd open my drawer in the shared bureau and it would be empty, wood-smelling, and dusty in the corners. Then he'd realise what I had done. Maybe he'd think I had gone to another house in the section. I had never talked to him about the others. Even if he had gone through my storage boxes at some stage before I'd left, and seen the old photographs and cuttings of Carhullan, he still would not associate what he saw with my leaving. He would have thought it too much of a leap for me to make.

He would wait a day or two, in case I came home, saying nothing to anyone, and if the factory sent word to ask why I wasn't punching in he'd say I was sick. Some old loyalty would extend that far. But then he'd have some difficult choices to make, about when to report me gone, when to move someone else into the terrace quarter with him, and when to have my name taken off the civil register, so that I would become ineligible for work, accommodation, and children. So that I would be an Unofficial.

I stood up from the concrete stand and looked around the village. As I moved something cat-sized flashed away into the ditch next to the cottages – a fox, or a badger, I wasn't sure which. I suddenly realised the hedgerows and trees were full of birds. They were not singing but every few moments one would flutter out of the greenery and flutter back in again. They were yellow-eyed, red-beaked. I did not recognise them. In the road ahead were two suitcases lying open on the ground. I walked over. They were empty except for the debris of leaves and dirt that had blown inside. It was unnerving to see the

34

cases. I tried to imagine the last person leaving the village, and what kind of scene there had been here. Perhaps it was harried, with Authority monitors standing alongside. Perhaps they had been told they were taking too much, trying to salvage too much of their old life. There might have been a fuss, a dispute, and their personal items had been abandoned or scavenged through. It was not unheard of for monitors to confiscate the best of what they found in the possession of civilians, to be sold later on the black market.

Up ahead the church doors had been removed, probably to burn, and a grey arched hole tunnelled back into the building. I didn't go inside. There was no point. All the pews and the pewter would be long gone, stripped out, split apart, and recycled by utilitarian locals or by the Authority. Not that I could have carried anything so large and bulky with me up to the women. But it didn't matter. I had not come empty handed.

The rifle had belonged to my father. I'd known its whereabouts for twenty years, since he had buried it in the garden of his house on the north side of Rith. He'd never had a proper licence; all he wanted it for was to take pot shots at crows when they went after his seeds. I could remember him lining up the sights and squeezing the trigger, the crack of the shots being fired knocked his shoulder back an inch, as if he'd been punched there. He had let me hold it, supporting it under the stock to lighten the weight. Once or twice I had fired it, and each time it felt as if my heart had been jolted loose. 'You'd make a good soldier, little tinker,' he'd said to me. 'Hup two three. Atten-shun.'

I was nine years old when the weapons amnesty was issued. I remember there had been a bizarre shooting in a school in Manchester. A mother had come into a classroom where her boy was in the middle of a maths lesson. She waved to him and then aimed the gun. Eight other children and a teacher lay dead before she placed the barrel under her own chin. Nobody knew why she had done it. I watched on television as they carried the bodies out of the schoolroom in black bags. Within a year all guns were banned again.

The evening news had said there were an estimated twenty thousand weapons that would have to be handed in from British citizens. 'That's twenty thousand minus one,' my father retorted, winking at me from his armchair. It was against tradition, he said, and he wasn't taking part in any soft-policy hand-in. 'Will they arrest you and put you in prison?' I'd asked him. He'd laughed and said not a chance.

He wrapped the rifle in oily rags, put it and ten boxes of cartridges into a steel container and shovelled them into the earth next to his leeks. 'Never know when it might come in handy, tink,' he said to me as I watched him dig. He rested for a moment on the handle of his shovel and gazed at me. 'It doesn't do to rely on those in charge completely. That's one thing the Yanks always got right. You've done a bit of history in school, haven't you? Well, now. Imagine if the National Guard had surrendered their arms, and the Germans had invaded after all. We'd have been fighting with broom handles and axes like hairy medievals while they ran over us with tanks. Your great-granddad knew that. This was his gun. He was at Osterley.' Then he had smiled and scruffed my hair. 'Come on, help me get this clod tipped in.'

I remember my father fondly. He was a good man, and his eccentric defiance stuck in my mind. My mother had not lived long enough to see me aiming at the black corbies on the garden wall. I was glad my father's bad lungs had let him escape before the next war, a decade later, that he had not witnessed the decline of his proud country. I knew it would have taken a piece out of his spine. It hit the oldest most severely. Their parents might have lived through downturns and wars, but they had only known stability, appliances, and readily available goods. For them it was simply madness to have to give up their homes, to be supplied with canned food instead of fresh global produce, and to be told that Britain was now little more than a dependent colony.

My father's generation seemed to die out quickly, though their lives had been lived in prosperity. The health system cracked apart. Epidemics swept through the quarters in every town and city. There were new viruses too aggressive to treat. Those who did not fall ill seemed just to fade away. It was as if, one by one, they made the decision that the present and the future were intolerable propositions. And maybe they were right.

I never forgot my father's gun. Remembering it reminded me of him, wearing his slippers and dressing gown out in the garden, bending to pull snails off his tomato plants, watching film after film on his satellite television with a cigarette drooping between his fingers. It reminded me of another era, a better time. I wondered if the rifle would be found when the house reverted to the council and was reallocated, but whenever I walked past it the garden was overrun with weeds and untended. Finally it was shut up, abandoned like all the others falling outside Rith's habitable zone, and it became a midden.

I'd known Andrew would not be home until much later. There were shipments of kerogen coming in from the Southern ports all that week and he was overseeing their handling. I had finished my shift at the factory and I walked over the hill beside Rith to the house where I had lived as a child. The stars were beginning to spark and glint but there were few lights glimmering below, as if life in the town had been blown out. Only the Authority barracks in the castle glowed faintly, running on auxiliary generators. The grid would not go on until six, leaving people to manage as best they could with candles and the glow of Mag-lamps until then.

The garden of the old house had looked overgrown and dilapidated when I arrived. It was filled with rubbish. By the gate there were heaps of electrical appliances, chairs, and bundles of rain-swollen papers, cast-offs from homes that had been thinned down or vacated. Beside one of these piles was a rotting dog. The muzzle was sodden and decaying and its jaws looked set in a wide snarl. The eyes and fur were gone. Its belly had distended and under its tail was a writhing patch of maggots. I stood over the creature until the smell that rose from it became unbearable. Then I walked away.

The wooden potting shed at the other end of the garden was coming apart through the planking, the walls leaning inwards like an unstable structure of playing cards. It was unlocked. Heaps of cans and plastic bottles had been flung inside. I kicked them to one side and found a trowel. I brought it out and began to cut through the undergrowth at the edge of what had been our vegetable patch, pulling up the sods with my hands. There were dead bulbs in the soil and the roots of drowned plants. Only the apple tree had fruited, and bruised globes lay on the ground beneath it.

The box was still there, slightly bent and discoloured by the wet earth. For the first time in weeks I felt optimistic. 'Thank God for Osterley, Dad,' I heard myself say. I lifted it out, banged the lid with a stone, and forced it open. I unwound the rags. The mechanism looked a little rusty, but not too bad.

I should have been afraid of the gun. I knew the risk I ran keeping it in our quarter, even for a short period, was high. It went well past civil disobedience. Reports of robbery and rape were seldom punished with more than a reprimand now; the prison system could manage only the most serious offenders. Even black market agents and dealers were not often threatened with prosecution. But nobody was permitted to have a gun. Any kind of weapon, any suggestion of militia, was considered a direct attack on the Authority and the security of the country. Opposition meetings were sometimes broken up, if there had been a tip-off, and everyone present was searched. There were beatings, but no arrests. No one was stupid enough to carry a weapon.

To be detained meant entering an unknown system. At the factory, it was rumoured that there was a holding centre in one of the industrial cities to the south, Warrington or Lancaster, where those found guilty of severe crimes were sent. It was said there were executions. But there was no way of knowing if this was true. Radio and television broadcasts in the allocation hours were censored. There was no verification of what the structure of government really looked like now, whether it was impenetrable, or whether it had vanished altogether, and in its place something else existed.

I knew all this, but I took the gun out of the box, rubbed the grease away, and put it in the soft shoulder bag I was carrying. I covered the hole with earth and looked at the patch of disrupted ground. Then, picking up two sticks, I went back to the refuse piles. I slid them under the rank body of the dog. I held my breath and lifted it up, brought it to the spot where I had been digging and lay it down. The hollow tunnel of its eye stared up at nothing. It was little more than a rotting pelt. I put the trowel back in the shed. Then I slipped home in the dusk.

The woman from the other quarter in our building was standing outside when I reached the terrace. I startled her as I came up to the door, the bag slung over my shoulder. She held a hand to her neck and apologised for crying out. In her other hand was a packet of cigarettes and a lighter. She waved them. 'Been saving these till I needed one,' she said. 'Thought you were on days this week. I heard you go out this morning. Clump, clump, clump. Bang.' I shrugged. I wanted to get inside before the grid was turned on and I would face the scrutiny of light bulbs. I hitched the bag further behind me. She seemed distressed somehow, and unaware that she was blocking the doorway. Her face in the grey atmosphere was agitated and twitching, though she was standing rigidly. 'What are you doing out here?' I asked her. She snorted and shook her head. 'Nothing. What is there to do? Can't get our tea on yet, unless we want a cold lump. Can't find out which poor cows have won the baby lotto. I hate this time of day. It makes me crazy.'

She shook her head. 'Sometimes I can't believe it. Sometimes I wish they'd just dropped a bomb on us after all. Put us out of our misery. Don't you wish that?' She looked at me and then looked away into the alley opposite. 'It would be OK if I couldn't remember how things used to be. We went to Portugal every year. We used to fly.' She laughed bitterly and then began to cough. With brisk motions she took out a cigarette and lit it.

For a minute I felt a rush of sympathy and I wanted to befriend her, confide in her, and tell her what I was planning to do, the way I had not been able to tell Andrew. We'd never talked properly since she and her family had moved in. I had heard them through the walls, the muffled conversations, voices pitching and subsiding, the bouts of morning and evening coughing, and I'd heard them together at night, he louder than she. In our shared bathroom their footprints muddied the shower tray along with ours; their hair stuck on the enamel sides and clotted the plughole.

Some residents in the old sandstone quarters had made the best of things, abandoning privacy, opening up the house rooms like one big happy family. All our doors were kept shut. I barely knew the names of the other residents. They were so close by, so familiar, but they were strangers.

I knew it was a stupid thought to have had, spontaneous camaraderie with this woman I did not know, and I abandoned it almost immediately. I told myself I was just feeling it because I was conscious of where I was heading soon, and I had ideas in my head about it all. But I had to remain discreet. Nobody else was to know anything.

The woman looked at me again with an annoyed expression. 'Oh, it's all right. I'm just in a bad mood,' she said. 'Turns out I've got TB. That new bloody strain. Aye, so. I'm away into quarantine probably and the kids will have to contend with their father. They say there are some drugs that will help. But I know it's not true. Besides, I've got no money. Who the hell has? Oh, but they've given me this – for all the good it'll do!' She reached into her coat pocket, took out a faith card, and tossed it to the ground. She rolled her eyes. 'These bloody Victorian houses. I might as well put on a corset, sleep in the coal shed, and have done with it, right?'

She took a draw on the cigarette. I told her I was sorry, said goodnight, and went inside to the bedroom. I put the gun in the cupboard and made sure the barrel was fully covered by my overcoat. The cartridge boxes I placed under the bed next to a stack of magazines. It was too tiny an area for hiding anything but I had little choice.

For the rest of the week, I was filled with paranoia. Every time Andrew got in and out of the covers, I imagined him kicking the shells and scattering the metal casings across the room. There would be no hope of denying any knowledge of them. Our possessions were few and all were accounted for. In the nights that had followed I seemed to wake with a start every hour, reaching down to touch them, making sure they were properly stowed, praying he would not find them.

But now I was safely away, beyond exposure and explanation. I was alone. Here in the empty Lakeland village I couldn't have explained to anyone exactly how secure I felt, even if there had been someone around to listen to me. The village reverberated with silence, with human absence. There was not a soul to be found and I liked it. It had been so long since I had felt that. Even on the Beacon Hill above Rith I could see people moving in the streets and I knew they were close by. Here I was breathing air that no one else's breath competed for. I was no longer complicit in a wrecked and regulated existence. I was not its sterile subject.

Standing opposite the gutted church, in the wet deserted roadway, something unassailable crept over me. I felt the arrival of a new calmness, an assurance of my own company. The only noises, other than the movement of wind through the trees and the trickles of water, were the animal sounds of my tongue moving in my mouth, and my boots grating on the ground as I adjusted my stance. I was aware of my own warm predominance in the environment, my inhabited skin, my being. I suddenly felt myself again, a self I had not been for so long. I remembered how I had experienced the same feeling in this place when I was young, when I had been here walking, before the restrictions.

The hikes had always been long and steep. 'Get on, lass, just over that brow,' my father would call back when I lagged behind, aching and winded. 'You'll live,' he would shout back to me. 'You'll live through it. It'll not kill you.' It was here that I had first understood I was stable on my feet, capable of direction and distance and stamina. It was here in the blue fells that I first knew I was strong, and that I had it in me to be stronger.

Now, once again, I was in that landscape, where human beings had always journeyed to feel less and more significant than they were. Where the mountains stupefied and emboldened them, bringing them high and to the edge of what they thought themselves capable. As I stood and looked in the direction of the summits I felt properly dressed in my own muscles, and ballasted by my sense of physicality, as if I belonged outside, away from the crowding, the metered artificial lighting, the ethics of a lost society.

Ahead of me the hills were disappearing under heavy cloud, another front of rain was moving in, obscuring the horizon. I took a deep breath, picked up my rucksack and put it on. Inside its material the butt of the gun rested firmly against my back. I didn't know how good a shot I might be – it had been years since I aimed through the sights – or even if the gun still worked. But I was pleased to have it, pleased that I could offer it to those at the farm.

I walked through the settlement and began upwards towards the fells. On the howse there were delicate purple harebells growing in the grass between limestone outcrops. It was too late in the season for them, but at that moment they were the loveliest thing I had seen. As the clouds drifted down, thunder rolled again, sounding loud in the hollows of the mountains, and after a moment or two, rain began to run down the soft cambers of the sky. I stopped, put the bag down, and stripped off to the waist. I put the damp bundle of clothing into the top of the rucksack, tied its neck, shouldered it, and walked on. The clean October air passed over my skin. Rain snaked down my shoulders and arms, dripping off my breasts. I knew I must look peculiar. But there was no one around to see me. The driver of the van was long gone, back to his lonely life at the draw-off tower. The closest human beings to me now were the women of Carhullan. By the end of the day I would be with them. I would be one of them.

FILE TWO

COMPLETE RECOVERY

I had first heard about the farm at Carhullan when I was seventeen. Even then it had notoriety, a bad reputation. Its lamb was being sold in Rith, its vegetables and honey, and char when the tarn on its estate held them. The women living there traded every month in the border markets, with organic labels and low prices. When they arrived in town conversation about them picked up, the way it used to when the travellers came for the horse-driving trials.

They were a strange group, slightly exotic, slightly disliked. I could remember seeing them in Rith's market stalls, setting up their tables, staring down the hostile looks of other farmers. They were odd-looking. Their dress was different, unconventional; often they wore matching yellow tunics that tied at the back and came to the knee. Seeing their attire, people thought at first they must be part of a new faith, some modern agrarian strain, though they did not proselytise.

They were always friendly towards other women, joking with them over the wicker trays of radishes and cucumbers, giving out discounts and free butter. With the men they acted cooler; they were offhand. People commented that they must be doing all right for themselves up there on the fell, if they were solvent and could still afford to drive a Land Rover all that way into town each week. When we went shopping my father told me not to buy anything from them. 'Give that lot a wide berth,' he would say, nodding towards the group. 'It's probably wacky butter they're flogging.' If I lingered too long near their patch he would hurry me back to the car, saying we were late for something. But if he wasn't around, or if I had come with friends, I would go and buy homemade ice cream from the women. 'Thank you,

Sister,' they always said when I handed them the money.

There had been a skirmish in the market once, not a fight exactly but a physical exchange of sorts. My father and I had only seen the end of it, as it broke up. There was the sound of scraping and a soft thump, and when I looked over I saw that three of the yellow-shirted women were standing over a young man. There were cabbages rolling on the ground around him. He was cursing them, calling them dykes. The expression on his face was one of shock and outrage. But their faces were utterly calm.

Among the locals, speculation about the lives they led was rife, and it was often cruel, or filled with titillation. They were nuns, religious freaks, communists, convicts. They were child-deserters, men-haters, cunt-lickers, or celibates. They were, just as they had been hundreds of years go, witches, up to no good in the sticks. A few years after they set up, the national papers got wind of the enterprise and Carhullan became moderately famous. Ambitious reporters made the pilgrimage up the mountain to interview the women.

It was one of the last working fell farms. And life there was hard. There were animals to deal with at the crack of dawn, there was lumber to shift, fields to crop. Some reports said the place was really a rustic health club, a centre for energetic meditation. As well as the agricultural efforts, there was other physical training; traditional sparring, eight-mile maintenance runs once a week. There were no men allowed, though some of the rumours said there were, and inferred what they were used for. The proprietors remained difficult to pin down on the subject.

Jackie Nixon ran Carhullan with her friend Veronique, a tall black woman from the American South. Jacks and Vee they were known as by the other girls. I had heard Veronique on the local radio station and she had the last hum of an accent, a soft drawl, when she talked. And it was mostly her who talked. She was the spokesperson, the one who gave interviews to the magazines and news crews. The place sounded utopian, martial or monastic, depending on which publication was inter-viewing, and what angle they wanted to push. Veronique's other half was more reclusive.

The number of women grew each year, though no recruiting was ever done. There were some complaints from men, that their wives and daughters had been kidnapped, brainwashed, assimilated, and bent. There were police investigations, but no formal charges were ever brought. The girls who went there had simply opted out of their old lives. Each time I came across an article in the papers I would cut it out and keep it. I fol-lowed the progress of the farm, discarding the criticism, and searching through the text for a clue to its real spirit, its philos-ophy maybe, until the newspapers switched fully to issues of state, then downsized circulation, folded, and I heard nothing more about the place.

I don't know what it was about Jackie Nixon that compelled me. Maybe it was because she was from my area, and that likened us. I felt I almost knew her. She was always depicted formidably; hard-cast, like granite. People in the region were wary even of her name, old as it was – stock of ironmongers, masons, and the bowmen of the North. In Rith it was issued like superstition from the mouths of those discussing her and her girls. 'Jackie Nixon,' they said. 'She's one of the Border Nixons. They were the ones who went out with bulldogs to meet the reivers.' I watched for her at the market, but she never seemed to come down from the farm with the other women.

Before he died my father commented that it would take only a small twist of the dial for Jackie Nixon to become a menace to society. The more he spoke out against her, the more intrigued I became. I remember asking him across the kitchen table one morning what it was about her that he thought was so objectionable. 'Don't you think she's some kind of heroine,' I'd asked him, 'like Graine Warrior? I mean, she lives up there completely independently. I've heard she doesn't take any sub-sidies. The others must trust her to stay on. She must be an amazing person. I'd like to meet her.' My father had raised his eyebrows high on his forehead. 'I think she's leaning on them lasses to do whatever she damn well wants, and she's messing with their heads,' he said, 'like a cult bloody crackpot. And you, my girl, are to steer clear.'

I had two photographs of her. The first was from back when the project began. She was standing outside the heavy oak door of Carhullan with an arm around Vee; it was held awkwardly up across her friend's shoulders because Veronique was much the taller of the two. The picture looked posed, agreed to, and as if the notion of what they were doing was a high-spirited challenge of some kind, like crossing the Atlantic in a coracle. The two of them were in their late twenties then and they looked full of vim and determination. The caption described them as partners and the article went on to speculate about whether or not they were lovers. They'd met at Cambridge University, it said, while completing postgraduate degrees; two like minds, two retro feminists. Before that Jackie had been in the military. Her rank was uncertain.

Jackie had tightly cropped hair, a lopsided face, and a broken jawline. Her eyes were the blue of the region's quarried stone. If she'd had a softer appearance she would have been called bonny perhaps. As it was she was handsome, arresting. In the picture she was wearing a tank top and army surplus trousers. She looked both slim and stocky at once. The second photograph, taken five years later, had her turning away from the camera. Her hair was slightly longer, she was much leaner, and there was a deep frown on her face.

Both picture cuttings were tucked into a metal box of possessions in my backpack, with my identification card and a few other personal effects. They were faded and creased, but I had kept them. If she was still alive, it would be her I'd have to address when I reached my destination.

And I could feel it already, that I was entering her country, her domain. It was a raw landscape, verging on wilderness. The thick green vegetation overrunning the lowlands was now behind me. Rock was beginning to show through the grassland; the bones of an older district, stripped by the wind, washed clean by fast-flowing becks and rain. There was heather, bracken, and gorse.

As I walked upwards on the scars I thought about her. In the early reports Jackie had always been depicted as a typical Northerner; obdurate, reticent, backlit. She seldom went on the record about anything, personal or otherwise. When she did, it was curtly expressed. Anyone coming to the farm needed good shoes, she said – boots, trainers – books, and nothing else. They should get their wisdom teeth removed first. Rarer still, she spoke about her beliefs. 'It's still all about body and sexuality for us,' she was once quoted as saying. 'We are controlled through those things; psychologically, financially, eternally. We endorse the manmade competition between ourselves that disunites us, striping us of our true ability. We don't believe we can govern better, and until we believe this, we never will. It's time for a new society.'

When it was suggested that she might be offering an empty alternative, a formula that had already been unsuccessful, she directed scorn at the governing politicians, asking if the environment they were creating was acceptable. She was often asked what it was that she had in her, making her do what she was doing, as if she were somehow afflicted. Interviewers commented on her impatience, her furious suspension of the conversation if the wrong questions were asked.

Jackie and Veronique were given plenty of titles, called plenty of things by different people in the years of Carhullan's publicity. But as they had it they were simply libertarians. As they had it, theirs was a culture moulded from necessity, formed, as Jackie described, to spean the lambs before they became sheep.

And Carhullan was Jackie's idea, that much was apparent. Her family were from the area, so she knew it like none of the other women ever would, though they worked the land every day, moving sheep and cows, panting across the rough terrain to break the eight-mile hour. This was her home turf. Her territory. She had either bought the place outright or taken it over because it was lying empty. Already by then people were heading into the town, driven out of rural habitations by the transport problems and the steepening fuel prices. Farming was considered a dying industry.

The buildings sat in total isolation, far from any conceivable thoroughfare. I knew I had hiked near there in the past, but I had never seen it. It was the highest farm in England, almost inaccessible, impervious to the flooding that would come in the years to follow, and the shifting of the water tables. It had a massive Westmorland kitchen, a cast-iron range, and any number of ramshackle outbuildings that would become dormitories. Until they wired it up, there was no electricity. It could be reached only on foot or by four-wheel drive via a convoluted upland route.

The land belonging to Carhullan covered hundreds of acres and took in moors, woods and fields. No one knew who originally enclosed it, but it had always been a private steading, not a tenanted farm belonging to the local lord. It was a vast, self-contained, workable place. Jackie had grown up in the valley below, and she must have wondered about its history, maybe trekking up the mountain and climbing in through the windows as a girl, lighting fires on the iron grill and sleeping there overnight. Finding the bones of martins and swifts buried in the soft floors of the byres.

Years later, looking at the photographs of her under the phosphorous Mag-lamp of our quarter, I imagined that she was visionary, that she had foreseen the troubles and the exodus from the villages and hamlets long before it became reality. She had sidestepped the collapse, and the harsh regime of the Civil Reorganisation. Every time I opened a tin and transferred the gelatinous contents into a bowl I thought of the farm's bright vegetables on the market stalls the decade before. I imagined the taste of Carhullan's crisp peppers and yellow lentils, the delicate flavour of the lavender ice cream the women made and sold.

At work in the New Fuel factory, with the noise of the conveyor deafening me, I had often imagined the benefits of being up there with Jackie and Veronique. The tedium of my job was excruciating: eight hours of standing on the concrete factory floor watching metal bolts roll past, knowing that the turbines were not being installed offshore, they were just being stored in the warehouse, cylinder upon cylinder, their blades fixed and static. There was a dead comb of them now built against the walls. I could get inside each grey shell, take out the lock-pin and turn the rotors smoothly with my hands. There were enough units to power the whole of the Northern region if they had been installed in the estuaries.

But for reasons unknown to us, there had been no green light for the operation, no deployment of the technology yet. Authority agents arrived at the factory and took inventories from time to time, as if about to ship the turbines out to the sea platforms constructed years before above the brown tides. The evening news bulletins broadcast still-reels of the New Fuel products, as if proving the recovery's protocol was working. But it was all a bad joke. Every day the pieces were manufac-tured and assembled, then left defunct. And like drones we added to the vast metal hive.

At first I had been glad of the placement. Work at the refin-ery was much worse; the manual labour was filthy and jeopar-dous. Those at the vats quickly developed breathing problems, shadows on their lungs. There were complaints from them that the credits earned were not as high as they should be. But they were higher than anywhere else. And the products were being used – the unconventional oil, and the bios – if only by the gov-ernment.

I had quickly realised our efforts at the factory were for nothing, and I hated the redundancy of it all. There was a per-vasive mood of despondency in the hangar, joylessness. In the restroom the men and women taking shift breaks removed their face guards and tried to sleep for ten minutes before resuming work. Some went into the washrooom and cracked open ampoules of flex. They came back onto the factory floor with wide pupils and no coordination. There had been several accidents. The previous year I had seen a man's arm torn off in the heel-blade of a machine. No one heard him shout out. He had simply picked the arm up with his other hand and walked towards the door of the factory, leaving a wet red trail. I saw him walk past. He stopped before he got to the exit and sat down and placed the amputated limb across his knees. I went over and knelt beside him. 'I was a teacher,' he said quietly. 'I was a teacher. A teacher.' There was a look of shock in his dilated eyes. I knew he could not feel a thing.

There was something better out there. I knew what it was and where to find it. Even if it meant looking behind me, to a venue that had long been forgotten in the aftermath of catastrophe, and the desperate rush to subsist. Like those who had brought pictures of better times to their workstations and tacked them up on the panels of machines, I had kept Carhullan in my mind throughout the recovery's dark years.

It had never been built with the outside world in mind. It was of another age, when utilities and services were unimaginable, before the light bulb had been dreamt of. They must always have known its potential, Jackie and Veronique. Within a year of it being inhabited the women had installed a waterwheel, harnessing a nearby spring. A year-round garden had been planted, and a fast-growing willow copse. There were sties, bees, an orchard, and a fishery at the beck shuttle of the tarn. There were peat troughs, filtration tanks. It was all grandly holistic, a truly green initiative.

It was, and had always been, removed from the faulted municipal world. It sat in the bields, the sheltered lull before the final ascent of the High Street range. There was a panoramic view of the surrounding valleys; it was the best lookout point for miles. The Romans knew it and they had raised a fort there that Carhullan's byres and pens were later built around. And before the Centurions, the Britons had a site nearby; five weather-pitted standing stones which leant awkwardly towards each other, west of the paddocks. The Five Pins they were called. It was a place for pathfinders and entrepreneurs, empire builders, priests, and survivalists; those with the determination to carry stone thousands of feet up, over rough water and inhibitive ground, those who could rear livestock then slaughter it, those who had something so true in themselves that they were willing to dwell at the edge of civilisation for the sake of it.

That was what Jackie Nixon had had in her. It was a spirit bred from the landscape I was now treading. And, as I ascended the brant slopes, I wondered if her ideas had first been formed around the farm, all those years ago when she lay beds of kindling in the sooty range and drank water from the cold stream. It must have been put into her head early on, that after technology and its failures, after the monumental mistakes of the industrialised world, human beings could still shelter and survive in rudimentary ways, just as they always had. Independent communities were possible. Alternative societies. Something durable and extraordinary could be created in these mountains.

By the time I reached the lower bields I was exhausted. I had never carried so much weight such a distance before. The straps of my bag were making my skin raw and tender and my feet felt as if every tiny pliant bone in them was broken. I stopped briefly and put my damp vest and jacket back on. Immediately I felt cold. I walked on again. The water I had brought was gone now and my saliva was thickening up; when I cleared my mouth, it looked like cuckoo spit on the ground. I'd been expecting a clear fast-flowing stream or a gill from which to fill up the canister but had not yet come across one, and I didn't want to wander off the thin sheep track. In the last hour, without really realising it, I had been talking softly, telling myself that it would be all right, telling myself to keep going.

The fell was covered with stiff gingery grass and droves of heather. Here and there my foot sank into small brackish wells, then sucked back out covered in mud. Every step was harder than it should have been. The smell of the grassland and peat was all around; open and bloody, burnt and aromatic. I'd been keeping the dry-stone wall I thought signified Carhullan's land on my right as I climbed, and it had led me through bogs and swales, up over outcrops of rock and loose bluffs.

My father had told me as a child that it was the Vikings who originally built Cumbria's dry-stone walls, and they had been more determined with their corridors than even the Romans. Here, now, I could believe it. In places the structures ran almost vertically upwards; each stone held tightly on to those surrounding it. They were modest, impossible feats of engineering. Over the years, while the district was occupied, they had been repaired and tended by farmers, shepherds, and hired hands, but some sections must have dated back a thousand years. A couple of times on the climb I wondered whether I'd been following the wrong wall, whether I might end up on the broad windy summits of the range, lost as the night came in. Now and then I thought I could hear the bleating of sheep, Carhullan's hefted flocks perhaps, but each time the sound was fainter, and further away.

Looking ahead I judged that there was perhaps just one final hill to scale and then I would be able to see the farm and its outer fields. I decided to stop and rest, and think about what I would say when I arrived. Suddenly it seemed stupid that I had not considered a speech, some meaningful words of introduction that would secure my welcome. I shouldered out of my rucksack, lay it down on the moor, and sat on a broken lip in the wall. I had gained considerable altitude. Below me was the tapering valley, and beyond it, in the next dale, I could see the sleek corner of Blackrigg reservoir.

All around, the wind stroked the tawny grassland; the veld darkened and lightened in waves as the air coursed over its surface. There were belts of dark yellow underneath the parted clouds, the oblique late light of autumn evening. I could smell gorse, blossoming sweetly against its spines. After the confinement and industrial stink of the town, the factory metals, human secretions, the soots and carbons of the refinery, this harsh and fragrant expanse was invigorating. It was the smell of nature, untouched and original, exempt from interference. For all my weariness, it made me feel a little more alive, both human and feral together, and somehow redeemed from the past.

I would tell Jackie and Vee the truth. I'd say nothing more than I felt. That I believed in what they were doing, now more than ever. That I felt there was nothing for me in the society I'd left behind. I couldn't condone it. I couldn't live within it.

Suddenly there was a burst of movement at my side. Three deer bolted past, almost silently, their heads held erect, their hides the colour of the surrounding moor, white rumps flashing. The hooves became audible on the wind for a few seconds, a dull thudding on the ground, and then they were gone over the brow of the hill. Their swiftness was astonishing. They had broken cover only because of their speed, as if pieces of the ground had come loose in a rapid landslide. A few seconds later I heard the hollow barking of a stag behind me, and then it flowed past after the hinds, darker and broader against the terrain, its antlers cast high, its neck thick and rough with fleece. I stood up to see if I could catch sight of it rising over the next hill but there was no sign, just patches of October light drifting across the moor. They must have heard my approach, or scented me as they grazed, I thought.

I sat back down on the wall. I wanted to take off my boots and look at my feet, expose them to the cool air. They were sore at the heels and under the toes and my socks felt as if they were sticking wetly to blisters that had already ruptured. When I'd hiked with my father this was the ritual always performed at the end of every trip. We would sit on the bumper of his car and wrench off our boots and the air would soothe our skin.

There was probably another mile still to hike, but I decided it would be better to patch any abrasions before continuing. Putting my boots back on would hurt, but it would be worse if I kept on with open sores, and I didn't want to spend my first days at the farm limping around, seeming incapacitated and weak. The women there must have come through much hardship, having survived for so long in that place. And I was determined to match their resilience, in spirit at first, then physically.

As I leant down to unlace my boots I felt myself pitching forward off the wall as if it had given way underneath me. The ground rushed up. There was no time to get my hands down to break the fall and I landed hard on my shoulder and face. My kneecap cracked against a slab of stone. A jolt of pain shot the length of my leg and another through my mouth. For a second I lay there, stunned, my cheek sunk in the wet ground and the blond grass swaying indistinctly across my field of vision. Then everything slowly came back into focus. An inch from my eye a spider was belaying down one of the stems on a pale rope. Its legs pedalled precisely on the descent.

I drew a shallow breath and as I did so my collarbone and back protested. All the air had been knocked out of me on impact, but my lungs had been strangely airless even before I hit the ground. I fought with my diaphragm to let oxygen pass, trying to stem the panic of being winded. I couldn't find and use my arms so I pushed against the ground with my chest, trying to raise myself. But I could not move. I was like a landed fish.

As I made an effort to get up again I heard a voice, not far away. 'Keep her down. Lock on tight.' I felt the pressure on my back increase. I stopped moving, and tried to say something, but it came out as nothing more than a cough. There was the gory taste of peat in my mouth and blood that ran from inside my nose. I lay still and looked into the moor grass. After a moment my lungs began to calm and fill, but my heart was hammering. In front of me the spider reached the base of the stem, cut itself free, and disappeared into the undergrowth.

'Check the duffel,' another voice said, closer to me this time.

Curling my fingers I felt the warm skin of a hand that had both of mine pinned together behind my back, midway up my spine. There was the sound of ratching and zipping, nails scrabbling quickly between the nylon folds of my bag. I heard the soft brush of clothing as it was brought out of the rucksack, the thump of my canister as it was dropped on the ground. Then there was a pause. 'She's got a bastard gun. Look.' The grip tightened on my wrists. A hand was placed on the back of my head and my face was pushed further into the damp earth. 'Shit. Good girl, eh?' I heard the last contents of the rucksack being turned out, the boxes of bullets being unwrapped from a bundle of T-shirts. Then the casings were rattled against the cardboard edges. 'No. Bad girl. Ready to get her up?'

The voices were women's. I could not tell how many were present, they were muffled and low, but I could hear that they were efficient. 'Yes. In a minute. Lynn, go and secure the ridge.' There was the sound of someone running. Then the hand on my head tightened into a fist. It took hold of a clump of my hair and lifted my face out of the wet earth. 'Anyone else with you?' The voice was louder now that my ear was out of the mud, and it was precise, leaving a small pause between each word. I moved my tongue against the roof of my mouth and my gums and spat out a mouthful of dirt. The inside of my cheek was stinging, and I knew I'd bitten it in several places. 'No,' I said. 'I walked here alone. From Rith.'

There was another pause. 'When was this?' 'Today,' I replied. There was a snort. The voice next to me had remained level, but now a note of annoyance entered it. 'Almost forty miles? No, you didn't.' I realised the inaccuracy of what I had said, and corrected myself. 'There was a man who gave me a lift part of the way. He said he worked at the reservoir. I got out at Rosgill.' Another pause. My head was lowered back down. No more questions were asked.

For a long time it was quiet. Then a dry whistle sounded across the fell. I could hear my possessions being shaken one by one and stuffed back into the bag. I was still being held down but the grip on my scalp had relaxed. The hand lay flat there, and at one point I thought I felt fingers combing gently through my hair. Then I felt another set of hands patting me down, reaching underneath me, pressing my hips and ribs, my ankles. Pain started to arrive properly in my mouth, my knee, and along my collarbone. I tried to cast the shock and discomfort away and get a clear reading of the situation. It must be them, I thought. They had found me first, before I'd seen the farm.

I was disarmed. I hadn't expected such an aggressive meeting and I wanted to explain myself, but all the things that passed through my mind were submissive and desperate, a reiteration of the position I was already in, so I did not speak. My shoulder was aching but I held as still as I could, was as compliant as I could be. They continued their search. I heard the small bag with my soap and shampoo inside being unzipped and investigated. There was a metallic rattle and the lid of the tin where I kept my few small personal items was popped off. Papers rustled.

For a time the women were so quiet it was as is they had disappeared, as if I were being held down by some supernatural force. The wind hissed through the grass. Then I heard dull footsteps coming towards where I lay. I could see a pair of broken leather boots. Grey tape had been bound round the toe and sole of one of them and it looked like a dog's muzzle. The hand on my skull was taken away. I twisted my head upwards as best I could and strained to see. The figure standing above was holding out a piece of paper to whoever was squatting over me. 'Jacks,' she said. 'Ages ago.' There was another long pause. From the corner of my eye I saw a hand gesture being made. Then I was released.

Slowly I knelt and ran the back of my arm across my face, wiping away the filth. The bones to the left of my collar felt cracked and pushed out of place, but I tried to block out the sensation and stop my eyes from watering. 'Come on. Get up on your feet.' It was the woman who had gone through my things that spoke. Her tone was as even as it had been through-out, but the voice seemed less taut now, less officious. I stood, keeping my weight on the knee I had not jarred, and as I looked at her I knew for certain she was one of Carhullan's residents. She was about my height. She was my size, and my sex, but she looked almost alien. Her face was brown and lined, and the eyes in it were pale green, careful but indifferent. On top of her head the hair was short, it looked oily and separated, like an otter's pelt. At the back it was longer; she wore it pulled away and tied at her neck.

She had on rough black trousers made of canvas or denim, a long thermal with holes in the sleeves and a padded body vest, the kind the old walking shops used to sell. Under her clothes she looked compact and athletic. The flesh between her bones was spare and seemed whittled back, dug out, but not unhealthily so. She was honed. There was a quality about her that seemed so vital and distinguished, so memorable, that I felt I might be gazing at someone I had met before, or had seen on the news a decade ago. More than anything, she appeared native.

In her hand she held the straps of my rucksack. 'It'll be better if you carry this in,' she said. 'Are you going to be able? You all right after that?' I nodded and she passed me the bag. She held it out with a straight arm as if it weighed nothing but when I took it from her it felt as if it had doubled in weight since the walk. I had a ridiculous thought that perhaps she had loaded stones from the moor into it along with my possessions. In her other hand she still held the tin box. Grimacing, I slung the bag onto my back again.

I turned round. The other woman was much younger, no more than a girl, sixteen at most. She looked too slight to have held me down, though her face registered no such concern. Her head was shaved, with only a few days' worth of red bristle on her scalp. There was a primitive blue tattoo on the raised skull around her ear. A thin piece of leather was wound several times around her neck. Her clothes were equally worn and practical, but they looked like burlap or hemp, homemade. She was as aloof as the other woman.

I glanced down and saw she had the rifle loosely trained on me. She held it low on her hip, casually, cradling the stock. I had not heard her load it, or test the mechanism, though I guessed she might have. She was obviously confident with its handling and unimpressed by what she was holding. She seemed to be waiting for direction of some kind. I looked back at her elder, who unzipped the body warmer, put my tin box inside and zipped it back up. 'Fifty–fifty who spooked the deer,' she said, 'but you were downwind, so I'll bet it was us.' She said this slowly and with deliberation, as if making a basic point, or speaking to a young child. Her lips were rolled inwards. It was an expression that could have been a smile, or it could have signified derision. Behind her a third girl was running back across the moorland. As she approached she nodded to the otter-haired woman and then ran past. 'Right. Away in then,' the woman said to me. 'You can tell us your name if you like, but you might as well save it for Jackie. She'll be the one you have to ask it back from anyway.' I felt myself being nudged forward by the gun barrel.

Nothing more was said as we walked. I fell slightly behind the two of them. The pace of my escorts looked leisurely but it was brisker than I could manage. I tried to keep up, but the weight on my back made me slow and clumsy; my knee was swelling and stiffening, and I stumbled over the uneven ground. From time to time they adjusted their stride, falling back a few paces, not enough to allow me to catch up properly, but I could see they were keeping me in their range. Their hostility had lessened, but they were making no moves to be friendly, to find out anything about me, nor were they inviting me to ask about them. A sense of disappointment began to creep through me.

It was not the reception I'd played out in my mind so many times when thinking about Carhullan. I'd seen myself striding up to the farm, looking fit and fierce, being welcomed, not with awe or amazement, but with quiet admiration by the girls working outside. I'd imagined an immediate sense of unity, the way it had felt to form a group of new friends at school, with everyone suddenly aware of the collaboration and trust involved. And there would be Jackie and Veronique, standing at the great oak doorway, just like they had in the photograph, as if that's where they had always stood, and would always stand.

But fifteen years was a long time to be left alone in the wilds. And in that time so much had passed. There had been terrible events, and responses that were almost as extreme. Though I had lived in it I often barely recognised the residual world. I wondered what they knew of this. How must it have been for them, detached and unaided as they were? Perhaps aware of the changes going on. Perhaps oblivious to them. As we walked I began to realise that I had come to a place now as foreign and unknown as anywhere overseas, as anywhere of another age. I wanted to press them for information, ask questions, and tell them about conditions in the towns. I wanted to try to negotiate, or ingratiate myself. But I didn't. Suddenly I was too tired, too weary almost to move.

Rain blew in from the summit of High Street, colder than before, soaking my face and clothes again. I tried to fasten my jacket but my fingers felt awkward and would not cooperate, so I held it closed over my chest. I peered into the squall. There was still no sign of the farm or even the outbuildings. All I could see were drifts of rain and the relentless brown withers of fell, appearing then disappearing. The adrenalin of the encounter had worn off. I had walked more than twenty miles to escape. And I had gambled with my life. Now I felt numb, and close to seizing up. All I wanted was water to drink, and to take the bag off my back, lie down, and go to sleep. It took all my energy to put one foot in front of the other and remain upright.

Ahead, the girl and the woman paused, but they did not look round at me. I wondered if they could hear my dry, laboured breathing, and if it had concerned them. I'd slowed almost to a shuffle as I moved between the limestone boulders and thorn trees. Before I could reach them they stepped forward again and the gap between us widened. It was a calculated move designed to keep me separate but corralled, and they repeated this behaviour all the way across the fell. Finally, I felt tears of exhaustion and self-pity stinging my face. I wanted them to stop, and take hold of me, and tell me it would all be fine. I wanted them to say that I had done well, that I was here now, with them, and it was all right. But they didn't. The fell wind blew damp and cold between us. They were moving me along impersonally, as if I were an animal they were stewarding, as if I belonged to a different species.

Eventually, through the gloom and darkening cloud, I could make out the shape of the farm. It looked smaller than I had imagined it. The outbuildings sat low on the ground, huddled around the main house like stone wind-breakers. Only the long slate roof and upper storeys of the central structure were unobscured by byres. The night was quickly closing in and from the top windows shone a dozen soft lights, loose glowing ovals like egg yolks. I was so tired that I had been almost oblivious to the surroundings on the final leg of the walk, trying not to amplify the pain in my shoulder and knee with every step taken. It was only when I heard dogs barking in the distance, and I looked up, after an hour watching the spry beards of grass passing slowly underfoot, that I saw the settlement.

It was almost lost in the shade of evening and the long shadow cast by the summit of High Street. Against the dull brown massif it looked like the last place on earth, defended and extraordinary, an outpost where all hopes and energies, all physical means, had been consolidated and fortified. It was Carhullan; the place on which I had pinned all my hopes for a new existence. As I peered through the swale of damp fog I was struck, not by the audacity of such a dwelling, cut into the high fells, but by its seclusion, the emptiness surrounding it, and the sheer girth of the landscape around its foundations. Looking at the paucity of illumination coming from the farm and the diminutive proportions of the settlement, I felt the shift of currents in my stomach, the gathering of nervousness.

In a country now so dependent on urban arrangements, the extremity and lunacy of this location were inescapable. In that moment, Carhullan could have been the gatehouse to Abaddon. But it did not matter. For better or worse, there was no turning back now. Even if the women had released me, I was too weary and sore to think about a return journey. I knew my options were reduced to this place alone.

As we approached the farm a ripe smell of silage began to grow stronger. It was an odour both offensive and rousing; that got right to the back of my nose and throat and smelled of decayed grass, fish and animal waste. The pungent tang of husbandry had long since been gone from Rith. Instead the air was filled with petrochemical emissions and the rot of uncollected rubbish. The agricultural spread held faint memories of the county in its old incarnation at this time of year, with sprays of yellow fertiliser jetting over the earth and heavy, silted tractors working behind the hedgerows.

We passed through a stone gate and the moor suddenly gave way to black turned earth, deep furrows of soil. It was soft and uneven to walk on, the limp piles yielded richly under my feet. After the austere expanse of the fells the farmland seemed peculiarly cultivated. In a small pasture to the right there were several rows of oddly shaped plants that looked like small palm trees. Next to them were taller growths with frothy white and purple flowers; I recognised them, they were Carlin peas, like the ones my father had grown. To the left was a little humpback bridge. I could hear the spatter and hiss of water in a rocky channel nearby but could not see the upland beck that I knew rose close to Carhullan and drove the waterwheel, powering the electrical generator. We passed three triangular-shaped hutches. At first glance they seemed empty. Then I made out the creatures kept inside, about six small birds in each, with stippled plumages.

My two guides stopped when they reached the first of the stone pens, waiting for me to catch up. I stumbled forward, hoping that I would not be seen arriving too far behind them. They looked straight ahead, towards the walls. I hesitated a few feet away from them and waited for instruction. They seemed to be rocking gently in front of me, from side to side, as if to music I could not hear. After a moment I realised that I was swaying on my feet. Nausea swelled in me and the back of my throat tensed and lifted. I leant to the side to vomit but could do no more than bring up a mouthful of sharp bile. I retched again, dryly.

I glanced upwards. The woman and the girl holding the gun had turned and were observing me. I folded over at the waist, put my hands on my thighs, and waited for a spell, making sure I wasn't going to be sick again. I spat a few times to clear my mouth, and tried to concentrate on breathing deeply and evenly, but I knew I was in trouble, that I had pushed myself beyond the limits of my fitness. When I'd bent over, the rucksack had slipped on my back, and it now rested heavily against my head, digging into my neck. I stood and it dropped back into place, pulling hard against my shoulders and sending a hot lacerating pain through my damaged collarbone. A sound left my mouth, a half moan, half whimper. My eyes swam to find focus, and unsettlement rippled in my gut. I felt desperately ill. Then the dizziness overwhelmed me and I lost my balance. I began to fall forward.

'Hey. Hey. She's going. Megan!'

I heard the voice only a second before I felt one of them take me by the arms. The grip was firm, insistent, and in my disorientation I found myself leaning against the support, unsure whether I was kneeling or sitting or lying down. It was the younger woman, the girl who had held me down. She had sprung forward in time to catch me and now she was keeping me upright. She said nothing but held me steady for a minute, then cautiously she took her hands away and stepped back. The older woman picked the rifle up off the ground where it had been dropped.

There seemed to be no one waiting for our arrival. We had not been greeted at the farm's periphery. None of the other women had been out in the fields as I'd expected they would be. Through a gap in the pens I could see that the farm's courtyard was also deserted. I listened for the sounds of talking and laughter coming from nearby or inside, anything to indicate that an interested crowd might be gathering, a welcome committee. But there was nothing. Even the dogs that I had heard a quarter of a mile away were quiet, silent rather than muffled, as if they had been taken inside. I wondered again how many women were left, whether just a handful ran the place now, a skeleton crew of some kind, rather than the eighty strong that had once lived and worked here.

The lights were on but the place was still and empty. It was apparent that we were waiting for something or someone. The two had turned their backs to me. From their posture they were making it clear that if I was going to faint again they were not going to catch me. I was responsible for my own conduct and I would have to summon the strength and coordination to keep my balance. I squeezed my eyes closed, opened them and blinked rapidly several times, fighting to maintain concentration and alertness. I knew that I had to remain standing, that for all their coolness and detachment they wanted me upright, aware of what was happening, and capable of representing myself. But I craved unconsciousness, and was close to passing out. What I wanted to do was give in, let the blackness and numbness claim me. I wanted to crumple to the floor and stay there until the sickness and pain and exhaustion passed, leaving me ready to face this strange and desolate community.

Inside the settlement walls, a door opened and shut. There were footsteps on the courtyard flagstones and I saw a figure walking towards us. The silhouette grew more distinct, then, from the middle of the buildings, a broad-waisted woman emerged. She had on a floor-length skirt and a waxed coat. Over that she wore a sleeved plastic apron, like a vet's. She paused for a moment in front of the otter-haired woman and the girl whose name I now knew was Megan. They murmured a few words together and the woman nodded.

As she stepped towards me I felt a last rush of panic. I was not ready to meet her. I was not composed, not cognitive enough. The long hike had taken its toll and she would surely think the worst of me for arriving in this state, for being too weak. But as she came into view I saw that it was not Jackie. Nor was it Veronique. I did not recognise this woman. She was middle aged, perhaps in her fifties, and stout. Her hair was long and loose, falling in thin dry curls to her waist. There was a deep groove above her nose where her brow pinched in. It was the mark of a perpetual frown, an expression that seemed to be worn perhaps even when she did not mean for it to be present. On her apron there were dark pragmatic smears.

'Take off the bag, please,' she said to me, pointing to my rucksack. 'Go on, it's OK.' I pulled the straps off my shoulders as slowly and carefully as I could, and tipped it to one side, catching it in the crook of my good arm. Then I let it drop to the floor. She could see from my face the distress caused by the manoeuvre. Her eyes were bright hazel and fast, taking in my level of discomposure and processing what she saw. 'Right. I'm going to check you out. I know you're hurt,' she said to me. 'Do I have your permission?' I did not reply. She kept her eyes locked with mine. I saw kindness in them. After a few seconds of her gaze, I nodded. She stepped in again and took hold of my jaw, opening my mouth gently but firmly. With her other hand she placed two fingers on my tongue and patted down. She turned them and touched the roof of my mouth, then brought them back out. I winced as she brushed past the bitten rim of my cheek.

'When did you last piss?' she asked. I shook my head, then remembered. 'This morning,' I said. My voice sounded cracked and hoarse, as if I had grown older since I set out.

'Have you thrown up?' I nodded. 'Well, you weren't carried so your feet can wait,' she said. There was a lilt at the heart of her accent, perhaps Westcountry or Welsh, but my mind was too disordered to place it. She sighed. 'OK. Now I've got to have a go at that shoulder. I'm sorry.'

Before I could respond her hands were working over my throat, pressing along the line of my clavicle, and in the hollow under my arm. She took hold of my wrist and elbow and raised them up. I tried not to shout out but the pain was too vivid and I made a strangled noise that sounded shrill and bird-like. She held tighter and moved the arm in a wide circle. The bone from my breastplate to my shoulder cuff felt as if it were grating and splintering as it rotated. I was crying openly now at the agony of her manipulations and though I tried to pull back, the force of her grip kept me from freeing myself. 'No, no, no,' she said, simply, as if talking to a stubborn animal. When she was done she placed the arm tightly back at my side, bent it up at the elbow, and pushed my hand between my breasts. 'Keep it held like this,' she whispered, almost too quietly for me to hear. Then, raising her voice to its previous level, she said, 'Yeah. It's fractured.'

The examination was over. As I waited for the throbbing in my arm to subside, Megan picked up the rucksack from the ground by my feet. Her eyes met mine briefly, then looked away. I saw that the blue tattoo above her ear ran all the way round her skull, down the median of her neck, disappearing at the hem of her jersey. I looked hard at it, focused on the orna-mental border to distract myself from the pain. I imagined the blue ink line running on under her clothes. I followed it as it snaked down her spine, across her ribs and her hip, down her leg and under her foot. I pictured the line continuing on and spilling into the blue twilight, like a river into a lake. Gradually the pain lessened. When I looked at her again she was shrug-ging the rucksack onto her back. It seemed huge on her slender frame, like an absurd beetle's carapace. She slipped between the outbuildings. A metal latch lifted and a door creaked. After a few moments she came back without the bag, and carrying instead a plastic container of fluid.

The woman who had inspected me in the half-dark took a few paces back and sighed heavily again. Her frown had deepened. She looked worried. She put her hands on her hips and her head dropped forward. 'It's not recommended,' she called out. 'Not bloody well by me!' From behind her, in the shadows of the courtyard, I heard another voice. 'Give her the water. Then put her in the dog box. She's fit enough.'

The women from the moor took my arms. As they led me away round the thick outer wall of the farm I glanced up towards the fells. There was now so little daylight that the horizon had almost disappeared. I squinted into the distance. The ground had lost its definition and the summit of High Street seemed to bleed into the deep teal of the night. The elements were combining darkly, but for a second or two I thought I saw a long row of black outlines, human figures, standing on the ridge against the sky. I could not be sure of it. But in that one glance, before I was pushed inside the narrow iron structure, there seemed to be a ring of people on the hillside above Carhullan. There were too many of them to count.

What followed was unbearable. I was kept in the metal tank for maybe three days, though I received no confirmation of how long it had been from the women who had left me there. By the end I had lost all track of time, and I did not know whether I had added the hours together correctly, or if I had forgotten some moments in between. There was no way to measure, no way to count.

The darkness was absolute. I only knew that the sun had risen by the temperature change inside the corrugated walls, the warming of the vault's iron sides and the smell of urine and sweat growing stronger in the heat. The dimensions of the cell were tiny, perhaps two feet square, and barely wide enough to sit in, let alone lie down or stretch out. In it was a single broken wooden stool. Its seat was flat and hard, too small to rest on comfortably. A single pole ran from the cross piece to the ground. It had not been hammered down securely, so the chair rocked and tipped in its shaft, moving whenever my weight shifted. Every few minutes I would have to adjust, and if I had drifted into shallow sleep I'd wake with a start, panicked by a sensation of falling, or by the clanging echo of the metal partition as I fell against it.

The container of water had been placed at my feet, before the door was closed and barred. When I reached to pick it up my head grazed against the rusty corrugation and I had to crane my neck to the side and put my hand on the wall to guard against the patches of sharply torn metal. It was the first fluid I had had for hours. I unscrewed the lid, upended it and drank thirstily, taking down great gulps of liquid until I choked. It was too much. My stomach heaved and I brought it all up in a bitter wash that spilled over my chin and down my clothes. For all my thirst, I knew I had to moderate my intake, making sure only to have small resting sips. After each drink I shook the bottle and tried to estimate how much water was left, how long it would last. No food was brought.

Every hour the containment became worse. I suffered cramp and had to move position constantly, rubbing my legs to try to stop them shaking. The muscle spasms in my thighs and calves felt uncontrollable. I had taken my legs to the point of convulsion after the long walk; they were starved of protein and the space to recover. My back ached from its carried load and the strain of being kept vertical after such exertion, from being bent and contorted as I tried to sleep leaning against the corners of the enclosure. I was desperate to sleep, and could not. The cell would not allow it. I tried curling in a ball around the stool, with my face on my hand, but the ground was damp and filthy; it reeked of piss and shit. I didn't know if it was animal or human. I was terrified that it was from other hostages, others who had come here. I tried not to believe it, I told myself there had not been people in here, kept like this for whatever

71

terrible reason, but deep down I knew that there must have been.

A few hours after I began to drink the water I felt the urge to urinate. I banged on the iron walls and called for someone to come and let me out, but it was futile. No one responded. No one even denied the request. Outside there was no sound, just the oboe of wind through the grass, and the strange nocturnal pitch of the moorland. After another hour my bladder began to burn and feel distended and I knew there was no other option but to relieve myself in the narrow space. I undid my trousers and crouched as best I could. Holding the water container on the seat of the stool, I tried to open my legs and squat back, but I began to shake violently again and the hot stream ran down my ankles. It happened every time I tried to piss. Finally, towards the end, I did not attempt to keep myself dry and clean. I let the neck of my bladder release while I was sitting on the stool and urine soaked over the wooden slat, down the legs of my trousers and onto the ground.

In the constant darkness I became confused about where I was. At times the room seemed bigger, wider. At times I felt that I could stand up and walk over to the other side, with my arms outstretched, or that I could even run the length of it, as if I were in a wide marble palace. I woke and thought I was back in the terrace quarter and I reached for the Mag-lamp next to the bed, only to cut a gash in my knuckles. Each time I came out of my reverie banging my hands or head against iron, the air forced from my chest as the walls rushed in.

I woke to the assurance of my blindness and hunger. In the pitched void images began to flicker. I saw faces I knew and did not know, visions of murder and rape. There were maggots multiplying in the wounds I had sustained. I tried to pick them out only find myself tearing at pieces of my own skin. I had never been claustrophobic in Rith's over-populated tenements, or as I crawled into the dead hubs of the turbines in the factory. But in the rancid air and relentless black of the dog box I felt hysteria boiling through me.

In the bouts of ragged sleep my bearings failed. I dreamt that my coffin was being buried in the peat gullies on the bields where I had lain face down, tasting the hag, my hands fastened behind my back. I dreamt that I was crawling through underground tunnels, pulling at cords of roots, only to have the soil cave in on top of me, filling my mouth and ears, the holes where my eyes had been. And I dreamt I was in the mouth of an iron woman. Her teeth were closed around me, and she was carrying me back to her den of wrecked metal in the mountains. I heard the creaking of her legs as she strode, like panels of metal beating in the wind.

I called out for someone to come, for someone to help me, please. When they pushed me inside I had not struggled, only tried to explain myself to the two women. I'd told them I had come because I believed in them. Because of how I felt inside. Because there was a coil in me, fury in me; something clawing to get out. I had come because what was left of the country was the disfigurement of its sickness, the defects left by its disease, and I would not let it infect me.

In the hours that passed I tried to find better, more accurate words to tell them why I had come, and who I was, who I wanted to be. I babbled to whomever I thought was waiting outside the narrow corrugated door. I pleaded with them, begged for their trust. I refused their silence, their abandonment, dreading to think I had been forgotten and left to die. There had been a mistake, I said. There had been a misunderstanding. I was here because I was like them. I asked forgiveness for not coming sooner. I battered the sides of the enclosure until I could smell my own blood turned loose over my arms, its scent like lead.

It was not torture. It was not torture because there was no one hurting me, no one peeling away my nails and salting the pulp beneath. The only presence in the iron box was my own. I began to understand that I owned the abuse; I was the only persecutor. They were not killing me slowly, methodically, with scalding instruments and wires. They were letting me break apart, so I could use the blunt edges of reason to stave in my mind, and the jagged ones to lance open the last blisters of sanity. I thought at times I might still have been lying on the fell, my skull cracked open on a lichen-pale rock as the deer raced past. I thought I must be dreaming all this up, waiting to be found. Then I thought of nothing.

There was the smell of fresh food. On the ground there was a warm heap of something. I had put it into my mouth before I realised it was shit.

I heard Andrew's laughter outside. I heard him knocking on the side of the enclosure, saying there was a letter for me waiting at home. The evening lottery had selected my number for reproduction. We could try and conceive now if I still wanted a baby. My mother walked towards me holding a lit taper. Both her breasts were missing and there were pegs along the mastectomy scars, holding the incisions closed. It was not the woman in the photographs I had been given when I was five years old, but the woman who had put her fingers in my mouth, testing to see how long I could withstand this place. She reached between my legs and brought out the decayed dog I'd seen in my father's garden. I held it in my arms and it felt like a piece of wet leather.

In the end I knew that if they left me much longer, I would not survive all the deaths of myself that it was possible for me to create.

FILE THREE

COMPLETE RECOVERY

She woke me by putting a hand on my forehead. I was lying on my back, finally able to unhook my joints and extend my body. The first sensation was feeling unfastened, so slack and comfortable that I could almost not come round, and if the hand had not stayed where it was, exerting gentle pressure, I would have drawn the soft layers of unconsciousness over myself again and fallen away. But she did not want that. She spoke a word and then a number and I reached towards them, half recognising them, but they slipped away.

I did not know how I had kicked away the iron walls and freed up enough space to straighten my legs and uncurl my back. My thoughts were slow to arrive and difficult to arrange. If the door of the dog box was open I could escape. If the pen was like a puzzle, somehow I had decoded it, made one sprung move, one solving turn, and the sides of the cage had released. I could sleep. The stool was gone and I was lying in the dirt. And yet it was smooth and there was the fragrance of soap.

I opened my eyes and for a minute had to fight the uncomfortable brightness. Above me the sky was whitewashed and cracked. It was a ceiling. A thin bar of sunshine ran the length of it, splitting into a pale green prism at one end that was too luminous and beautiful to look at for long. The last finger of a woman's hand was sitting like a pink visor over my vision. As I turned my head to face her she took it away and I felt the plush of a pillow underneath my cheek. I was in a bed. I was inside the farm.

'Long walk,' she said. I waited for my eyes to focus on her properly. They felt scratchy, and sore, as if surgery had been performed on them. 'We're near where the eyries used to be,' she went on. 'It's not clearly marked to scale on the maps.

They call it a reservation null. Supposedly it stopped people from stealing the eggs.' She gave a low laugh. 'Not very helpful for visitors though, is it? But here you are anyway. Shangri-La.'

Her accent was close to my own, less town-bred and more mobile over its vowels. It was the county's rural equivalent. I looked up at her face, finally able to see her. She was older of course, in her forties now, but immediately recognisable. Her jawline was thicker, though still slightly misshapen, crooked, with the smile worn higher on the left, as if she had always favoured the teeth on that side when she ate. On the lower inert cheek there was a strange fold of skin, a tucked-in line, like a suture tack. In the newspaper pictures I had never noticed it. Her hair was long; it reached her shoulders and there were colourless strands woven into it. It softened her features slightly, and it looked wrong.

But it was the eyes that gave her away. Jackie Nixon's eyes were the colour of slate riverbeds. The photographs had never been able to moderate or alter their lustre. Even in black and white she looked out of the pictures clearly and coldly, and I knew that the territory had somehow gone into the making of her.

She was looking at me now with an expression both curious and patient, as if keen that we should communicate but conscious of my disability, aware that we would need some lesser form of exchange. She watched as my eyes filled up, her gaze flickering to the side of my face as the tears ran across the bridge of my nose, over my eyelid and down onto the cotton. I blinked and squeezed out the gathering fluid, embarrassed not to have controlled my composure in front of her. My brain suddenly ignited then. It was her. It was Jackie. Not three feet from me. Alive in the flesh.

I tried to sit up but an aching stiffness ran the length of me and I found that my arm had been knitted up into a gauze sling, so I could only use the other elbow as a prop. After a few attempts I brought myself ungracefully to an upright position.

She did not try to assist me, but let me struggle against the soreness and the inhibition of the bindings. She was sitting on a wooden chair next to the bed, leaning forward, with her elbows on her knees, her wrists lopped over and crossed like paws. She had on fatigues and a long-sleeved vest. A thin silver chain fell down below her neckline. I wiped my eyes but the tears still came. The cut on my hand had been wrapped and it smelled sweet when I brought it up to my face, almost sickly, as if there was a floral ointment of some kind under the bandage.

Jackie lifted herself up a fraction, reached down and inched the chair closer in. 'Don't worry about it, Sister,' she said. 'You're just hungry. You're probably ready for some porridge now. I'll get the girls to make you some.' She smiled again, sympathetically, as if I were a child who had woken from an illness and would naturally be starving and eager for sustenance. The texture of her face seemed almost burned. There were smooth patches and areas where the skin looked crisp. She stared at me a while longer, then stood abruptly, scraping the chair back along the floorboards. She walked to the door, and though she was relatively short I saw her duck under the low oak beam of the lintel. Then I heard her boots on the stairs.

I found I was holding my breath. My lungs fluttered as I exhaled. I looked around. On the dresser next to the bed was a glass of water. The underlying thirst of the last few days had not left me, so I reached over, took it, and drank it down. My mouth nipped and stung as the liquid passed. The abrasions where I had bitten into the flesh had become ulcers; I could feel the sore little holes with the tip of my tongue. The sickness had passed, but there was a sulphurous taste at the back of my throat. I knew I needed something in my stomach. The rest of me was clean, but my mouth was furred and stale from the risen acid. I took stock of myself. I felt battered and bruised, weak rather than weary, but less confused, and less frantic. The delirium and fear of the metal tank where they'd kept me had gone, but I could sense them flashing around my brain, and I suspected that if I closed my eyes for long enough the terrible images and the feeling of restriction would come slipping back.

I tried to concentrate on the present. They had obviously washed me and dressed my injuries. My upper body was naked except for the sling and underneath the sheets I had on clean underwear from my backpack. The heels and toes of my feet were taped and when I moved them they felt moist and creamy under their stiff plasters. I pulled back the covers. I saw that my knee, where it had struck the rock, was dark purple and grey.

I could hear muffled voices downstairs, banging and general movement, doors opening and closing. Outside there were more sounds, dull thumps and the nickering and lowing of animals. I had met only a handful of the women so far, but I knew there must be more. The shapes framed against the skyline on the night of my arrival had not been a trick of the light or my eyes beginning their false projections. It was likely the farm had been evacuated before my arrival.

I climbed out of bed and hobbled to the window. Below, the courtyard was filled with slanting autumn sunlight. Brown leaves and tufts of fireweed were blowing across the granite slabs. Someone had left a book overturned on the stone steps to an upper door where a pulley hung from a bracket. Its pages fluttered. Two women were standing talking at the entrance of one of the barns. The strong breeze flattened their hair, parting it in white lines along their scalps. One held a box full of what looked to be root vegetables: turnips, carrots, cabbages. The other had a bundle of material in her arms. She shifted the weight a fraction and a tiny hand reached upwards from the folds. The woman next to her cradled the box of tubers and greenery against her hip, took hold of the little fingers with her free hand and leaned down to kiss them. It took a moment for me to comprehend what I had seen. My eyes were still watery and smarting, but

80

they were not mistaken. There was a newborn at Carhullan.

The women below parted company, walking in opposite directions across the yard, and I looked out beyond where they had stood. Through the gaps between the outbuildings I could see the expanse of fields and ditches that I had been escorted through. There was a high three-walled enclosure where a dozen fruit trees were rocking in the wind. Grazing underneath the lowest branches were four white and brown goats. One of them was being milked.

Beyond that I could make out a column of about twenty prostrate bodies on the ground. They were dressed in shorts and their legs looked pale against the turf. After a while I could see they were moving up and down, alternating position every few seconds, their arms spread wide at first, then held tightly in at their sides.

When I turned back from the window Jackie was standing in the doorway of the bedroom. I had not heard her mounting the stairs. In her hands was a tray with a steaming bowl placed on it, a jug, and a dish of apple pieces. 'You're up. Good lass. Feel like a run, since you're not pointing heavenwards any more? I'm about to send my unit out.' I felt my eyes widen. 'God, no,' I said. She laughed a quiet throaty laugh. 'That's all right. I'm just fucking with you. First things first, we'll get you mended.' She nodded at the tray. 'It's poddish. With a little bit of sago thrown in. You'd be forgiven for thinking it was frogspawn, but we'll not tell Sister Ruthie that. It's her department and she doesn't like much feedback.'

She jerked her head to the side, indicating that I should get back into bed, and I did so. Then she walked over to me and held out the tray. I took it from her with my free hand, gripping it unsteadily. The bowl and the jug skittered close to the edge. Feeling feeble and clumsy, I righted it and set it on my knees.

My stomach griped with hunger. The white substance in the bowl smelled starchy, and a little bit salty. It reminded me of the cones of popcorn that used to be sold in Rith's cinemas when I was very young. There was an oily yellow pool in a crater in the centre of the mixture. In the jug was thick, creamy-looking milk.

Jackie sat in the chair next to me again. 'Might taste a bit funny to you,' she said, 'but it gets better the longer you eat the stuff. That's butter on it, for a bit of winter insulation. You look OK to me, but the girls here have to put on a few pounds this time of year or they start getting run down.' I nodded, picked up the spoon, and began to eat. It was scalding hot and burned the roof of my mouth and the tender spots inside my cheeks, but I was too hungry to care. I worked air into the mouthful to cool it down and swallowed. Jackie leaned over and poured the milk into the bowl. As she did so her arm brushed past me. Her vest smelled of utility, like the proofed fibres of a cagoule. She put the jug to her lips and drank the last inch.

I felt self-conscious in the bed, eating so hurriedly, and only half dressed, with one breast covered by the sling and the other exposed. I was aware of how vulnerable I must appear, and had already proved myself to be. I'd been run through the mill because of it. We were now in civil proximity, Jackie Nixon and I, and the atmosphere was one of diplomacy, but I also understood that it had been her choice to incarcerate me initially; it was her voice I had heard in the darkness, committing me to my term in the hot, stinking shed.

She had been ruthless then. Now she was giving me a reprieve, making a truce perhaps. She was even waiting on me. Her actions were not designed to intimidate, but nevertheless I felt nervous in her company. She was a woman I had wanted to meet for a long time; a woman who was indigenous, who had built up an extreme rural enterprise and kept it going for almost two decades, while all around her things had broken down. Face to face, I could see there was a durability to her appearance, a worn and coarsened exterior. And she had poise, the look of someone in power, someone to whom others would bow.

She raised one leg onto the chair, bringing the boot into the back of her thigh. 'Well, where to start, Sister? I'm sure there's a lot you can tell us. But you've probably got a fair few questions to ask too.' She raised her eyebrows, waiting for me to respond. I finished the oatmeal first, unable to stop eating it, and set the tray to one side. The lethargy I had shrugged off came warmly back as the food hit my system, but I was determined to stay sharp. 'How many of you are there?' I asked. Her eyes narrowed. 'Sixty-four,' she said. 'As of eight weeks ago, that is. You saw our littlest one out of the window I take it.'

She did not wait for me to confirm that I had before continuing. 'She's called Stella. The second generation is bigger than we'd imagined it would be. You've met the oldest of them already – Megan. She knocked seven shades out of you apparently. Bit excitable. We've not had anyone to try out the system on before you. She'll no doubt apologise at some stage, or maybe she won't, it wasn't personal, was it? That tough little bitch is trained as well as it gets.' I saw a shine in her eyes, the glitter of pride perhaps. 'So, you'll go to her if there's a problem between the two of you. Don't come to me with it. The way it works here is everyone resolves their shit at source, face to face. That's just how we run things. OK?' She crossed her arms and the chair creaked as she leant back into it. 'All the births have been manageable, thanks to Sister Lorry. We only lost one, and that was before she came.'

I took a slice of apple from the dish on the tray and bit into it. It was sweet, crisp and full of juice. It was the most delicious fruit I had tasted for years. Jackie noticed the pleasure on my face. 'Yeah, that's an Egremont russet. Aren't they lovely? It's warm enough up here to get them now. We've a good crop this year. And look. They've cut it up for you in case you can't chew, busted up as you are. They're good lasses.' She reached over, stole a slice and winked at me. 'We'll all be sick of them come December. But not the *wine*.' She drew out the word, letting her voice hum over its cadence. It was a swift and playful

83

change of tack, and her whole demeanour altered. I felt suddenly charmed by her. Then as quickly as it had arrived, the banter was gone and her face hardened again.

There was a fierceness about her, something amplified and internalised, an energy that my father would have described as Northern brio. Growing up in Rith, I had seen girls with this same quality. They had carried knives and had scrapped outside the school gates with little concern for their clothes and their looks, and there was an absence of teasing when they flirted with men. Jackie looked like a more mature and authentic version. Sitting beside me she seemed too inanimate for her voltage, too kinetic under her restfulness. It was as if her skin could barely contain the essence of her.

I wondered what the other women at the farm made of her. For all its equalities, and whatever formula the place ran on, it had been apparent from the first night that Carhullan operated a system of control; a hierarchy was in place, and Jackie Nixon's orders were obeyed. She was the superior. The alpha. As she sat watching me in the bed, I thought about all those who had walked up the slopes, a decade and a half before, knowing her name. Over the years she must have achieved some kind of mystical status as one of Carhullan's founders. I had still not seen the other.

It surprised me that they had not come in together to give me the low-down on the place. I swallowed the last piece of apple and wiped my mouth. 'Where's Veronique? Can I meet her?' Jackie's chin was resting on her hand. She dropped it an inch and pressed her knuckles to her mouth. Then she clenched her uneven teeth. A wave of tension ran though her forehead. 'No. She's dead, Sister.'

Jackie met my gaze for as long as it lasted. I could not hold her eyes. I shook my head and looked towards the window. 'She's been dead three years.' There was an uncomfortable pause. 'I'm sorry,' I said, looking back at her. I wanted to say more, but the grin she had on her face jolted me from making anything but the briefest of condolences. It was a terrible expression and I couldn't tell if it was genuine or not. I thought that she must be joking, and at any moment she would apologise for having a black sense of humour and say that Vee was out on the farm with the others. But she did not. The smile held, becoming gross and manic. Her cold clear eyes held no mirth in them. 'Life goes on,' she said, 'beloved or bastardised.'

I knew then that she was serious. I felt a shiver pass through the pores of my skin, though the autumn sun shone into the bedroom with a warm cidery light. The nipple of my breast felt tight and hard against my inner arm, and the flesh of my chest was suddenly chilly and damp. I tried to pull the sheets up around me but they were trapped under the tray.

Jackie observed my discomfort. Her face relaxed out of its grimace and she stood up. 'You'll see how it all works soon enough. We're strict, but things are pretty straightforward. We're all sticky up here. I know you know that, Sister, and I know that's why you're here.' She paused, as if to let me register what she had just said, but her words seemed oddly confidential and coded, as if she was speaking to someone else, someone who knew more than I did about the place I had come to.

She went on with the cursory induction. 'If you're after it, your shampoo and roll-on are in the pokey with our soap supplies. I'm afraid they won't last long once word gets out. We're not a heavily deodorised institute. The hole is last on the left, spare paper's in there. Three sheets max for a shit. Take a tub of Vaseline from the pokey too, and don't forget to use it. Sister Lorry is going to come in and look you over later today. She'll talk to you about getting that bit of rubbish out of you.'

Her attitude fell through another revolution again. She put her hands on her hips and stood squarely in the room. 'Listen. I don't care if you are a murrey, just don't put it about, eh? I don't need these bitches squabbling over new cunt. Not now.' She licked the corners of her mouth and stepped towards the door. 'It's fine if you want to go back to sleep for a bit,' she

85

said, nodding her head, and it did not seem like I was being offered a choice. Then she left the room, closing the door behind her, and this time I could not hear her footsteps moving away.

Once she had gone I stared at the stripped knotted wood of the door panels. My shoulder felt sore again and I realised I was completely tense. I tried to relax. But somehow I felt upbraided. And I was perplexed by Jackie Nixon's many faces. She had passed through arrangements of humour and pragmatism, lightness and invective, as she presented herself, as she covered those matters she wanted to discuss. There were gaps in her elucidation of the farm's fellowship, and I wanted to know more. She hadn't mentioned my gun, or the photographs of her I had kept in my tin. And she hadn't apologised for my being locked up.

No. She had not welcomed me exactly. But what she had done, without my having to apply officially, was make it clear to me that I could stay at Carhullan. At least for the time being.

From the bedroom window I had been watching small groups of women running furtively up the ridge, scaling its steep sides and attempting to gain the summit without being seen by the two sentries stationed at the cairn. Some of them appeared to be carrying wooden shafts in their hands. Others lay back behind stands of gorse, waiting for a signal. It seemed an impossible objective, such extreme sniping, until one figure managed to cross a craggy overhang of rock, skirt the summit, and tackle the guards from behind. I wondered if it was Megan. Those who had broken cover and been picked off were made to kneel with their hands linked behind their heads.

Closer, in a field by the metal structure where I had been kept, another small group of women worked in pairs, each having to wrestle her partner to the ground. I could not tell if they were practising a martial art, or whether what they were doing was some kind of combined skill. At one point I saw

Jackie enter the group and demonstrate a move. A woman stood up and volunteered to spar with her. They set their legs wide and gripped their wrists behind each other's backs. After a brief engagement, and the vying of heels for ground space, the woman found her footing gone and I saw her body arc through the air before she was slammed onto the grass. I winced as her head rebounded off the turf.

I might have become bored with my convalescence were it not for the fascination of these activities. It was as if I had been granted access to a private training camp. There was a meticulous quality to the exercises being carried out. The effort put in was acute, and even when they were not engrossed in the action themselves the women remained vigilant and observant, squatting on their haunches in a circle around the arena. It did not take long to realise how easily they must have picked me off on the bields as I made my way up towards Carhullan, slowly and in full view.

There was constant movement in the courtyard below too. I heard the rumble of barrels being rolled on the wide uneven cobbles, and the chock-chock of wood being stacked. Sacks of feed were taken in and out of the storage sheds. At one point a pack of dogs spilled into the yard, their tails wagging stiffly. They roiled around and then were let out. Over in the paddocks, ponies necked against each other, or frisked their tails and cantered about as the high wind caught hold of them.

Jackie had not given me permission to leave the main house or walk around the farm, so I stayed put in the white stone bedroom, sleeping a little, then sitting cat-like on the wooden window seat and observing the drills and agricultural routines. I'd wrapped the blanket from the bed around myself, knotting it under the sling. My rucksack and its contents were still absent.

Once or twice I had walked quietly down the long landing to the bathroom, shyly passing door after door, afraid of running into someone else. I'd felt like a ghost moving through the quiet loft of the farmhouse, undressed and trailing a sheet; a wisp, little more than vapour. It was almost unbelievable to think of the crowded noisy terrace quarters in which I had lived only a few days earlier; where people streamed ant-like to and from work; where they queued to use the bathrooms and the oven; where they fucked and argued and cried, and the floors creaked under the weight of so many penalised bodies, and everywhere the atmosphere was of human pressure.

Towards evening Lorry knocked and came into the room. I had begun to feel edgy and discarded and I was pleased to see somebody I recognised, even though our previous encounter had involved a painful examination. In her hand was a folded yellow garment. She laid it on the bed, and told me to put it on whenever I was ready and wanted to come down. 'Standard practice for new intakes,' she said. 'We're a traditional bunch of so-and-sos really.' In her other hand she held a black leather case, like an old-fashioned doctor's bag. As she opened it and brought out a wrap of instruments I thought about what Jackie had told me, that Lorry had been responsible for all the safe births on the farm. Like Jackie she seemed to possess authority and confidence.

I wondered how Veronique had died, and whether Carhullan's midwife and medic had tried and failed to save her. Perhaps there had been an accident, something too wounding to treat. The thought of it saddened me.

I wanted to ask Lorry for all the information I had not managed to get from Jackie during our brief exchange. Of the women I had met so far she had been the most amenable and kind, and I knew she had objected, at least on medical principle, to me being tossed into the dog box. I decided not to try my luck on the subject. I was not in a position to pry and I did not know how much inquiry was acceptable yet and how much would be discourteous. I had seen already that the place ran reasonably smoothly and with considerable collaboration among the women. I was still an outsider.

'You're looking bright,' Lorry said. 'Considering.' She sat down on the unmade bed. 'I hope you're OK with everything.

I know it must have been a blow, getting slung in the box right off like that.' She shook her head. 'Jackie wanted to be sure – we thought we were off the radar by now.' She smiled at me, and the crease in her brow deepened. 'She probably wanted to see what you were made of too. She can be a bit of a sod that way. But it is her department.'

Lorry had on the same long skirt that I had seen her wearing previously, and a woollen cardigan that looked baggy, stretched out of shape at the cuffs and elbows. I shrugged as best I could in the gauze sling. 'Someone shows up armed and with a picture of me, I likely would have done it too. She thought I was an assassin or someone sent by the Authority, right? And I was supposed to confess in there? I would have confessed to it if I'd thought it was the way to get out.' Lorry chuckled and gestured for me to sit on the bed next to her. 'You would have, if it had been the truth.'

She ran another quick check of my shoulder and then lifted the dressing on my hand. I saw a row of neat black stitches in the flesh. 'No tetanus shots here, I'm afraid,' she said, 'but I irrigated, so you should be OK. Just keep an eye out that it doesn't start to go green.' I nodded. 'There are no shots down there either any more,' I replied, 'At least, not for free.' She glanced up at me and I noticed the caramels and greens that made up the strange marbling of her irises. There was more grey spun into her hair than I had seen in the dusk outside. 'No, I know that,' she said. 'But they do have the means to inoculate against some things, don't they? The utter bastards.' Her tone was quietly aggrieved, but she was still smiling kindly, tacitly, and I could see the criticism was not directed at me. It was bitter sympathy that she was expressing.

My eyes stung and began to fill with tears again. I felt like hugging her, or putting my face in her lap and crying myself quietly back to sleep. Exhaustion had left me too sensitive, too emotional. I bit my lip, caught hold of myself. She took a glass jar out of the case, unscrewed it and gently thumbed a waxy salve over the cut. It smelled of honey and witch hazel and stung a little. 'Yes. We're up to speed on the Authority's anti-breeding campaign. But, you know, it might be good if you talked about it to the other women during one of our meetings. If you feel you want to. We've reached a bit of an impasse on the subject.' She taped a new patch of lint over my palm. 'So, now then. What do you want me to do about it?'

I had been undressed, washed and administered to, presumably by Lorry herself. It was obvious that she knew my situation, as Jackie did, and I was glad of it. Sitting there with her rough hands on my arm I felt understood. On the face of it Jackie had seemed convivial, but there was something calculated about her manner, a note of restraint perhaps, that went with her position. The woman tending to me now had a different role. She was a healer. I realised that in her years at the farm Lorry must have dealt with every kind of female complaint, every kind of harm to the body. I did not have to explain myself to her or inch in to a difficult topic. I did not have to try to justify my discomfort, as I had to Andrew.

Since the regulator had been fitted I'd felt a sense of minor but constant embarrassment about myself, debilitation almost, as if the thing were an ugly birthmark. I knew others around me were fitted too, and on the surface they seemed unchanged and able to accommodate the intrusion. Now, in Lorry's company, the device felt exactly as it was: an alien implant, an invader in my body, something that had been rejected all but physically. It was like a spelk under the skin; it had stopped pricking, but I had not for one day forgotten it. And I was not wrong to hate it.

'I want it gone,' I told her. 'Really, I don't care how much it hurts. Just get it out.' I rubbed my arm above the blanket. There was so much more to say. I wanted to talk to her, wanted to tell her how bad it really was, all that had been done to me. I managed a short outburst. 'There are fourteen-year-olds with these things in, you know. And grandmothers. What right have they got to violate them?'

Lorry sighed and clapped her hands on her thighs, squeezing

the meat of them with her fingers. 'Yes, I know. Listen, don't worry. It'll be fine. I can't promise you a wonderful time while I'm down there, but I think you'll cope.'

As she stood I noticed a kink in the way she raised herself, a favouring of one hip. I had guessed her to be in her fifties perhaps, but now I was not sure that she wasn't older. 'I'll go and get ready,' she said. 'We might as well get on with it and get it over. You just sit tight.' She paused at the end of the bed, then took hold of the folded yellow cloth and shook it out. It was one of the tunics I had seen the Carhullan stallholders wearing all those years ago. 'Ha! Just like old times!' she said. 'It's going to be good to see someone wearing this again. You know what, I'm looking forward to it. What we need is some of the old passion back.'

It was not until the next day that I finally made it downstairs, into the massive kitchen of Carhullan. I was sore from what Lorry had done to release the hook and the wire, still bleeding and cramping a little. Up in the room she had given me a draught of something sweet and syrupy which made me drowsy and thick headed, apologising when she handed it to me for the homespun nature of the sedative and explaining the difficult choices necessary when dispensing their meagre store of painkillers and anaesthetics. She apologised again, and said she hoped I wouldn't suffer too much. Last year she'd had to remove a finger on one woman's hand after an accident at the oat mill – it was mostly gone anyway, crushed to hell – and even that call had been a tough one. In the end the woman had gone without. They used the old wooden-spoon method a lot. Teeth got pulled that way too, she said. But that was the nature of things at Carhullan. Supplies were limited.

Then Lorry had set to work. She'd been quick and determined about me, forcing my knees apart when I tensed and resisted, and she'd given me a soft rag to put in my underwear to absorb the flow afterwards. But still I felt stretched and scoured. I had tried to sleep for the rest of the day. She'd left another draught beside me on the dresser and sometime during the night I'd woken with a deep griping in my belly and I'd taken it and it had knocked me back out. In the morning there had been dark brown blood on the sheets. I'd bundled them up and gone down to the bathroom to clean myself, and I'd put the stained cottons in the old copper bath to soak. In the mirror opposite the tub I had looked deathly pale. It was odd to see my reflection after days of not looking. I almost did not recognise myself.

Towards midday Lorry had checked me out again, given me new presses. 'You'll do, but take things easy, OK?' she said. 'Let yourself heal. And I don't just mean physically.' I had tried to get her to stay on a while and talk to me, but she'd excused herself, saying she was really busy; a couple of the ponies needed looking over, and she had a sow to dispatch. She was also the farm's vet and butcher.

I did not want to remain confined much longer upstairs. I had begun to feel like a bird that had flown accidentally into the rafters through an open window, then lost its bearings and been unable to leave. Though I half expected her, Jackie did not come to see me again, and there were no more initiations or welcomes, no more meals brought to me on trays, just the muffled sounds of people below and outside getting on with things, signalling my exclusion. The second herbal analgesic had worn off, leaving me thirsty and quaking, and I was aware of how empty my stomach was again. I knew the decision to leave the room was now mine alone. Hunger rather than courage would drive me out. It was late afternoon when I finally found the desperation to move. By then the spasms in my abdomen had lessened and I felt able to face all those who must know about my presence but had yet to see me in the flesh.

The woollen tunic seemed strange when I slipped it on, like a rough borrowed shirt, an item taken temporarily from a friend until wet or damaged clothing might be returned. In its weave was a mustiness, and the lingering scent of someone else – I did not know who – perhaps the last person to have worn it, whenever that was. But it was comforting to have been given it, and as I fastened its ties in a knot at my back I began to feel less solitary, less alien. I knew this was the first official step towards inclusion.

I came nervously down the stone stairs, barefoot and careful on the cold steps. There was a door at the bottom of the hall-way and a hum of activity in the room beyond it. I opened it to find upwards of thirty women sitting on benches at a long wooden table, taking a small meal of dark brown meat and kale.

They turned when they saw me and stopped eating, and for a long minute I endured their full scrutiny, uncivil and raw. I scanned the rows for a face that I could recognise – Megan, Lorry or even Jackie – but there was no one I could quietly implore to rise and seat me, introduce me, or serve as my guide in this unfamiliar realm.

Facing me were women of all ages, some with grey in their hair, some with long braids, and others with eccentrically cropped styles. They were mostly dressed as the women I'd met on the moors had been, practically, with thrift and a cer-tain bespoke artistry. Some had overalls that seemed extreme and invented, tribal almost. Others had panels and shapes shaved into their heads. They wore straps of leather around their wrists and upper arms, and stone pendants: their smocks and shirts were cut down, resewn, and there was a small girl among them with her face painted blue, and blue stains on her jumper. No one else had on a yellow tunic. The bright item I was wearing suddenly seemed more like a convict's uniform than it did my banner of belonging. I tried to smile and greet them but my mouth was paralysed. All I could do was remain still, silently waiting for someone to tell me what to do.

I heard whispering along the bench. Then, one by one, they stood up, as if about to change shift. I thought perhaps they were leaving, because my presence had somehow triggered offence, because I was not wanted here. But instead they picked up their knives and began knocking the handles on the tabletop, quietly at first, then louder. They looked straight at me and banged down on the wood, and the plates in front of them jumped and clattered. Bits of food spilled off the earthenware onto the scrubbed oak. The knives flashed silver in their hands. The little girl leapt up and down on the bench.

I blinked fast and involuntarily in the racket. The sound rang through me as if I were made of glass and might shatter if it continued, so brittle and thin was my spirit. I was rooted to the floor, afraid to move forward, unable to turn and leave, not knowing whether to ask for mercy or somehow stand my ground against them. The drumming went on and on, and I felt its tattoo echoing in the hollowness of my body.

I knew then that I was nothing; that I was void to the core. To get here I had committed a kind of suicide. My old life was over. I was now an unmade person. In the few days that I had been at Carhullan nobody had called me anything other than Sister, though they had seen my identification card and knew my name, and I had shouted out my story over and over from behind the metal walls of the dog box, trying to engage their sympathies, trying to tell them who I was. The person I had once been, the person who had walked out of the safety zones and up the mountain, was gone. She was dead. I was alive. But the only heartbeat I had was the pulse these women were beating though me.

It was not until the first of them left the table, came forward and took hold of my neck and kissed my mouth, while the others continued to knock their cutlery, and when the woman next to her followed suit, and the next, and the next, that I began to understand what was happening. I realised what the noise was. It was not a clamour intended to drive me out or to let me know I bore some kind of stigma. It was the sign of acceptance I had been waiting for. It was applause.

The following morning Jackie waited for me after the breakfast shift, gesturing for me to get ready, and I hurried upstairs to put on warm clothes and went out with her onto

Carhullan's land. After my appearance in the kitchen, my boots had been given back to me together with my clothes, cleaned and dried and folded. I had the use of the indoor bedroom until otherwise notified, Lorry had told me, until I got well enough to handle something less luxurious. Then I'd be moved out into one of the dormitories. 'Make the most of it while you can,' she said. 'It's no fun dotting over that stream to take a piss in the middle of the night. Believe me, I know. I did it for years. And the other girls will keep you up gabbing, I have no doubt about that.'

I noticed the other women watching as Jackie and I passed by on our way out of the farmhouse. They had not been unfriendly; I had shaken hands, learned a few names, but for the time being they were mostly steering clear of my company.

We did not go far. My legs were still sore and I was light-headed from days of undernourishment. I apologised to Jackie for my condition when I had to pause and rest, but she said not to worry. 'You'll be right soon enough,' she told me. 'Back when I served, I saw people come out of the box and never get well. It kills your head. You're stronger than that. Keep eating what they give you. And keep taking butter on it, like the others do.' I warmed at her compliment but I knew it was too generous. At least once or twice a night the terrors of that confinement woke me in a sweat, and I would cry out as if still trapped there.

As we walked around the estate's inner fields, she listed the illnesses that I should watch out for, and could probably expect to get. Anything that brought a fever with it was a real problem, and I should tell Lorry immediately. Anaemia was a risk. When she heard I didn't eat red meat Jackie scowled and shook her head. 'That's going to have to change, Sister. I'm going to get Ruthie to give you liver this week. It'll do you more good than anything else.'

There were gastro-sicknesses occasionally – the outside toilets were old and bugs got passed around. I should clean up well after myself, she said, put the sawdust mix down after a shit, boil my cloths clean every month, and adhere to good rules of hygiene, though it would mean braving the cold outdoor showers every day. Some of the girls had warts; not much could be done about that. Constipation; after four days something had to be done about this. There was a bit of cockie about, she said – I did not know what she meant but I made a note to ask Lorry later. Women had thrush. There were ringworms. Parasites. I'd get giardiasis if I drank anything other than water piped from the well. Even then it might happen. It was an inconvenience. But eventually I'd be immune, she said.

We crossed the soft earth furrows. The small irregular trees I had been marched past on entering Carhullan were sago palms; they thrived better in the new humidity of the summer than the traditional plants did, Jackie told me. Corn and rye too. There had been years when the wheat crop had failed completely, and they had been hard years to endure. The oats and the potatoes seemed to manage in the wet conditions. These were the farm staples.

We collected a batch of eggs from the quail coops, then ventured a little way out onto the fell, and Jackie showed me how to set the hillside snares at the lips of the burrows. 'Can't eat rabbits too often,' she said. 'Not enough nutrition in the buggers to do you any good – but they're OK for filling up the gut now and then, and that's half the battle won. They make you fart like nobody's business, the table empties pretty quickly on smoor night, I can tell you.' She said this seriously, smiled a crooked smile a moment later, and caught herself chuckling. Then her face altered, recomposing itself. She would not allow levity to remain with her long.

The next morning I felt stronger and we went higher on the mountain. The November sky was ash-blue and the clouds moved fast above us. The wind never let up on the fell. Though it was in the lee of High Street, Carhullan was still exposed. The shapes of the trees on the ridge were distorted; they leaned hard to the east. I turned to look at the farm and felt the air kiting at my back. From above I could see why the walls and hedges of the growing plots had been built so tall around the farm, and why the central house stood protected by its barns and pens. It was savaged by the elements. But the upland weather felt cold and clean, and I relished it.

Jackie wanted to show me the hefted flocks; the farm's first true success, she called them. They were close to the summit of High Street. As we climbed upwards her hair blew lankly around her face, across her eyes and mouth, but she did not bother to fasten it back, as if the feeling of it were inconsequential. Under her body warmer her arms were bare, slightly reddened and chapped. She was more lean than brawny and I could see that for all her middle age she was still strong, still vital. When I looked down at my own hands they seemed pale in comparison, and starkly veined.

I fought for breath as she talked. 'The lambs are threatened by seagulls now as well as the corbies,' she said, 'even this far inland. They come and pluck out their eyes and their arseholes, anything soft they can get hold of. There are no fish for them to catch, so the bastards come for my heafs. I have to sit up here in lambing season and scare them off. I'm a bloody scarecrow, Sister, that's what I am.' Her voice was not loud, but it carried well outside, and even in the strong breeze, with me falling behind, I could hear every word.

We were heading into a small half-valley tucked away at the bottom of the ridge. I caught up with her. 'Sister, you see that river over there?' she asked me. Her arm was raised, indicating a small waterway ahead. I nodded. 'That's Swinnel Beck. It feeds the mill further down. I once saw a hare get stranded on a piece of ground in the middle. It was grazing there and then it started to rain like murder, a really bad flash rain, you know the kind we get now. The thing froze right where it was. It didn't move. And the water rose up so fast it cut it off from the banks.'

She paused, then spat on the ground and wiped her mouth. 'Christ! I've got a bad stomach today. It's all Ruthie's bloody garlic. She goes howking through the woods for the wild stuff.

That crazy bitch thinks it keeps us protected from everything on the planet and douses the scran with it any chance she gets.' She held a hand to her chest. 'I need some goat's milk or something to settle myself. Come on, let's away back.' She turned on her heels, abandoning the walk. 'What about the sheep?' I asked her. 'We'll do it tomorrow,' she called over her shoulder. I followed after her, back down the slopes. 'So what happened to the hare? Did it drown?' She glanced back at me. 'No, no, it did not, Sister. It swam to the banks and got the fuck out. All animals can swim if they have to.'

We walked on a few more paces, with her a little in front. The mountain air was buffeting past us. Suddenly she swung round and I almost walked into her. She put a hand on my shoulder and leant forward as if pushing me away. Her eyes were rocking with water. 'There are girls here in love with me,' she said. 'I only have to put my hand on them and they want to lick me out. I can't even look at them.' She cocked her head to the side and squinted back towards the river, and I passed out of her focus. I could feel my face burning. I did not know why she had chosen to say this to me, or what to say to her in reply. I did not know why she left her hand on my shoulder so long. Her eyes, usually oily and flammable, were glassy and clear. There were times I'd felt sure her temper was about to ignite, though it never had. Now she looked rinsed of her energy. I said nothing and waited for her to snap back to life, knowing she could disarm me as suddenly as she could make me her ally.

On the way back to the farmhouse we passed through the paddocks and stopped to stroke the manes of the ponies, and the deathliness seemed to leave her. 'There's no written constitution here,' she said, rubbing behind the ears of a small brown mare. 'We thought about it for a while, when Vee was alive, setting out something formal. But it wouldn't have worked in the end. We'd have been paralysed by it, I'm sure of that. Constitutions are hard to change. And we're going to have to change.' Her fingers worked through the mane, pulling out the tangled knots. 'I can't say that I didn't expect I'd have to fall back on myself during all this. People might think I'm an extremist, but it's for everyone's sake. They've not tried to cut my throat yet.'

She laughed her low inward laugh, swung a leg up onto the pony and mounted it. I watched as she heeled the mare gently in the flank and took off at a brisk canter across the field. She rode without much grace, her back slouched over slightly and her legs drooping long. Travellers at the horse-fairs in my youth had ridden with postures similar to hers, I remembered, bareback and untidy, but with similar control.

She turned the animal about a few times as if testing it, and brought it back. 'Cumbrian fell pony,' she called to me. 'Bonny, eh? They're the hardiest of all the breeds. They're even tough enough for me. It's how we get to the towns when we go down on rec. Saves diesel. And they like a good run out across the tops.' For a moment she looked as if she might be about to spur the pony into a gallop, but she reined the animal in with her knees and slid off, then bent down and felt along the length of one of its legs.

I knew she was not trying particularly to impress me, but right then her capabilities seemed unlimited. I felt that if she told the mountain we were standing on to get up and move it would. There was something remarkable about her company, electric almost. I wondered if that sensation would ever fade, if one day she might walk into the room as just an ordinary woman. I knew it was unlikely. The other women responded to her with respect; I could see it. As she checked over the animal I tried to picture her as a gentler woman, less martial, less dominant, before she had enlisted, or as Veronique's partner. But I could imagine no other woman than the one in front of me.

'You've seen the girls out training, haven't you?' she asked. 'That's my unit. It's what they've chosen to do, and they're good at it. There are some here who disapprove of us having a defence council. It'll get talked about in the meetings – you'll see. We all get along though, at the end of the day. Everyone has a specific role in this joint. In the copse. Or the dairy. Or the fishery. Each to her own corner of expertise. We're a bit like a monastery that way.' She snorted. 'But not in other ways. Now, let's go, I need that milk.'

She did not try to describe Carhullan as any kind of Utopia. Even on my first day in the house, when she had referred to Shangri-La as I lay recovering in bed, it had been with a note of irony. She was visibly proud of the place. But I wondered how much she felt she might have failed in her original plan, how much she might have had to compromise. Perhaps she had tried to leave behind her past, as the others had, and found that she could not, that even in this most remote of places she could not escape human conflicts. She excelled in managing them. I wondered how much the absence of her partner had affected her. I did not understand her grief, with its dark humours, its tripwires and awkwardness, but I knew she must have suffered in the bereavement.

I waited for her to finish with the pony. I reached out and put my hand on the forelock of the creature and it nudged against me. Its coat was coarse and greasy, but it smelled sweet and there was something pleasant about the odour, something reassuring.

She did not come for me the next morning; nor the one after. I was disappointed. Instead of walking with her, I hung round the kitchen, helping Ruth and a woman called Sonnelle prepare the evening's food. I drained the bowls of Carlins that had been soaking overnight and tipped them into a huge cast-iron pan on the stove, ready to boil. Their black eyes shone. I'd not eaten them since I was a child. The stitches in my hand had begun to itch and feel tight, and when the cooks were done with me I went to find Lorry and she took them out with a pair of scissors. I did not know where Jackie had gone, or what she was doing, and when she found me the following day she did not say anything about her absence, merely continued familiarising me with the farm's layout and calendar. Much of it revolved around food, growing it, harvesting it, consuming it.

We entered the soft air of the greenhouse. The panes had crosses taped over them to keep the cracked glass in place. On the building's roof were three solar panels, and the interior was warmed by a circulating hot-water system. It had cost a fortune back when she bought it all, Jackie said. But it had been worth it. The women ate tomatoes from May to September. There were soft fruits that came out of season, soya beans and citrus. 'The Victorians called places like this forcing houses,' she said. 'It's not hard to learn from the past and apply it to the present, Sister. That's all we've done.' In the corner of the structure, a woman was bending down behind a rack of seedlings. She righted herself and smiled at us. Her pale haunting eyes were familiar. 'This is Benna. My green-fingered cousin. What would I do without her?' 'You'd get rickets,' the woman replied, and Jackie smiled.

In the stone outbuildings hung racks of smoked char and trout, sides of beef, mutton, venison, and pork. There were straw drays of eggs. They tried not to waste too many bullets on the local deer, Jackie told me. Usually that meant her or Megan or one or two others went after them in the winter, when they were easier to pick off. Whichever sharpshooter got the kill also got the tongue, prepared in vinegar and thyme by Ruthie. 'It puts a spring in your step,' Jackie said, rocking up onto her toes. 'Come on, I'll show you.'

We crossed the courtyard into another small stone building. It was the slaughter room. Lorry was already inside, steeling a blade and preparing to skin a deer. It hung from its bound back legs on an iron hook, limp through its full length, a young hind. I put my hand on the fleece of its belly. The body was vaguely warm. There was the coppery smell of blood lingering in the enclosure and the fust of animal hide. It was all done too quickly to turn my stomach, a few fast shaves of the bowing knife, a hissing cleft, the pale blue and burgundy sacks of organs removed from the cavity of its belly and dumped into a bucket. Only the undigested grassy cud bothered me, its green fronds twisted together and steaming on the cool stone floor.

Lorry took out the tongue and gave it to Jackie, who placed it on the scored game table, took up a smaller knife and slit it neatly in half. She pinched the scrap and put it into her mouth. Lorry shook her head. 'I take it you got this one, then,' I said. Jackie swallowed. 'I did,' she replied. 'But it was your Number Five that dropped it. I thought the mechanism might have fused, but it's cleaned up all right. Good scour and a bit of oil. So. Go on. Fair's fair.' Her mouth lifted at its good side but she held her poise. The invitation was serious. I looked down at the puckered strip of meat on the marble slab. I knew if I thought about it too long I'd never manage it. Whatever minor challenge was being issued, I did not want to fail.

The tongue was softer than I thought it would be and tasted of soil. I did not chew but forced it down whole. My throat made a clucking sound and I brought my fist to my lips. The two women laughed loudly and Jackie took hold of my elbows and shook me. 'Hell's tits! Revolting, isn't it?' She reached into a side pocket of her fatigues and took out a hip flask. 'Here. Quick. Better give it some alcohol before it starts tasting your breakfast.' Lorry laughed harder and leaned on the red-smeared marble for support. I felt my stomach pitch and I shook my head and walked into the fresh air of the courtyard.

It was not just game that was hunted at Carhullan. Crayfish and snails were collected from under the beck rocks and the garden's leaves. A local delicacy, I was told. They were fried with butter and garlic on the big griddle of the range. The vegetable plots were extensive. They were tended every day by a group of women who were more worried about insect netting than anything else they ever had been in their lives, Jackie said. And they were happier for it.

What was not taken and used fresh was pickled or dried, preserved for the harsher months when less was growing. Nothing edible in the vicinity went unharvested. Nothing was wasted. There were full casks of autumn nuts, apples, and mushrooms. The glass jars on the larder shelves looked old and domestic – saved from the time before the mass importation began. There was a small dairy where the milk was strained, separated, and churned, made into cheese and butter. Nearby, in the meadows, were the beehives. The honey was speckled with black. It tasted floral with a slightly tropical note from the gorse blossom and the heather. Lorry used it as a mild antiseptic, I discovered, and when it was available the royal jelly was divvied up among everyone. Meals were small and basic, but mostly they managed, Jackie told me.

The driest of the sheds contained salt and sugar, oils and seeds, provisions brought up in great quantities before the place became autonomous and sustainable, though some of the containers looked new and when I saw them I began to suspect that Jackie's visits to the town were perhaps raids, and that she lifted items out from under the Authority's nose from time to time. In the terrace quarters we had been told that our rations were low because of stealing that had gone on while the food was en route, but no more details were ever given out. When I told Jackie this she said the first rule of population control was that enemies of the state had to be played down, never described as a serious threat. Otherwise people might get ideas. Though the Authority seemed forceful and despotic, with the bulk of the army gone the country was weak. It would only take a small uprising to punch holes in the fabric of government, she said.

The crates of fruit were laid out carefully, with none of the pieces touching, so that blight and mould could not spread. Anything rotten would be given to the animals, or composted. It was a serious and honest existence at the farm. There was no external support system. Carhullan had burned its bridges the day the women failed to show up for the Civil Reorganisation. They were on the blacklist, illegals. But the more pressing concern was how to survive.

One hundred years ago, Jackie said, I could have walked up the fells and found the same sort of industry as this, with the same severe penalties for mismanagement. There was a purity to the existence, a basic sense of solvency, that the country had long since discredited. And I could already see the satisfactions of such a way of life. After so many months of tin openers and foil packaging, reconstituted food and dependence on the foreign shipments, this was as honest and raw as I could get.

'It's incredible,' I said to her as she lifted the latch on the door of the largest byre. 'You own all this.' She paused before going inside. 'No. We've never owned anything, Sister. The lands of Britain belonged to the Crown, ever since the Norman Conquest. The government has always had the power to nationalise land, and declare it state-owned. It never did until now. Crisis management. That's how they've been able to move people into those rat holes they call quarters. The flood zones just got the ball rolling, made it all seem reasonable. A wet run for the real thing.' I stared at her, amazed. She shrugged. 'No one knew about any of that. And ignorance leaves people vulnerable, doesn't it?'

She pulled open the wooden door of the barn and it grated on the ground. A slanting light fell in through the narrow windows. Inside, under tarpaulin covers, were the Land Rover and the army wagon. The huge deep-treaded tyres of the Bedford stuck out from under its sheeting. Next to these was a substantial supply of diesel in heavy plastic containers and metal drums. I was right to have assumed Jackie Nixon had predicted the economic spiral. She had removed from civilisation those things that she needed to assist her enterprise, her brave new world, and then she had become self-reliant.

She sat on a drum, crossed her arms and pointed at me. 'I've seen a lot of what's gone on, Sister, just as you have. I've even been down to the so-called capital. It's in a bad state. You would not believe it if I told you. But I'm not interested in London. London's finished. We're no longer the nation we were. If you think about it, there's no central command. We're back to being a country of local regimes.' She paused, put a hand to her face and rubbed her jaw. 'Sister, you've been on the inside, I want you to tell me everything you can about Rith. I want to know exactly how the Authority operates. And I want to know where the weaknesses are.'

There were two meals at Carhullan: breakfast and dinner. And most evenings there was a gathering of some kind in the large downstairs kitchen. If the generator was switched on there was power for the CD player, bickering about whose turn it was to select the music, and if not, those with instruments usually played for a while. There were a couple of guitars and a fiddle, a flute, and an accordion. Some of the women could sing very well, Benna among them, and I liked it when the tallow candles were lit and the musicians played.

I had begun to put more names to faces. The otter-haired woman in Megan's patrol was Cordelia. Everyone called her Corky. I had smiled at her a few times across the room, but she remained distant, perhaps suspicious of me. Most of the women were Caucasian; there were a couple of Asians, and a black girl called Nnenna, who had been the most recent arrival at Carhullan before me. The rest of her family had been deported. The mother of Carhullan's newborn was Helen. Every time I heard a new name I said it a few times to myself in order to remember it. Katrina. Sil. Tamar. Corinne. Maia.

People came and went, to and from the dormitories, so it often seemed chaotic and crowded, but there were always routines in place to ensure everyone was fed and comfortable. The apple cider was in plentiful supply and it was wonderful to drink. There were batches of sloes from the year before that had been turned into a sweet spirit. I was passed a cup of the purple syrup. I soon realised it was what Lorry had dosed me with before taking out the coil, and when I smelled its aroma of cloves and berries, it brought back that memory and I couldn't sip it. I handed the cup back to Sonnelle and she shrugged and drank it herself.

The atmosphere lightened after the dinner shifts. The work of the day was done, though the unit was still on duty, and

Jackie posted a four-woman patrol every night to keep a look-out over the surrounding area. I found this out from Megan one evening when she wasn't on the night watch. She did not mind usually, but the temperatures had dropped in the last few weeks, and she was glad not to be out in the boggy dark, she said, freezing her arse off.

Megan was fourteen years old. She was the most confident girl I had ever met. Where some of the other women held back at first, glancing at me across the room, and leaving space around me as if I were a frail being in need of air and insulation, she was not so shy about finding a spot on the bench beside me. She shoved the women closest to me along the wooden seat and straddled it. Her arm rested against mine as she sat down.

'Took your time getting up, didn't you? Nice togs. I never had to wear one of those,' she said, tugging the strings of the tunic. There was a directness about her, but no trace of hostility in her smile, and I knew in her mind I had ceased to be a problem. Then, as she had done on the moors, she reached up and touched my hair. 'God. It's so fluffy it could blow off, like a dandelion clock.' 'Yeah, well, maybe I should get a buzz cut like you then,' I replied. She reached up and rubbed her own scalp. Under the ginger bristles the blue tattoo stood out. Up close I could see the intricacy of the line pattern. It looked Celtic. I wondered who had done it for her at so young an age. 'I had lice last year, didn't I? So, it had to go.' I pulled a face. 'Not very nice for you.' She shrugged. 'I like it like this. I've got a good shaped head. The Sisters are all copying me now. You should do it.'

I liked Megan's company and I was glad of it. She was tough and easy in equal measure. She was keen to tell me her story, and proud of her status as the oldest of the second generation. Her blood-mother had walked up to Carhullan, bruised from her father's fists and seven months pregnant, she told me, instantly putting my own journey to shame and confirming the rumours I had heard that the place had in part been a sanctuary for abused women. Megan's tone became prideful. Her mother had been beaten once too often by him, and fearing not only for her life now but for the baby's also, she had stolen his car and driven the breadth of Ireland. She had taken a ferry from Dublin to Holyhead and buses from there to Kendal, where she had had a cousin, holding a suitcase of nappies and a stuffed toy on her knee. Then she had made her way on foot, up through Mosedale and over the pass, to the Sisters at the farm. She had thought it was a convent.

She'd died in labour – this was only just before Lorry's time – and she was now buried in the small graveyard, by the Five Pins. 'Is that where Veronique is too?' I asked. Megan ignored the question and continued outlining her own biography. 'I'm multi-mothered,' she declared, and went on to say the women had all raised her among themselves, as a community daughter. She had been an experiment in a way, she told me. 'To see what they could do without the influence of nem.' 'What's a nem?' I asked her. 'It's men turned around and made to face the other way,' she said. 'Ha-ha-ha.' She delivered the explanation flatly and tonelessly, as if reciting a standard expression of which she had become bored. 'So, have you been a success?' She shrugged nonchalantly, and without shame or uncertainty reached up to my hair again and felt a lock of it.

She did not seem like any teenager I had known. But neither was she fully an adult. There were qualities of youth about her; a greenness to her personality, but she gave the impression of practical maturity, durability. I could see the strong influence of Jackie in her. She handled weapons with skill, I had witnessed it myself, and she had easily 'neutralised' me on the fell. But she was playful and open too, and fiercely considerate. At dinner she gave me one of the three potatoes on her plate in order that I be better sustained for winter. She was worried that I might find it too hard in the first year. It was colder up here than in the towns.

Two of her fingers were still taped together. 'That's from

bringing you down off the wall,' she said, holding them in front of me. They looked swollen and blue but she seemed not to register the pain as she retied my tunic. It was clear that there was no remaining dispute between us over my introduction to the farm. She had just been doing her job. I wondered what schooling she had had and when I asked her if she could read and write she looked at me as if I were an idiot. 'I'm not backward,' she said. 'I've read every book here.' I had not seen much literature at Carhullan – there were a few volumes on the alcove shelves in the parlour next to the kitchen – well thumbed and cracked through their spines, mostly classics. But Megan's statement sounded boastful, as if it had been some feat or other.

We ate our food and then she began to interrogate me. 'Which do you like best, prick or pussy? Everyone wants to know. There are bets on.' I imitated the blasé shrug she had just given me. 'Not much of the former up here, is there?' I said, and she grinned.

Megan was curious about my life, and my experiences in a society that she had never been part of. But she was not bemused or awed, or afraid of its ugly side. There seemed to be little attraction or repulsion to the outside world. It was more a question of pragmatism. What she had learned at Carhullan had been second hand and subjective. She had watched the towns from afar, and it seemed she had not been taught to despise or fear, or wish for some other way of life, some earlier existence. When I told her about the recovery efforts she described the government as temporary and misguided. I knew they were not her words and I was not sure how much she comprehended of the system in place, or whether she realised she still fell under its power. She talked about the Authority as if it were bad weather, something that had to be taken into account, and could be endured, until it passed.

If she had been created on a philosophical specimen dish then her genetic beliefs had been altered to make her more resilient and assured of herself, more companionable to her own kind. She had not been exposed to a world of inferiority or cattiness, nor male dominance. She was, in a way, an idealised female. When she spoke of the outlying world it was with disapproval but not with trepidation, and I could not help wondering whether she might be more vulnerable or more fortified because of it. There was something gallant about her. She considered that most of the women left down in the zones were in need of her assistance. They were like slaves, she said. They needed to be freed. And I had been very sensible to come here. She admired me for it. 'You should shave your head like mine though,' she told me at the end of our dinner together. 'That fluff won't last.' I laughed and said I would think about it.

Towards the end of the second week she found me in the kitchen helping those cleaning the plates and rinsing them in the sink. She handed me a piece of blue stone looped at the ends with wire and attached to a lace. She had on a similar necklace. 'You don't have to wear it if you don't like it,' she said. 'There won't be any offence.' I thanked her and asked her to fasten it behind my neck but she refused, saying it would be inappropriate and that I should do it myself. She moved back into the crowd and began drinking with the rest of the women. In the corner I saw Jackie watching me, a bottle of spirit stowed next to her on the hearth, the contents glowing in front of the flames.

Not all the evening meetings were given over to entertainment and carousing. There were formal discussions and debates that ran to order. There were at least two of these a month I learned. I could remember hearing some of the debates in the old Houses of Parliament on my father's radio. They were torrid and wasteful affairs, conducted by obtuse politicians, interrupted by jeers and barracking, and filled with disparaging comments. In the weeks preceding the collapse they had ceased to be broadcast and the public had been left to speculate about whether the dysfunction had increased and paralysed the mechanism altogether, or whether representatives were belatedly getting down to the business of trying to prevent the country's ruin. Not long after that, the Thames flood barrier had been overwhelmed and tidal water had filled the building.

At Carhullan things were startlingly different. Disagreements were expressed through uninterrupted statements and anyone butting in forfeited her right to speak that night. Women took turns to put forward an idea or a problem, one after the other, and then there was a rebuttal or agreement. Occasionally something might be put to a vote. The speakers presented their views concisely or at length, depending on who was speaking and what was being said. Meanwhile a hush from the others was expected. The room listened. Whoever chaired the meeting did so with a firm but fair hand. Jackie did not host the gatherings, but she had an almost presidential right to comment, to approve or veto. The influence she carried was quiet and pervasive. It was not that she out-argued her opponents. She did not have to. It took only a slight nod from her for an appeal to be granted. Usually she accepted whatever was being said. If not, her disagreement would be carefully couched and resolute. Over the next months I would find that there were only a few women willing to go up against her in earnest about the running of the place, or challenge her fundamentally on the nature of what it was she was doing with her unit.

The first meeting I attended, though I had agreed in principle to speak, I was granted a pass. I heard Lorry and Jackie discussing me in the kitchen the morning before as I came down the stairs. Through the open door I saw that they were hanging a yellow swatch of cloth above the lintel. 'Give her another couple of weeks,' Lorry was saying, 'until she gets her strength back. There's no need to rush things.' Jackie seemed less keen to have me sit it out. 'It'll be better if she's still sick with it. Better for them all to see it in her. They need to see it.' Lorry sighed. 'That may be, but she needs rest. She's still not sleeping through.' Jackie nodded, and when I came into the room she told me curtly not to worry about speaking that evening, and she left the house.

Instead I sat quietly and listened to the proceedings. There was a brief request for people to stay off the growing furrows when they walked to the bothies; the plants were being trodden down and damaged. Soap was being used up quicker than it could be made again. One of the dogs was ailing and might need to be put down. After practical business the floor was opened up to other things.

If Carhullan appeared on one level to be efficient and united, it was also fraught on others. I could see that there were old areas of conflict, matters that had been worried at again and again by the inhabitants without resolution. There were several men nearby, I discovered, in a lower lying hamlet on the other side of the valley. They were involved with the farm's running, but remained at a satellite location. Whether to include them at Carhullan seemed to be a matter of continual debate. How many of them there were I could not glean from the discussion. But one of the men was married to a woman at the farm, and I could not be sure where the others fitted into the scheme of things.

There were also two boys who had been born in the second generation that were now absent. They had been sent to the settlement at puberty, because of their sex. It was a startling piece of information, but I kept my mouth shut throughout the meeting. The laws of the place were still foreign to me. My heart quickened as I watched one woman stand, begin speaking and then quickly break down, saying through her tears that she wanted her son to be with her, that he was spending more time among strangers than with his own blood. He had just turned twelve. He had been moved to the settlement the day after his birthday.

The night I was due to speak I felt sick with apprehension. I was told that all the women would be present for it. And I could have the floor for as long as I wanted. I had been at Carhullan for almost a month and had met perhaps a few dozen of the Sisters so far, and though I'd begun to form relationships with some of them, others were still strangers. The thought of having to be articulate in front of so many people was terrifying. In the past I could barely hold up my end of an argument in front of Andrew. I imagined myself fumbling over the retelling of how the last few years had been in Rith. Or simply being struck dumb.

Jackie had said she wanted to see me before I spoke. She asked me to go to her room at the end of the landing an hour before the meeting. I'd glanced at the door many times on the way down the stairs but had not seen inside. Sometimes I had been tempted to knock on the door. But I never found the nerve. Since my arrival I'd laid down strict routines for myself, had tried hard to fit with the way of the farm, modestly helping out wherever I was directed, trying to find my skills, and not straying into any of the areas where it might seem that I was interfering.

Lorry and Ruth had allowed me to assist them in their tasks, and I had cut vegetables with Sonnelle in the kitchen, and cleaned the oak table after meals. I'd even learned how to paunch rabbits and cut strips from the aged carcasses hanging in the cool stone larder. Though my clothes were returned, and the tin with my possessions in, I still wore the yellow tunic over my jeans, and was uncertain about how long I should keep it on. So much at Carhullan was self-initiated, self-decreed, but I had not yet found my footing. In truth I liked the feeling of it, the rough texture on my arms, and I liked the brightness of it reflected in the windowpanes when I walked past. Every day I wore Megan's necklace, tied at the base of my throat, like a charm.

Jackie's bedroom was the largest upstairs and it overlooked the mountains to the west. Whoever had built the farm four centuries ago had fashioned for themselves a chamber of suitable status. When I knocked she did not call out, but I heard the squeak of a mattress and then her heavy-soled footsteps crossing the boards to let me in. She had on wire-framed reading glasses, and they tempered the hard aspect of her face, made her appear scholarly. I felt as if I had disturbed her, even though she had asked me to come. But she motioned for me to enter, and I went in.

I had not known what to expect of her private space. When I'd looked in on them, the dormitories were small and crowded. The bunks were sometimes separated by curtains, but mostly through the day they were left open, even if shared by two women, and they were immaculately tidy. The beds were made, many with matching khaki blankets – army surplus I guessed – or carthens, and the floors looked swept. On the first visit I had thought perhaps they would be strewn with items of clothing and bedding, that a natural dishevelment would prevail, but it was as if they had been prepared for an inspection. I did not know if this was on my account, whether Jackie had prearranged it, knowing that she would be taking me there that day, or if this was one of the expected standards at Carhullan. Military neatness.

Her bedroom was not as chilly as the rest of the house, though the window was wide open. There was a cast-iron grate in the corner of the room. It was empty and there was no wood stacked beside it. The temperature was still falling on the mountain, but it was not yet cold enough for Jackie to need the heat, and perhaps she never did. Every wall was lined almost from floor to ceiling with books. Where they would not fit on the shelves they sat in loose piles or were slotted into the gaps above the rows. They seemed to absorb the light and distort the angles of the room, and probably went some way towards insulating it.

Her bedroom was as tidy as the barns, but it contained much more. It was Carhullan's library. Suddenly Megan's boast of having read all the farm's books seemed worthy; I stood in the centre, surrounded by them. 'Are these all yours?' I asked her. 'There must be thousands.' 'Yes and no,' she said. 'I brought most of them. But they belong to us all. It's quite a collection now. You fetched nothing up with you. Do you want something to read?'

She sat down in the chair by her desk, pushed a stack of written papers back against the wall, and removed her glasses. She handled them with great care, folding them back in their case gently, as if they were the most precious thing she owned. I couldn't remember the last time I had read a book. Even though there had been enough time between work shifts – the only public television now ran during the hours of allocation and it was pitiful and full of propaganda – I had never found true solace in reading; I had never turned to it as an escape. 'Honestly? I wouldn't know what to ask for,' I told her. 'I don't know what I'd enjoy really.' She nodded. 'OK. There are a couple of things I'd like you to look at though.'

She stood and walked across the room, bent to one of the lower shelves and searched out a thick volume. On the cover was a grey photograph. I could not see what the picture was, perhaps a man in a long coat carrying something, but the image was hard to make out from where I stood. She opened it and removed a thin pamphlet from between the pages and then she handed it to me. 'Why don't you start with this?' I took it from her and looked at it. It was flimsy and old. The sheets had been stapled together in a couple of places and the words looked typed rather than printed. Its title was 'The Green Book'. 'What is it?' I asked. 'Let's just say it's a limited edition,' she replied.

Jackie put a hand on my shoulder. I could almost feel a current passing from her body to mine. 'Look. You know why you got the hood, don't you? Well, you'll never go back into the box without first agreeing to it. I promise you that. If you read this, it might give you a way of dealing with it. It might give you some context. And some company.' Her voice remained gentle, but I felt a flutter of panic in my chest at the thought of ever returning to the blackness, the stench, and the abrasive metal sheeting in that tight solitary space. There were moments in daylight when I closed my eyes and I could still see the iron-jawed woman carrying me off, still feel the rotting shrunken dog held in my arms. And when I woke from my dreams I sometimes thought I had not yet been released from the cage and I'd yell out in the dark of the room.

I held the pamphlet in my hand. I wasn't sure what Jackie was asking of me, or telling me to do, past reading it, but I knew there was a subtext. I felt she was again crediting me with more understanding than I possessed, expecting more of me than I knew how to give, and I felt out of my depth. She took her hand away from my shoulder, stepped back, and lowered herself into her chair again, folding the energy of herself away. I was standing above her and through her thin hair I could see several raised red marks on her scalp. 'Sit down, Sister,' she said. 'We'd better have a quick run over matters before tonight. There are things you need to know.'

Her bed was the only other place to sit, and I could not move to it, so I remained standing. I already knew there were tensions at work in the farm. It had not taken long to realise the smooth operation of the smallholding countered an opposing gravity, and that something separated the women in their beliefs. It was why the meal shifts always contained the same faces. And why some of the relationships had broken up. 'Is this about the defence council?' I asked her.

'Yes it is,' she said. 'But it's not just about that. Listen, the beauty up here is that we can disagree, we have the space, we have the time. And we do disagree, Sister. Especially when it comes to the outside world.' She sighed and crossed an ankle over her thigh, held the knotted laces of her boot. 'But I don't blame the Sisters for shutting it out. Truly, I don't. They've come up here to make a better life, and not make the same mistakes. They've . . . Let's say they've washed their hands of the past.'

Her expression darkened. 'Fine. Yes. Women were treated like cunts back down there. Like second-class citizens and sex objects. They were underpaid, under-appreciated. Trust me, I know all about being told you aren't suitable for a job. Fifty per cent of the world's female population was getting raped, the fanatics had the rest bound up in black. We were all arguing over how women should look and dress, not over basic rights. And in this country, women have treated each other just as poorly. Fighting like cats and dogs. Competing for men. Eating our own young. No solidarity. No respect. No grace, if you want to call it that.'

She let go of her bootlace and spread her arms wide. 'And here, we'll we've more or less cracked it, haven't we? Everyone's employed. No one's made to kneel in a separate church. No one's getting held down at bayonet point. We're breeding. We're free. Why would anyone want to risk this, Sister?' I gave a small brief nod, but I don't think Jackie noticed. 'And the government down there now? Well, it would be madness to interfere with it and draw attention to what we've got here, wouldn't it? Sheer madness. Too much of a risk. What possible kind of campaign could we run? Surely it's better to just bolt the door. Hole the fuck up. And pray to be left alone.'

There was a smile on her face. It was not derisive but it seemed somehow mannered, and patronising, as if she were acknowledging a moderate and rudimentary opinion presented by a child, like the reciting of a basic commandment: *Thou shall not kill.* Her sympathy was so great it almost looked like disappointment.

Suddenly, she leant forward on the chair. 'What do you think, Sister? Do women have it in them to fight if they need to? Or is that the province of men? Are we innately pacifist? A softer sex? Do we have to submit to survive?' I was still standing in the middle of the room. I felt the air around me, wide and open at my sides, and wished I had something solid to touch. 'Yes, of course we have it in us,' I said. 'Ah. Attacking or defending though?' I frowned and thought for a moment. I could not tell if she was seriously engaging with me, or just warming me up for what might occur in the kitchen. 'Both,' I said. 'But it depends what scale it's on. I think women are naturally just as violent. Especially when we're young. But we're taught it's not in keeping with our gender, that it's not feminine behaviour. Men are forgiven for it. Women aren't. So it's suppressed. We end up on the defensive a lot of the time. But I think we're capable of attacking when it's something worth fighting for.'

Jackie nodded. 'All good points, Sister.' She sat back and recrossed her legs. 'Then let me ask you this. When you went in to get that tag fixed up your tuss, why didn't you fight then? Why did you let them do that to you?' Her brow was lifted and heavily lined. She had summoned up incredulity and I did not know if it was for effect or if it was genuine. I felt as if I had been punched in the gut, and I gaped at her, appalled by her ruthlessness. I had become used to her bad language, her often taciturn moods, but the onslaught when Jackie Nixon launched a hard line of enquiry was impossible to withstand. I could feel my back teeth clenching and grinding over each other, a prickle in the ends of my fingers. I did not know if I was upset or angry. 'What choice did I have?' I finally managed to say. 'It's the law. I was surrounded by the system, and . . .' I stumbled over my words, '. . . and they have these places where those who refuse are sent. I've heard about them.'

She nodded again. 'Yes, I know they do. They're in the old county prisons. It's a scandal.' There was an undertone of sarcasm in her voice. 'So, tell me. Was it fear that stopped you? Fear of reprisal? Fear of what else they might do to you? Sister, how bad does a situation have to be before a woman will strike out, not in defence, but because something is, as you say, worth fighting for? Weren't you?' I searched her blue eyes for compassion, then I looked away. The bedroom window was lit by the red western light of the setting sun. The withers of the fell wore the same vivid stain on them. I could see women walking over the fields towards the main house. I had no worthwhile reply.

'OK,' she said. 'It's difficult, I know. You think I'm cruel. You think I'm a royal bitch. Maybe I am. Shit, I won't lose any sleep over that. I just want to get to the bottom of why these things go on. I'm a dark fucking tourist, Sister, I like going to these places. It's interesting to me. I'm interested in what holds people back. And what doesn't. And how far these things extend.' She paused. 'I've got one more question for you – would you mind hearing it?' I looked at her again. She had one hand on her hip and the other was resting on the tabletop holding her chin. She looked restful now. The vibrant dismay and the actor's posture were gone. I shook my head. 'It's fine.'

'Suppose you had that old gun I've fixed up. Suppose you had it in your hand and the doctor asked you to lie back and open your legs wide. Suppose if you said no, he was going to make you. Would it make any difference, that gun?'

I nodded. 'Yes, it would.'

Downstairs there were tallow candles burning on the windowsills and the table. The paraffin lamp had its wick turned up and it threw out a buttery light from the hook in the middle of the ceiling. The wind had picked up; it moaned across the courtyard and rattled the farm's window frames, and the sound of it in the hollow of the chimney breast was mournful, its register almost human. Orange flames blew through the iron fret of the range, reaching out towards the wood stacked in the recesses and glinting off the firedogs. The dinner plates were gone, the table had been pushed back against the wall and the benches set out in front of them ready. Those who could not sit on chairs stood to the back or squatted on the floor. Sixty-four women. Sixty-five, now that I was there.

I took my place in front of them. They faced me, quietly, patiently. Some sat with arms around each other, or arms hooked through the legs of a partner. If there had been talk or banter earlier in the gathering when they first arrived from the fields and the dormitories, it had lulled the moment the stair door opened and Jackie and I entered the room. In the candlelight the women looked gaunt and sculpted, their eyes shadowed. They did not look like girls, middle aged and older women. They seemed to be sexless, whittled back to muscle by toil and base nourishment, creatures who bore no sense of category, no dress code other than the one they chose. Their differences in age dissolved against their bones. I knew they were strong, resilient, perhaps braver than I would ever be.

My voice trembled as I began to speak, but the words came more easily than I thought they would, and I did not feel afraid. The heat of the fire at my back warmed the red embers inside me. I knew they already understood something of the conditions in Rith, and the events of the last few years, but I talked about everything. The floods. The collapse of the market and the recession. The state of emergency declared and the Civil Reorganisation. I described the terrace quarters, the deprivation, sickness, the Authority abuses. I told them what had happened to my marriage with Andrew. And then, without knowing I would, I described my own humiliation, at the hands of the doctor, and the monitors in the back of the cruiser.

I took the metal device from my pocket and held it on my open palm. Then I passed it to a woman in the front row. She looked at it for a long time and handed it on.

After I had finished speaking I felt airy inside, and my mouth was dry. My forehead ached and I realised that I had been holding it in a furrowed expression for almost an hour. I rubbed it with the heel of my hand.

The room remained silent. I invited questions, but nobody raised a hand or called out. Then from the back of the room Jackie told me that a discussion was not going to be opened that night. It was the privilege of each new speaker, she said. During the next meeting, I might be called on to continue, and if there was anything I wanted to close with now, the floor was still mine. I thanked them all for listening. I half expected them to clap, or shout out something, moved perhaps by what they had heard, but there was nothing. Just the darkly cast eyes turned on me, and my hands clasped over my belly. It seemed anti-climactic.

The gathering broke up. A swell of noise rose as women filed out and began to talk among themselves. Those who had been sitting on the cold flagstones rubbed their rumps to warm up. Some of the women stayed in the kitchen, as usual, to drink cider, and Lorry brought me a glass. 'You did well,' she said. 'Not easy the first time, but you did well.' I shook my head. 'All I did was tell them what they already know. They've probably heard it all before. Their stories are probably far worse.' Lorry lowered herself onto one of the benches. I sat with her and drank quickly to the half-way mark of the glass. 'No, that's not true,' she said. 'You're of interest to most people. We all got out before things really deteriorated, more or less. It's hard to appreciate it when you're up here. It's still hard to believe of this country. I think some of them still imagine things are the way they were when they left. We thought we were unlucky when we came. But we weren't.'

I shrugged. She was being kind and I knew it. 'Anyway. How's your shoulder?' she asked. 'A lot better now, thanks,' I said. 'It only hurts when I roll onto it at night.' Lorry ran her hand along my collarbone. 'It's good it didn't break or dislocate. Never would have healed right without being set, and you'd have been left with a weak spot.' Her eyes in the flickering of the candles glimmered between brown and topaz. They looked flawed and lovely. She cleared her throat and her tone became more confidential and earnest. 'Jackie's picked up the Authority's communications before, out on patrol. She's good at tracking frequencies; hell, she's had years of practice at it. There are things we've known for a while. But it's quite another thing to hear what they are doing from someone else, first hand. It makes a difference.'

She stretched her legs out in front of her, under the long pleated skirt, and placed her elbows back on the table behind her. I had never seen her not looking tired, but she often stayed up late in the kitchen. 'So what's your story, Lorry?' I asked quietly. 'You mean why did I come here?' I nodded. 'Oh well, it was a long time ago now. I was in my forties, divorced, and pissed off at work – everyone in the health industry was back then. It was in bits, about to go bust. I was doing more bloody paperwork than anything useful.' She paused, took a sip of her drink. 'You were a doctor?' She shook her head. 'Nurse.'

She took another sip and continued. 'There was one little atrocity too many for me to stomach I suppose. Domestic abuse. I was on duty. Nothing I hadn't seen before. But . . . I had to hold this little girl together while she told the social worker her father had attacked her and her mother. He'd just got back from service in South America. He had Clough's syndrome and wasn't being looked after. Not a very popular diagnosis with the Ministry of Defence, you see. He was in the next room, yelling away; he'd had a go at himself with the knife too.' Lorry paused and then grimaced. 'Angharad, her name was. I remember it. Poor little thing. Six pints of blood she took and it all pissed away out of her. I suppose that was my tipping point. You just know when the world is about to break apart. I think you just know it, don't you?'

She patted me on the leg and smiled. 'I'm glad you came, Sister. But be careful, won't you? And be sure about what you want. Jackie is a brilliant woman, but she has her demons. She's seen more terrible stuff than everyone here put together. She's had to do things you couldn't even imagine. Some days I pity her. Other days . . . oh well.' Her voice trailed away. She lifted her glass and drained it.

I stayed up with her and a couple of other women. They were careful not to ask me too much about anything I had said, as if it were out of bounds, or they were keen not to pry. Instead, perhaps to show camaraderie, they swapped memories of what had been topical in the years before they had come to the farm. There had been a spate of poisonings in London. House prices had started to drop as the insurance companies refused policies. The Red Paper on climate change had been published. Funding for the new Windscale reactor had been approved. And another wave of terrorist attacks had hit. It was news almost two decades old.

I drank more cider from the flagon before it was put away in the pantry. After the tension earlier, it felt good to drink until I was unsteady on my feet and the evening's events blurred with the halos of the candles. A woman called Carla brought me a spoonful of her latest batch of lavender cream. It was home-made, she said, and it was great on chapped skin. She rubbed some on the backs of my hands, circling my knuckles, working the lotion in. The aroma of the flowers and the motion of her thumbs pushing into my palm and in between my fingers made me feel drowsy and loose inside. I closed my eyes and felt my head fall forward. After a few minutes I heard Lorry telling her something quietly, and though I didn't want her to stop she took her hands away from mine.

The tallow wicks and the paraffin lamps were blown out and the women drifted back to the dormitories. It was only when I stumbled upstairs to bed that I realised nobody had given me the coil back. Somebody had kept hold of it as it was being passed round.

FILE FOUR

COMPLETE RECOVERY

Megan had been right; the first winter was hard. The refreshing coolness of autumn gave way to bitter cold and damp. Early December brought freezing rain and low cloud. The farm fields were often lost in a mire of fog, and sleet drove down from the fells. In the worst weather the free-ranging animals were brought in to the byres. The cows seemed stupefied by the cold. But the goats did not care what kind of environment they were kept in. They chewed on everything in sight, even the wires of the farm pens, and gave plenty of milk. Lorry told me that a couple of them had escaped a few years back, and now there was a wild herd living on the other side of High Street. They were impossible to catch.

Jackie worried about the sheep most of all. They were not the main source of food and they were the most resilient of the farm's stock, but she was loath to lose any of their number before time. I watched her bringing them in with a couple of collies, the dogs weaving skilfully at the edges of the flock. I could not imagine how hard it had been, training the sheep to remain faithful to a portion of the uplands. It was an extreme and difficult thing to do, almost a lost craft, and one of the oldest ways of farming in the region. Lorry told me that Jackie had stayed up on the tops with them for months, like a shepherd. And the yellow tunics had been made from the first few shearings. The wool had been carded and spun, and dyed the colour of the moorland lichen and gorse.

By then I had moved out of the main house and into one of the dormitories. A low wooden bed was quickly made for me and I kept my clothes in boxes beneath it, much as I had in the terrace quarter. But here, among the others, I felt happier and less confined. It did not matter that there was so little space or privacy, nor that I had so few material possessions.

Each little domestic burgess within the dormitory had its own personal touches: photographs taped up, a box of effects, borrowed books, candlesticks, and sometimes there were little wooden effigies made from thorn branches and wrapped with scraps of cloth. I had seen these left out by the Five Pins also. It seemed a pagan thing. There was no real talk of religion at Carhullan, except within the forum of the evening discussions. If there was faith of any kind then it remained personal; a discreetly practised creed. The votives were never mentioned and I could not guess what purpose they served.

The women in the dormitory were cheerful and practical; they let me sleep near the stove where it was warmest, keeping my spirits up when the temperature fell at night and I hunkered down under the covers, half dressed and inhaling as little of the frosty air as possible. They would call over to me, asking if I could still feel all my toes or whether some had snapped off, and they made me laugh despite the frigid discomfort. It was odd at first, so many women sleeping in the same room, but I was used to hearing close-by neighbours, and in a way I was glad there were now no walls to separate me from my fellow humans. Sometimes in the early hours I could hear two women together, moving under the sheets, whispering, and I listened until they were finished. It made me feel both lonely and reassured.

I had known it would be colder at this altitude than in the town. I could remember hoping for snow as I set off, but I soon realised there was less romance to the idea than I had imagined at the cooling end of summer. The reality was brutal. There was little insulation in the outbuildings other than a lagging of hay chaff in the lofts, and the stone walls glowed with dampness and cold. The wood-burning stove was stoked up in the evening, but if it had gone out by morning the air in the dormitory was gelid and painful to breathe, stinging the inside of my nose and throat, blocking my sinuses. I could not get warm until I had eaten a serving of oatmeal.

At the side of the building was a lean-to shower, with a rain-chamber above it. A back boiler heated it in the mornings and evenings, but only to the level of tepidity, and I became used to washing with furious haste, barely bringing up a lather from the slab of lanolin soap before rinsing myself and running back out to dry and dress. I washed my hair as infrequently as possible, and tried to shower at the end of the day when I was already hot from work. The pot-hole toilets were bitterly cold. I'd visit them after someone else had been, while the wooden seat was still warm.

There was a tradition at Carhullan, a custom that had been implemented early on, as soon as the numbers began to grow. Each woman was allowed to bathe indoors on her birthday. For up to an hour she could lie in the deep green-stained copper bathtub surrounded by hot water and steam, undisturbed, and look into the mirror opposite. When I heard this I realised how lucky I had been to have access to the indoor bathroom for the weeks I was recuperating. It now seemed like the most luxurious place on the whole farm.

I began to wear the yellow tunic as an undershirt, with my heaviest jumper and a waterproof over it when I worked outside. I still did not want to discard it and the warp and weft of it was tight and warming. As soon as I was well enough to do more than clear the plates and help prepare meals I volunteered to work, and I was placed with a contingent of women shifting and storing peat bricks. Swathes of turf had been cut and were drying under long canvasses stretched on the fells. With the weather turning it needed to be brought inside, to be burned slowly and aromatically through the winter months along with wood from the willow copse. There were even plans to heat tar out of a portion of it, and refine the distillation into paraffin oil. It was amazing to me that so much could be culled from our surroundings, and that such knowledge was put into practice by the women as a matter of course.

I was happy to help move the fuel but it had not been my first choice. I had asked Jackie if I could join her unit. After our talk before the meeting I felt sure that she would agree. The day I was deemed fit to join the others sleeping out in the converted barns, I went looking for her. I found her feeding the dogs in the courtyard, and told her I had decided that this was what I wanted to do at Carhullan. As usual her smile was crooked, pulling the unmarked side of her face upwards. She shook her head. 'No, Sister.'

Naively, I had expected her to be pleased. She had given the impression of beckoning me to her those past weeks. And, as if to keep my interest piqued, she had left another book on my bed, Lawrence's *Seven Pillars*. I had read it quickly and left it propped against her bedroom door. Instead she seemed amused by my offer. 'Ask me again in spring,' she said. 'I don't think you're ready to walk through fire just yet. Not while you think you've still got scores to settle. Besides, they're going to want to see you pulling your weight here first. And I can't use someone who isn't built up. I can't afford any accidents.'

In her hand was a plastic tub. The dogs writhed around her legs, yapping for the food. She emptied the red chunks out of the container into a trough and they butted heads over the scraps. I was taken aback. 'Jackie,' I said, 'I understand what you did to me and why you did it. And I swear I'm not harbouring any bad feeling. I feel great.' She looked at me, through me. 'I don't mean up here, Sister. I mean back down there. There's no room for vendettas in what we're doing. You'd be a liability. Chloe could do with some help at the gullies. You know where they are.' I went away disappointed and confused.

The cutters looked up from the black trench when I arrived. They had scarves wound round their faces or hoods gathered into small openings to keep out the strong wind, and it was hard to see them properly. 'Need some help?' I called out. They were quiet for a moment and then one of them came forward. Under the wrappings of her head I saw her eyes, a rich sorrel, and the skin surrounding them was dark. 'Sit,' she said. 'No, really, I'm fine to help you,' I told her, 'I'd like to. I've been doing nothing for weeks.' Her eyes shone. She seemed amused. 'Sit down. I need to wrap up your feet. Otherwise you'll get trench foot.' I glanced down at her legs and the legs of the others. All of them had plastic sheeting over their boots. I sat down on the coarse moorland.

She walked to a barrow that was half filled with slabs, and took out two old carrier bags from the canvas satchel hanging on it. She came back and knelt beside me, lifted one of my legs onto her knee and slipped the bag over my boot. She tied the handles at my ankle. Then she repeated the procedure for my other leg. 'Got to look after your footwear,' she said. 'It's like a bog out here when it rains.' She reached into the pocket of her coat, fetched out a spare pair of gloves and passed them to me. 'I'm Shruti. This is Chloe, Katrina, Fish, Lillian, and Maud. They're all imbeciles. Just ignore them.' The women cawed with laughter, shouted a few expletives, and started lifting the squares again. Shruti picked up a spade and passed it to me. She held her hands apart. 'About this big,' she said. Then she pointed to a row of dun slabs under a tent of canvas. 'When you get bored you can help turn those ones.' I couldn't see her mouth under the tassels of her scarf, but I could see from her eyes that she was smiling.

The group of cutters was friendly. The women were hard working and used to each other, and they did not mind having me along with them. I liked Shruti as soon as I met her. She was kind, sombre looking under her work gear. She put me at ease and had a serenity about her that gave way from time to time to a droll wit. The other women always called her by one of her nicknames, Shrooms or Titty, and they teased her accent, but she gave as good as she got. 'If you bunch of white-bread bints have nothing better to do than stand around all day copying me that's your problem,' she would say to them. 'Take your time. Sister and I will keep things running.'

It was the tamer end of the banter at Carhullan. At first the jokes among the group seemed shocking and vicious to me; little was taboo, too impolitic or too rude, and they called each other terrible names, referred to their gashes and snatches, as if it was nothing to them to use such language. They insulted each other about their sexual proclivities, but no one seemed to take offence. I had heard the harsh way Jackie talked about the women at the farm, describing them as bitches and twats, and I had thought it was just her rough policy, but it seemed endemic to the place.

Shruti was about my age, and had come to Carhullan when she was twenty. There was a shiny patch of skin on the right-hand side of her neck that I saw when she took her outdoor clothes off for dinner. She wasn't in my dormitory, so I had never seen her undress, but Nnenna, whom I bunked next to, told me the disfigurement ran on down her shoulder and breast, all the way to her thigh. She'd had acid thrown over her by a member of her family, a brother, an uncle, for some cultural transgression – a marriage refusal or an illicit relationship. But this was not why she left her home and headed north. She had been standing trial for a revenge assault. The charge had been downgraded, taking into account the provocation and the state of her mind, but she was looking at fifteen years' detention. The Ministry of Justice had not managed to track her. Now, like the rest of the women up here, she had ceased to exist altogether, and that was fine by her.

It was a good group to be on the fells with. They worked outdoors all year between the gullies, the willow copse and the orchard, and they were bronzed and lively. Because I was new to them, and curious, they seemed to enjoy the opportunity to retell their stories, discuss old war wounds, and boast about their early misadventures. There were fewer victims at Carhullan than I had imagined. Often it was the women themselves who had committed a crime or were misfits: they had been violent, outspoken, socially inept, promiscuous, drug-addicted, and aware they needed some kind of system to bring them in to line. They all agreed that Carhullan was the best thing to have happened to them. That coming there was the best decision they had ever made. Not that they weren't sick of the sloppy hare stews, the arse rashes, stinking loos, nipple-pinching showers, and lack of tampons.

They were all in their thirties, but they had the frisky spirits of girls. They took up handfuls of the peat bog and threw it at each other, and got through the days of heavy manual labour in the half-light of winter with high morale.

I liked them, and I liked being with them. There was a camaraderie on the moors and in the dormitories that I had never experienced before. It went beyond tolerance or the absence of men. It was the sense of basic usefulness and dependence, feeling active and real and connected. Only half the girls were local to the county. The rest were from further afield: London, Glasgow, Birmingham. One woman, Katrina, had even come from Russia. If they had been raw or ragged when they arrived, abused or abusive, now, years later, they were older, reconciled, comfortable to be who they were. 'There's nothing like this place for rehabilitation,' Shruti told me. 'It's working with the land that does it. Getting back to basics.' The key to it, she said, was communing with the actual ground and not being divorced from reality any more. It was therapeutic; it gave a person perspective. 'You'll see, Sister,' she said, and squeezed my arm.

By the end of the first day, after hours spent shovelling the black loamy earth, laying it out, and stacking the already hardened bricks, I felt more satisfied than I could recall feeling before. I did not mind the cold air and the rain. Working in the kitchen had not been as natural to me, and when I had helped Helen with Stella I had been slightly uncomfortable, as if my hands were the wrong shape to hold the baby. I rested more than the others, my arms and back aching, but I kept at it until dusk, until Shruti slapped me on the back and said it was time for food. 'Think it's mutton tonight,' she said, pulling a face. The plastic wrapped round my feet was grotesque with mud, and the gloves I had been given wore a thick layer of black so stiff I could not bend my fingers. I looked back as we wheeled a final barrow load to the farm and admired the rich gaping seam in the earth that I had shovelled.

To celebrate my first official day of labour, the cutters arranged for a musical session after dinner. They took a bottle of Jackie's whisky from one of the storerooms and passed the dusty decanter around, letting everyone take a tug on it. 'You thieving mutts,' she said dryly when she came into the room, but then she waved them off. I had never liked whisky but I drank from the bottle with them. It was a little sour, and the smoke and soil notes brought to mind the earth I had shifted that day.

The accordion was brought out and a violin, and the women sang an old prison ballad. I had never heard it before but the tune was similar to the Border songs I had sometimes listened to in the pubs after walking with my father. It was lovely to hear and I felt moved by it, and I didn't want them to stop singing. Some of them sang solo verses. Toward the end of the song Jackie stood up. She was unabashed and she sang confidently, her voice strong and melodious, and for some reason I was surprised by it, not thinking her capable perhaps.

The lyrics of the verses had begun to bleed together, there were so many of them, but, perhaps because it was Jackie singing, or perhaps because the accordion and fiddle suddenly let up and allowed her to sing unaccompanied, I remember the words of hers: 'In a female prison, there are sixty-five women, and I wish it was among them that I did dwell.'

My sleep that night was as deep and as restful as it had ever been, and I dreamt of nothing. The next day I woke up so stiff I could not bend my legs. But I got up and got dressed. It was like that every day for the first month. I hobbled to the kitchen and took a place on the bench with the others and I ate the bread and eggs, the black pudding or oatmeal, ravenously. The days passed by the same, and only the weather changed, from filthy rain and heron-grey skies to cloudlessness and the white abeyance of frost. One day, on the way out to the gullies, Shruti passed me a handful of walnuts and dried fruit from the bowl on the dresser, and told me it was Christmas.

*

For all their differences of opinion and different roles, the women at the farm were a tight community, respectful of each other and mutually helpful. Within the work groups there were firm friendships. But those in Jackie's unit seemed locked together in a way the others were not. They had an almost unspoken bond, and they could often anticipate each other's moves, arriving in the kitchen at the same time, laughing privately about something. Even in the biting wind and rain, the flurries of hail and the squalls, there was no let-up in their training. As I stacked the dark, charred-smelling squares on the agricultural barrow, I could see the women running the ridge carrying heavy bergens, their hair and clothes drenched, mud caking their legs and sprayed up their backs. On the steep ascent some of them would turn and vomit, or stumble and fall, but they never stopped. They got up or were lifted by another and carried on. And Jackie was always with them, not beasting them as a drill sergeant would, or shouting slogans, but simply running alongside the last woman in the pack.

Sometimes the unit went missing for a few days. We would see them rounding the summit and then they would disappear. By dark, if none of them were back at the farm, Ruthie knew not to waste their servings. In the bitterest spells they camped out in the stone bothies on the top of the mountain range. They would choose the worst days to decamp, always in gales, mist, ice, or in pouring rain. The masochism of their regime was alarming. It was as if any hardship or obstacle was useful to them. It could be harnessed, turned to their advantage, used to build resilience, and they always met it head on.

The others working in the gullies told me that what the unit got up to while away from Carhullan was more extreme and depraved than the behaviour of the old British Army Specials. That what they did out there amounted to torture, either to themselves or to the livestock. They would often come back covered in gore, carrying deer heads and pelts. They liked to parade the trophies around in front of the others. 'How long have they been training?' I asked Shruti. 'Oh, maybe three years,' she said. 'That's when Jackie got serious about everything. You know, if they weren't on our side I'd really worry. But since they are, I sleep much better in my bed. Doesn't mean they're not complete maniacs though. You've got to be crazy to put yourself through that.'

It was true. When the unit returned after a few days away many of them were bleeding, dirty, and blood-poisoned. Lorry stitched them back up, and they would be given extra rations of food. There was a subtle rift between the unit and the workers. It was not expressed in hostile terms, but in small separatist gestures – a line at the dinner table, a preference for drinking alone in the parlour room. I supposed it was typical of any community. I saw less of Megan while I was out loading the fuel. In her mind I was probably in another set now. I wore her necklace, only taking it off to shower. Other than my wedding ring it was the only piece of jewellery I possessed. She teased me when we saw one another in the kitchen, saying I'd gone for the soft option, but otherwise she left me to those I was stationed with.

They still called me Sister. Corky, the woman who had brought me in to the farm with Megan, had told me then I would have to ask Jackie for my old name back, and I had not forgotten it. I could have inquired whether this was true, whether it was another of Carhullan's rituals, but for some reason I did not want to find out. When I thought of it I remembered too much of what had passed and I was content to have the others call me by a name they often used for themselves too.

Time passed quickly with the routine of work. The days were measured equally; by the length of daylight and the quantity of lumber or peat moved. I did not mind the repetition. It shaped me, and was the apparatus with which I restored my confidence. The days when something unusual occurred were more unsettling. One morning there was a buzz in the kitchen, rumours that information had been picked up on an Authority transmission. As I was about to leave the farmhouse Jackie swaggered in and took one of the small russet apples from the counter. She threw it up in the air, caught it in her teeth and bit into it. Then she climbed up onto the table between two of the women, her boots cracking apart the empty plates as she walked the length of oak. She was acting crazily. I had seen her behave theatrically before – she had once taken a turkey from the hook of the marble game table in the meat house and made Ruthie waltz with it in the courtyard before letting her resume her plucking – but I had never witnessed such flamboyancy.

She spread her arms out, the bitten apple in one hand. 'The King is dead!' she announced. 'Killed in active service – God bless his bloody bones. Long live the revolution.' The mouths of the women fell open. It was rare to hear news of the outside world; rarer still for it to be of such magnitude. Jackie knelt and kissed the woman nearest her, almost pulling her out of her seat. I watched as she jumped down off the table and left the room, the brown apple fastened between her teeth. I followed her down the hall, and heard her laughter outside the front door. It was laughter that sounded loose and wrong. There were the fumes of whisky in the passageway; she had either been drinking through the night or early that morning.

We were stacking peat bricks when the group of men from the settlement approached; five of them, bearded, and thin about the face. Walking over the grassland in the drifting rain they looked like apparitions, the ghosts of the navvies who had walked the region decades ago, tall and slender and dishevelled. I could see immediately that they did not have the vitality of the Sisters and I wondered in what conditions they lived, whether their existence was poorer, and how much they depended on the women for their survival. As they picked their way across the bields, I wondered why, knowing they would be excluded from the mainstay, they had come to this place. I did not understand their affiliation. Even if they had followed their wives or girlfriends, to have stayed nearby, whether through love or weakness, or even habit, seemed ludicrous. But, like the rest of us, there was no turning back for them now.

Already I had become accustomed to seeing only women, and it was strange to watch them approach our group and shake hands, and for a few couples to exchange embraces. Chloe kissed one of the men and he held her hips. Shruti introduced me to them. Their names were Ian, Richard, Calum, Dominic and Martyn. They had heard I'd arrived, they said. A few of them thought it had been a wind-up. Nobody new had ventured to the farm for years and they thought anyone trying to leave town would certainly have been picked up. I nodded but said nothing. Then, one of them, Martyn, asked if a load of peat could be spared for their fire. If so, they would take it back to their settlement. In return they would help repair the fishery nets, which had been damaged by the high water of the last month. Or honour one of their other existing arrangements.

It was a polite request. I wasn't sure what I had expected the men to be like or how the women would act around them, whether the tensions of the evening meetings, where there was often a storm of scorn and disapproval directed towards their gender, would translate into unease or resentment. But it was not the case. Lillian and Katrina gave them some pieces of fruit they had in their pockets. The conversation was amicable; it had an undertow of negotiation to it but it seemed there was an old alliance at work, and even some flirtation.

In their presence, the dynamic on the fellside altered subtly. I felt as if I were watching two species of animals drinking shoulder-to-shoulder from the same stream, aware and alert to each other, but only temporarily compatible. No assistance was needed at the tarn, they were told, but the group would help them bring back the peat when they were finished for the day. The men glanced at me and agreed to come back later. Martyn leant forward and kissed Chloe again. It was a soft, intimate kiss.

'You don't have to go if you don't want to,' Shruti said to me as they walked away. 'Nobody will care. And it's a fair old slog over the pass.' I shrugged and said I didn't mind. I was tired, but I was curious to see where the men resided and how they lived. And I did not want to be separated from the group. I had grown used to eating meals with them, listening to their loud, exuberant conversations and mock insults. Shruti observed me for a moment with her dark placid eyes and smiled. 'Yeah. OK then. You come too.'

The rest of the day the women worked quietly and quickly, switching into some higher gear. At about two o'clock the men came back. They had a couple of rucksacks with them, some old fertiliser bags, and a wooden shoulder hod. They fitted as much peat in as would go and between us we carried it round the side of the ridge, to a lower knoll, then up and over it.

On the other side was a grassy plain. It was flanked by bracken and gorse. We walked for about forty-five minutes, and as we began to drop down into another valley to the south I heard the sharp call of a bird of prey. I looked up and saw a single hawk turning broad circles in the air above us. It was a haunted stretch of land, windswept and barren, the bracken was dark red and dying on the slopes of the hills on either side, but the slender path we followed was trodden down, and clearly used often. Through the cut of the pass I could see another mountain range, in the heart of what had been the national park. Several rocky needles stood out against the horizon and behind this was a jutting mass of pikes. Once my father had probably told me their names, but now I could not remember. It was hard and rugged country. I wondered who was left out there, which abandoned souls might also be trying to survive away from the tight restrictions of the safety zones, lost from sight like us, in the mountainous territory of the North.

Calum walked beside me on the path for a while and asked a few questions about Rith, about oil supplies, and whether conscription had been introduced yet for the civilian men. He

had left for Carhullan when it looked likely it would be implemented. He'd not been down towards the town for seven
years. 'I'm a lover, not a soldier,' he said. He laughed when he
told me this and his gums looked red and inflamed. I was careful with my answers, more guarded perhaps than was necessary, but I felt a little on edge around him, suddenly uncertain
how to behave, and his grey eyes seemed too keenly fixed on
mine.

He smelled strongly of sweat and tobacco. There was little
to smoke at Carhullan. Now and then a carton of cigarettes
turned up and was quickly divided. Jackie had a supply of
Golden Leaf, though I rarely saw her rolling any, just now and
again when she returned from a training drill, or when she had
a glass of whisky to accompany it, and I wondered if perhaps
he traded with her. His hair was brown and collar length and
the tendons in his neck were raised and knotted, faintly purple
under his skin. I could tell he was underweight, that his diet
was poor. Even so, he looked healthier than the silverflex
addicts in Rith.

Martyn had fallen in to step with Chloe. Between them they
held a heavy sack, and from time to time they leaned into each
other and kissed.

The path dropped down and became broader, volcanic looking, a riverbed of dark glassy rock. Then the ground flattened
off. To the right were three small stone crofts with turf roofs. A
faint wraith of blue smoke curled from a chimney stack.
Standing outside was another man – older, white haired – two
boys and a dog. The youths came forward when they saw us,
embraced the women in the group, and then, after a moment,
turned and embraced me. I was startled by the gesture and
almost pulled away when the first boy put his arms round me. I
had never met them before but they seemed to accept me as one
of their familiars. They had something of Megan's candour
about them, her blunt affection. They were small and wiry; one
might have passed as barely ten years old, but already around
his eyes there was mottling and signs of aging.

We unloaded the peat bricks, stacked them in a lean-to, and went inside the largest of the cottages. The boys and the old man remained outside and I heard the dog barking from a distance, as if they were leaving the settlement.

It was more basic inside than the farmhouse: a single room, with a table and chairs, a small sooty fireplace under a hood, and two ladders on opposite walls leading up to alcoves where there were flat beds. There was no electricity and only two slit windows. The low structure was full of elongated shadows. Red cinders glowed in the fire's cradle. The place smelled of clay, charcoal, and animal fat, and there was a musky odour too that I couldn't place, something mushroomy and decayed, like a forest's interior. Underfoot it was soft. There were no boards. The women at the farm often decorated rustically, with flowers and green cuttings, bowls of fruit, or they made spirals with pebbles on the mantels and window seats in the parlour. But here there was little in the way of ornament. It was utilitarian and sullen.

There was an awkward pause and one of the men gave an airy bronchial cough. Then Calum seemed to liven up. He filled a metal kettle from a barrel of water and hung it on a curved rod over the fire, asking who wanted tea and pulling off his jumper. As he raised it over his head I saw his stomach, hairless and deeply corniced by his ribcage. Underneath, his T-shirt was faded and torn and there were pale yellow stains under his arms. No one answered him. There was another silence before Martyn and Chloe stood up and walked towards the door of the croft. The other women exchanged glances. 'Oh come on. No need for niceties,' Chloe called back. 'We're going to have to leave in a few minutes or it'll be dark.' The two of them disappeared and I heard a few softly spoken words, laughter, then the door of one of the other cottages opened and closed.

Calum stood looking at me from the fireplace. His hair was ruffed up on the back of his head where he had lifted his jumper over it. The bone surrounding his eye sockets was too prominent and his face was long. He had raw, equine features. I held his gaze for a few moments, then looked away. Somebody made a joke about conjugal visits and the others in the group began to move around the room, seeking each other out and pairing off. It was not a casual procedure but there seemed to be little discussion or etiquette. Katrina and another woman headed out of the croft cottage with men, leaving Shruti, Lillian and me with Calum and Dominic. I could still feel Calum's eyes on me, resting expectantly, curiously. I felt stupid not to have known what was going to occur. The back of my neck tingled and I felt a flush of heat. I wanted to stand up and leave, but I knew I could not.

The kettle began to shrill from the fireplace and steam rattled its lid. Its pitch carried on for a minute, and then Shruti stood and walked round Calum, picked up a cloth from the table, and removed it from the iron hook. She took it to a dusty sideboard and poured water into two cups and brought one to me. I took it from her, grateful for the gesture and the calm surrounding her. Lillian nodded and smiled. 'Well, it looks like I got the best end of the deal this time. Lucky me.' She walked to one of the ladders and began to climb up. The two remaining men followed after her.

'Want to drink this outside then?' Shruti offered. I nodded and we made our way to the door. 'I can't really believe it,' I said to her quietly. 'Yes you can,' she replied. She latched the door closed and we sat on a low crop of wall beside the crofts. I could see the boys and the dog further down in the valley, bending over in the furrows of a ploughed parcel of land. The elder was pulling a large container towards the edge of the field. 'What are they doing?' I asked, more for something to say than out of genuine interest. 'Turnips,' she replied. 'For the sheep. And for us.'

She nudged me. 'Look. Chloe and Martyn are married,' she said. 'They're pretty tight about it. He doesn't sleep with anyone else. Nothing wrong with screwing your husband, is there?' I sipped at the hot water. It tasted of iron. 'No. Of course not. Why doesn't she live down here with him though?' Shruti smiled again and shrugged. 'I don't know. That's between them. Just something they decided, I suppose. That's how they work it. Maybe he's not her main priority. They see enough of each other to get by. And, well, Martyn is a good guy. There have been blokes who set up a tent outside the farm, and then a week later they were gone. Not exactly what you'd call loyal or flexible. But I suppose it's understandable. Would you stay?'

I leaned back against the croft wall. It was uneven and uncomfortable, digging into my spine in several places. 'No,' I replied. 'So what about Calum and the others?' Shruti sighed. 'A couple of them came here with women, I think, and then stayed on and adjusted. Calum didn't. I don't know what brought him exactly, avoidance of the real world perhaps, but he's been here a long time. Longer than me. He feels useful.' She took hold of my arm. 'Look, they don't just stay on for the reason you're thinking, like our little harem. It isn't like that at all. They don't want to be in town any more than we do. They farm as well and we help them out because we can. Maybe there were romantic ambitions to start with, but not any more.' She paused. Her dark eyes looked almost apologetic. 'It's strange maybe. But up here it's difficult. You think you might be programmed a certain way but you soon find out you aren't. You just make do. And yeah, of course Calum likes it. I would too.'

She let go of my arm. We were quiet for a moment and I could hear muffled noises coming from the croft opposite. I did not know which of the women had gone into that building, but her voice was high and abandoned. Then I heard the man climaxing. The situation was still uncomfortable, but my body responded and I felt a bloom of heat between my legs. I pictured the occupants together, two faceless forms, moving steadily against each other, moving in a local and exaggerated way. I saw the man pulling out, hard and glistening, and imagined the soft slippery space in her closing again.

A sensation of breathlessness came over me. I had not felt

anything like passion for months. Since the incident in the cruiser I had not wanted to. If Andrew had recognised the trauma in me he did not broach it. He left me to myself. We had not slept together for months and if he had made arrangements with anyone else I had neither known about it nor cared. The women at Carhullan knew more about me than he did. Maybe it was the clear air, the days of physical exertion, or the sense of freedom and exchange between the residents, but here I suddenly felt ready for this part of myself to be opened again.

Shruti sat quietly, not saying anything, staring straight ahead. She was resting cross-legged on the wall, holding the chipped cup in her hand. I glanced over. Her dark hair was tucked in loose curls behind her ears. The patch of flesh on her neck looked shiny and faintly raised in the outside light. She was slight, fine-boned, but curved. If she had not been there with me I might have walked away, alone, back across the pass to the farm, leaving the women to their pleasures. But she was next to me. There was a peaceful containment to her, as always. I wondered what she was thinking, whether she was moved too.

Something about the tiny hamlet seemed rationally sordid, oppressive, and melancholy. It was unlike anywhere I had known. And I did not understand what had stirred in me, or why the proximity of others coupling had excited me in this environment. All I could think of was the movement of those within, the cries I had heard. I was no different from them.

I began to see images of Shruti in my mind. I imagined reaching over to her and unzipping her coat, lifting up the layers she was wearing and touching her nipples, taking them into my mouth, feeling the shape of them against my tongue. The dull ache in me intensified. It was gently painful. I set the cup of hot water down and stood up, looking into the valley below, and I took a few deep breaths.

The sky was darkening, but a band of pearly light edged the horizon. A low winter moon hung in the sky above it, shining with minor luminescence. It looked stranded and frail. The wind was cold against my face and neck, taking little bites and nips at my ears. I thought about how it would feel on my skin if I had stripped inside the croft, if I had lain down, naked and exposed in the draughts in the unwalled alcoves, and I imagined how a warm body would have felt covering mine. I was thirty-one years old. I was standing in a place that had taken millennia to grow. I knew it would cast me off without registering my existence. Suddenly I wanted to matter more than I did.

I turned and looked at Shruti. Her face was unreadable, her eyes drawn back. I did not know what it was that had overcome me. All I knew was what was impossible to return to, what my body felt, and what I wanted then.

She saw it in me. She stood up and gently pulled me a few paces back towards her, into the shelter of the cottage. Her arms dropped to her sides and she waited. I looked at her mouth, at the small, bowed shape of it, and then I leant towards her.

She broke away and led us round the corner of the building, so that we would not be seen by the others coming out. We kissed again, pushed against each other, and unfastened and lowered our trousers to our knees. When I touched her she was as wet as I was. Then our mouths were quick and gentle, our tongues copying whatever our fingers did. She broke off only once, to bend and push my jeans down further so she could open my legs, and bring more moisture out. The air blew around us, coldly on our legs and waists, and the sensation of it cooling the glaze where our hands moved was more erotic than anything I had ever felt. When I closed my eyes I could still see the white slit of moon in the violet sky.

When we were finished we pulled up our trousers and walked back to the front of the building. No one else had emerged. I picked up the cups of water, passed her one and we drank. They were still warm.

*

The journey back up the pass seemed much shorter without the load of peat to carry. The light was fading fast, and the rust-coloured bracken on the banks looked like a tide of scrap metal. It was a clear evening and the starlight was bright enough to cast some illumination on the path. On the way the women joked about what they had done. Lillian, the girl who had gone upstairs with Dominic and Calum, laughed when Chloe asked her who she had ended up with this time. 'Didn't have to choose,' she said. 'These two girls were very generous and abstained. Want to know what it's like being with two men? It's like being with one man, only twice as good. Nothing has to wait its turn. Except for them.' Her laughter tapered off into the twilight. Chloe seemed subdued. I had watched her and Martyn with curiosity as we left the settlement. He'd held her hand tightly, leant his face into her wheat-blonde hair, and asked her quietly to stay the night, but she had refused, and pulled away.

Shruti and I were also quiet. I don't know if she had been surprised by what had occurred between us. I don't know if I was either. We walked together on the path and a couple of times our hands brushed and once she took my fingers briefly and squeezed them. 'Look,' she whispered. I directed my gaze where she pointed. An owl was flying over the grassland, sweeping down towards the ground and then up. Its white, clock-like face hovered gracefully, while its wings worked hard and silently in the air. For a second I caught a reflection in its eye, a weird flash of yellow-green, like a battery light flaring on then off again.

My mind felt clearer and more focused than it had in months. I could see the details of the moor as we walked over it, the sprigs of heather and the pavements of limestone. I had not felt so sharp since the morning I'd left Rith. I was conscious of other life forces beyond us, out on the hillside, hunting with nocturnal vision, watching for movement.

The ridge separated our group from the pass. The others had picked up their pace, trying to get to the farm before darkness overtook us and the last supper shift finished, but I stopped for a moment and let them go on ahead. I stood still as they walked away, willing them not to turn and call for me to hurry up. When they were far enough not to hear I turned and walked back the way we had come, keeping my tread light and rapid, watching the outline of ridge as I did so. After a few minutes I paused and knelt down in the coarse swathes and kept still. I heard the voices of the others getting fainter and then there was nothing, only the gusts of wind hawing through the grass and past rocks, the low hum emitted from the mountains. I flattened myself on the ground and waited.

It was cold lying down but I did not move to get up. I pulled the hood of my jumper over my head and kept my eyes turned to the earth. Ten minutes passed. Then fifteen. The last blue smuts of light faded and in the murkiness the lamps lit in Carhullan gathered their energies and formed a beacon in the distance. Under my hands I could feel the beginning of a frost tautening the stems of grass, and the sting of thistles on my palms. I remained still.

Then I heard gentle cracking footfalls on the ground nearby, snapping down the heather root, and the wisp of fabric rubbing against itself as the patrol stole past. There was a murmured command that was lost in the wind before it reached me. I waited another minute before moving. Keeping low on the moorland I crept after them, pausing every so often and hugging the earth. I strained to hear the slightest sound and if I heard nothing I stopped and extended myself in the foliage until I was sure that they had continued on. Wetness soaked into the fibres of my trousers and they began to feel heavy on me as I moved. The broom and gorse scratched me when I crawled beside it, but exhilaration pumped through me and the sensations felt exact and good.

The patrol was only twenty feet ahead of me. The spines of a whin bush cut into my scalp and my wrists where my coat had dragged up, but I held still. We were close to Carhullan now. I heard a quiet clicking noise, as if someone was slowly turning the dial on a safe. I kept my eyes covered. Then they moved forward again and I could see the four of them silhouetted in the lights of the farm. I drew myself out from under the bush, rolling to the side. Its needles had hold of my clothes and I unfastened their grip cautiously, biting my lip as I handled the thorns, and I began after them again.

They had reached the courtyard gate. I heard raised voices coming from inside. At ease, the patrol went in. I had a wild feeling then, not of triumph but of satisfaction in what I was doing, the stealth, the patience, and being the last person on the moor that night. I moved to the wall of the courtyard and inched down.

As I got closer to the gate I could hear Shruti's voice. Mild alarm rang in it. 'She was with us, all the way. I thought she was. Didn't you pass her?' I heard another voice, Corky's, clear and scornful. 'No. You were all out getting laid. Your heads are full of quim spit and you didn't notice she was gone.' I heard Chloe chip in then. 'Fuck off, Cordelia. You don't have to follow us around all the time like the bloody inquisition. It isn't your job.' 'No, fuck you, Chloe, but apparently I do, since you can't keep it together. Now I'll have to go back out there with Lynn and find her. Which is going to go down a real treat, isn't it? You want to tell Jacks the probie's out there, probably with a busted ankle and exposure, or shall I tell her?' 'Be my fucking guest.'

Before the argument could escalate further I walked between the outbuildings and into the yard. 'It's all right, I'm here,' I said. 'Sorry, I got a bit turned around in the dark. That's all. No damage done.' The group stared at me, caught between astonishment and annoyance. Corky was shaking her head slightly. 'Turned around. Funny. I didn't hear you calling after the others, Sister.' She narrowed her eyes. I could tell she did not trust what I had said. Beside her I could see the relief on Shruti's face. I smiled to show her I was fine. 'Any chance of dinner or are we too late?' She rolled her eyes and jerked her thumb at the front door. 'If we're quick.' I felt her hand pressing the small of my back as we went through into the house. I heard Corky's voice behind us, and it was discomposed for once. 'A nice report this is going to be. I'm not sure who looks worse, you lot, us, or her.'

They had already begun clearing the table but Ruthie had saved our portions; she had five bowls sitting on the skillet of the range under a cloth. 'Carrot and ginger,' she said. 'And you can bloody well wash them up after. I'm done for the night.' The women all went to her and kissed her and made a fuss and when they let her go she left the kitchen, feigning exasperation. I sat with the group and we spooned down the soup and ate the leftover oatcakes, which had gone cold. Though the light-hearted mood had evaporated after the spat with the patrol, I still felt mildly elated. I apologised to them again for my disappearance but Chloe shook her head, saying it wasn't my fault, she just hated being spied on by the damn unit all the time, as if she was the enemy in some war game.

While they talked about the health of the two boys in the settlement, I tore a cake into pieces and swabbed the last of my soup with it. I wondered where the patrol had been watching from while we were at the village and whether they had seen Shruti and me behind the cottage. I knew it didn't matter. The women obviously made trips to see the men as and when they wanted; it was standard practice. Half the women at the farm were in relationships, and everybody's business was known: who was arguing, who was solid, and who had begun sleeping with a new partner. But I was still a fresh face, and I couldn't help feeling exposed.

As we were scraping out our bowls, Jackie came into the kitchen and sat on the bench a little way down from the group. She rested her head on her hand and watched us, her fingers massaging the folded cleft above her jaw. Her presence did not seem to affect anyone else greatly, but I was edgy and excited, the way I always was when she was close. I wondered what the unit had reported of the afternoon's events. She had not exactly issued an order for me to be celibate during my induction, but she had warned me not to cause trouble between the women. I wasn't sure how she would react to news that I had gone with them to the crofts and been late coming home, or that I'd given her patrol the slip.

She cupped a hand over her nose, rubbed it, and sniffed loudly before speaking. There was something about her timing that always seemed disconcerting and meticulous. 'Martyn's well, is he?' she asked. Chloe looked up from her dinner. 'He's OK. Better than he was.' Jackie nodded. 'And the slake's all in now, is it?' I could not help reading a slight note of rebuke into the question, as if Jackie did not wholly approve of Chloe's visits to her husband. It was Lillian who responded. 'Yeah, just about, thanks to Sister. We've turned another step in case we need it. Be better to dry it inside but we're full up already as it is. It's been good having another pair of hands this year.'

Jackie's pale piercing eyes ran over the group. When they reached me they stopped. She stood up, still looking at me. 'Well done,' she said. The comment was not directed at the others, and I knew she wasn't talking about the peat.

FILE FIVE

PARTIAL CORRUPTION

[Data Lost]

Shruti had just left my bunk and I was falling through the first stage of sleep when the unit ran the mock raid. I had calmed her down after the fight, holding her head against my chest, stroking her hair and trying to ease the images out of her head. It had disturbed her to see Chloe's face so bloody and swollen. There were few such altercations at the farm, and if Jackie had not broken it up, it would have been much worse. I barely registered Shruti moving when she got up. She leaned over and brushed my cheek with her lips. 'See you tomorrow,' I managed to mumble.

The doors were suddenly kicked open and before I knew what was happening there was noise and commotion, instructions were yelled out and the women in the dormitory found themselves lying face down on the floor with guns pointing at their heads. Confused and clumsy, I wondered if the Authority had arrived.

I could still taste Shruti in my mouth as I lay with my cheek pressed on the boards, and my heart pounding. A few people were whimpering. A cold shank of metal, maybe the barrel of a gun, came to rest gently on the back of my skull. Then it was lifted off. I could hear the baby crying in the barn next door, and the younger children who slept with their mothers were being told to hush.

The drill was carried out expertly, almost in darkness; the eerie glow from a hand-held light-stick was the only illumination as the covers were torn off each bed. Then the lights were switched on and Jackie walked into the room. I looked up. She had on fatigues, a thick padded vest with loops across its placket, and her hair was tied back. Her backbone looked completely extended, she stood erect, and her face was stern and remote, as if every person on the floor were a stranger to her. There was a haughty magnificence to the way she positioned herself in the centre of the dormitory, looking down on those held captive and kneeling at her feet.

The others in her unit wore balaclavas over their faces and black clothing. There were eight of them in the room, stationed at different points, holding short black rifles that I had never seen at Carhullan before. I could not tell who was who under the woollen helmets. I knew Megan and Corky would be among them, stationed either in our dormitory or another. They ran through the motions of what seemed to be a well-planned ambush.

'Give me a count?' Jackie said. 'All in,' replied one of the unit. Jackie nodded and the women tipped their guns down a fraction and filed out. She held up her hands. 'All right, ladies. Thank you for your cooperation. You've been very helpful. Sorry to disturb you. Try and get some rest now and I'll go over all this with you tomorrow.' She turned on her heel and left, closing the dormitory door behind her.

For a moment there was absolute quiet. Then people began groaning and swearing as they climbed back into bed. 'What the hell was that about?' I asked Nnenna. She looked distraught. She shook her head, rolled over and pulled a pillow over her face. I went to the door and opened it an inch. Out in the damp courtyard the cobblestones shone. There was nobody there, and the lights in the main house were off. It was as though nothing had happened.

The women complained into the early hours about the treatment and in the morning the yellow banner was taken out of the dresser and hung above the fire, and a meeting was called for that evening. I had lain awake a long time afterwards going over the details of the incident. It was the second time I had had a rifle trained on me by one of the Sisters. The first had been an empty threat, though I had not known it then. This time the weapons were of a different calibre; they looked heavy-duty and I wondered where they had come from, and whether they were loaded. I wondered why Jackie had chosen that night in particular to test us. I knew there was little she did without reason. I had not noticed the absence of those in her unit from the dormitory earlier on, and nothing had occurred in the main house at supper to indicate something was afoot. They must have gotten out of bed, I thought, without waking anyone, after Shruti had gone. Or perhaps it had all been staged from within. I felt less shaken and insulted than the others in the byre. I was used to Authority checks and searches. Instead I was curious about the purpose of the raid.

Breakfast was a sullen affair. As if in compensation, Ruthie put slices of ham and cheese out. No one said anything to Jackie when she entered the room and if she was braced for criticism she did not show it. She appeared pleased with herself. She stood under the yellow swatch hung on the lintel, eating a slice of the hock and some bread. Next to me on the bench, Chloe snorted. 'God, look at her!'

That day we ran through the usual routines. My work group had moved from the gullies to the willow copse. As Shruti and I sawed through the trunks I asked her what she made of the drill. 'Something's going on for sure,' she said. 'Even before you got here it was like this, not as bad, admittedly. They weren't kicking down the door in the middle of the night. And they aren't just playing around either, like some people think. Jackie doesn't play around.' 'So what is it?' She winced and removed her gloves, gently rubbing a blister on her hand. I took a roll of tape out of my pocket and handed it to her. I watched her picking at the end of it, trying to get hold of the edge so she could wind it back. 'Well, we'll find out tonight, won't we?'

Against the pale flaking tree-bark, in the low sun, she looked burnished and glossy from the outdoor air. I felt strongly towards her. It was not infatuation or yearning, like I had felt for Andrew and the other men I had slept with. But I felt close to her, an attraction that was complicated when I thought of it apart, but simpler when we were together, touching each other.

She sometimes teased me, saying I was intrigued by the novelty of her, and underlying it was a gentle worry. I knew it was not so very different from what I had associated with love before.

Since the settlement we had been together a number times, in the dark storerooms, against the walls of the nearby cave where Carhullan's mushrooms were grown in moss troughs and it smelled of underground spores and mould. We had gone wherever there was a private space, wherever we could undress enough, and not be heard. We had risked each other's curtained berths once or twice at night, and the outdoor shower, and there the cold had not mattered as I cupped my fingers inside her. And in the warm drying room of the farmhouse, with the women's wet clothes hung on wooden dollies around us, dripping steadily on the flagstones, she'd knelt over me, her tongue slow at first, then frantic as I pushed my hips towards her mouth.

I knew her body now. I knew that the burns on her skin felt like chalk. She was a soft-hearted woman and she had fallen for me. She'd looked after me through the violent sickness and aches of giardiasis, for ten days bringing me nettle teas and small dry pieces of bread, apologising all the while for letting me drink water from the croft barrel, and waving Lorry away when she approached my bed.

The temper she had once had was now held firmly in check, though when she came she clutched my hair and hissed my name. I knew she felt something more than just fondness for me, and I liked that. She had heard my own confessions, my account of life in the town with Andrew. But I hadn't asked her history, whether it had included the men at the crofts or some of the Sisters. Whom she had last been with, and the crimes of her earlier life, did not matter to me. She had killed, but it was clear there was nothing of that fury left in her now.

The others were in another part of the spinney, tossing logs onto the wheelbarrow and barracking, but she lowered her voice when she next spoke. 'Honestly? I think Jackie's restless.

It's always better when there's something for her to do, when there's something going on. She wasn't as hard-nosed when I first came here. She had Vee for company. She was more relaxed. It's almost like she wants to start again, differently, you know?'

I sat on a tree stump. There was a fresh smell of sap. 'She implied when I first came that the women should act different-ly, that we might need to.' Shruti laughed. 'Yeah, she implies that to everyone. Maybe it's true. But. We're still here, aren't we?' I nodded and bit the dry skin on my lip. 'What do you make of her?' I asked. 'Who, Jackie? Well, she's not crazy. I know that. No matter what some of them say about her when she's not around to hear. She isn't crazy. She should be though, she really should be. You're very interested in her, Sister. Careful. I might start getting jealous.' The tape creaked as she uncoiled the adhesive strip. I smiled at her. I knew now was my chance to find out more about Carhullan's history. I decided to press her on the one subject I had so far been unable to broach with anyone else. 'Nobody's told me how Veronique died. I haven't really asked. But it seems to be off limits.'

Shruti tore off a length of plaster, wrapped her finger with it, and passed me the roll back. She crouched on the ground in front of me and tucked her hands in the folds of her knees. 'Yeah, I know,' she said. 'No one talks about it. I knew you were going to ask me. That's what I get for being good to you, eh?' She smiled sadly. 'Vee got cancer. She found a lump. They knew what it was, straight away. But it was after the Reorganisation, and she wouldn't go down into the town and ask for treatment. Jackie wanted her to, so did Lorry, but she said there was no point – they'd just be turned away and it might ruin things here in the process. None of us are listed on the census, we all made that choice – well, you already know that.'

She paused, untucked her hands, picked up a twig and snapped it. 'They argued like mad and both were as stubborn as each other. God, the house practically came down around us all. I heard Jackie yelling at her upstairs once. She said she'd served her fucking country by killing as many sand niggers as the coalition wanted and now her country could serve her by keeping her nigger alive. Shit. You know how she talks. Well. This was one argument Vee won. They didn't go.' Shruti sighed. 'It took about eight months for her to die. She was in agony. Lorry did everything she could. She even cut her open and tried to get it out, but you can't treat something like that up here.'

She sighed again and blinked. Her eyes were bright with emotion. She swallowed uncomfortably and looked at the ground. 'In the end Vee started begging. For them to help her finish it. She just kept asking, over and over, saying if they loved her they would help her. So they did. They carried her out to the Pins, because she loved that place, and they shot her. Jackie did it. Everyone was there. Everyone loved her, you see. She was an incredible woman. My God, she was so full of optimism. Nothing fazed her. Not even Jackie. I wish you'd met her. I really do.'

She put her hand into the debris of the copse floor as if searching for something under the brittle leaves and twigs. When she brought it out there was a small brown kernel on her palm. She dropped it. I knew she was finding it all too difficult, trying to compose herself. She took a deep breath and continued. 'And Jackie . . . She kept hold of the gun. She wouldn't put it down afterwards. We thought she wanted to kill herself too. There was that crackle around her, you know, that feeling you get when people are a danger to you, and to themselves. When anyone tried to take it from her she pointed it at them. Even Lorry. It took about a dozen people to get it off her. They knocked her out cold.' She paused and swallowed again. 'I've never seen love like that before. Never in my life. I know I couldn't have done what she did. You see now why nobody talks about it.'

Shruti stood up abruptly and shook her head. There were tears spilling from the corners of her eyes. I stood as well, made a move to comfort her, but she waved me away and forced a smile. 'I knew you were going to ask me,' she said. She wiped her face with her gloves, picked up the saw and fitted it into the pale gash in the trunk. I took the other end and drew it back and forth with her. We worked in silence. I tried to concentrate on the task at hand but my mind would not cooperate. All I could see was a picture of myself, holding a gun to Shruti's head and the redness in her spilling through her hair onto the ground. I let go of the saw and stood back. 'That's why people put those little idols out there by the stone circle, isn't it? For Veronique?' Shruti nodded. 'Yes. Something like that.'

That evening, the meeting did not run with its usual smoothness and civility. For most of the day the women had been ruminating on the events of the night before, working themselves up about it. They were tired and they were shaken. Those who spoke out did so with anger, interrupting, chipping in over the top of one another, breaking the rules of the meeting.

Jackie stood beside the fire, listening to the comments of each woman who took the floor, and she did not object to the swell of voices, nor to the disorder. She nodded a couple of times whenever a new protest was shouted out. It was loud in the kitchen, and full of unrest, and she made a point of turning her left ear to the speaker, as if she was partly deaf and was trying to hear what was being said on her good side. It occurred to me that the scar on her face marked some internal damage. There was nothing of the previous night's swagger about her, though she still wore her fatigues and stood tall, with her chin held high. Instead she seemed every bit the mediator, collecting up a list of grievances as if she might be planning to pass it on to an arbitrating body. But I could see she was acting a part, it was simply another rotation of her personality. Her eyes were focused on nothing and no one.

I did not know how she could stand there, confronted by so many angry women, and not be intimidated by them. At that moment she was colossal, more incredible than even the iron-jawed woman I had dreamed in the dog box. But the mystery of her was less profound now. Before, I had wondered what had gone into the creating of her. I knew her stock, her inheritance. She was part of the old North, the feuding territories, and those antagonistic genes rubbed in her, creating the friction that fired her pride. And perhaps her time in service had aggravated that configuration, contracting with it, organising it; eventually making her unbreakable.

But there was more to her than regional spirit and vocational strength. In a book she had lent me there had been a quote, written out in her own hand at the beginning of the first chapter. *It is not those who can inflict the most, but those who can suffer the most that will conquer.* And I could see it now – the portion of her that had been immolated the day she pulled the trigger and took Veronique's life. She carried a piece of dead self with her always, and still she lived, and it was this tumour, this mass, that gave her system the supreme immunity it had. It was this that gave her a shield, that she could better blunt her enemy's sword, and drive in harder her own. She had killed her love with her lover, and cured herself of human weakness.

When the women had finished talking and the murmurs of discontent faded, she stood up, tossed a few more logs into the range and closed its grate. She cleared her throat. 'How long?' she asked. Her voice remained low key, moderate as ever, but the question was clearly audible. The room was quiet but for the cracking and spitting of the fire. 'How long have we got?'

When nobody spoke she surveyed the women in front of her. There was a resinous stillness surrounding them. They were all waiting for her and, if they understood the question, they were unwilling to answer it. Only she moved, bringing her hands from the pockets of her breeches to her hips. Her arms looked like skinless wings. 'I picked up a transmission this week on the radio,' she said. 'There's to be no succession to the throne. The Authority is working on a new land charter. They're setting up a commission to evaluate the current level of jurisdiction. In the next eighteen months they're going to sweep the unofficial zones, and readministrate the areas not under their control. They're going to come up here and they're going to take us apart. So. We have a year and a half before this place goes.'

Only Carhullan's children went to bed that night. The Sisters stayed up, keeping a vigil, keeping the fire banked and trying to manage what they had heard, and as the dawn began to dispel the greyness in the east, Ruthie began work on a breakfast that would feed every person in one shift. At first no one knew how to respond to what they had been told. There was disbelief, and upset. It was rare to see tears at the farm – ordinarily the women were resilient – but some broke down and leant on the shoulders of their friends and partners. Others drew back into themselves and stared blindly at the flagstone floor. And there were those less willing to accept the proposition.

The debate resumed. Jackie answered every question that was thrown at her, rebuffed allegations that she was lying, twisting the facts, or overdramatising the situation. This was not some elaborate and cruel hoax, she said. It was the truth. She called on those in her unit who had been on point with her the day the broadcast was intercepted to stand up. They did so and vouched for her veracity, relaying the same message, almost word for word.

I watched Megan, wondering how she would act, how she would feel about the matter, and about potentially losing the only home she had ever known. She stood to the left of Jackie and she seemed composed. If I saw anything in her it was pre-paredness, resolve, and loyalty to the clan's principal mother. If she was anyone's progeny, then she was Jackie's. I knew that she would follow her to the ends of the earth; she had been made in the crucible of this wild place, she was a daughter of its brutality, and the overriding influence in her upbringing was the woman in charge. After the news had been confirmed, Jackie leant close and whispered to her. Then Megan and Corky left the kitchen. Through the window I saw them exiting the courtyard, with rifles slung across their backs. A soft snow was falling from the sky. It was the first day of February.

Among those speaking out, Chloe stood and made an address. Her face was lumpy and there were bruised crescents beneath her eyes where Corky had laid into her. We had not got to the bottom of why they had fought, what had kicked it off. Of the two of them, she had come off much the worse. But her spirit still seemed strong, and there was a recklessness to her tone, a note of challenge in it, as if she had nothing to lose. 'So what do you propose, Jackie?' she asked. 'You've got something up your sleeve, obviously. You've got a plan.' Jackie gave her a measured look. 'I do,' she replied. 'But first, why don't you tell me what you're thinking, Sister?' Chloe tipped her head and crossed her arms. 'There are weapons here. Everyone knows that. This is our home. We must have some sort of claim. We've surely got a right to stay, and to disagree with the government's policy. It seems to me we're well equipped to defend ourselves if we need to. So. Why don't we just sit it out and see if your forecast is right?' Helen was rocking baby Stella in her arms. 'Yes, that sounds like the best thing to do,' she agreed. 'We could refuse to go. We could hold out long enough for them to lose interest in us. We're no threat to anyone.'

Jackie was quiet and though she looked to be calculating an answer, she must already have prepared it. 'I'd give us about a month. It depends when the American satellites pick us up, if they haven't already. That won't take long. Once they know who they're dealing with.' She paused and nodded, then went on. 'We're in a good position here, hard to get at. It's to our advantage in a ground assault. But we'd be on our back foot. And they could wipe us out with a single air strike if they wanted.'

'Be serious!' Chloe cried out. She laughed incredulously, but her laughter quickly died in her throat when she saw the face of her opponent. Nothing in its aspect was light. 'You think we're a small operation, Sister?' Jackie asked quietly. 'You think we're not consequential enough for those in charge to worry about, tucked away as we are? Do you know what grading we have? We are category-one insurgents. All of us, on the same hand. Finger through to thumb.' Her right arm was raised, the digits on it spread wide apart. She let the words hang in the air. 'No, Chloe. I'm not going to waste ammunition on a bolt-hole. The only real chance we have is to go out and disable the Authority's mechanism in Rith, rally the people there. And that is exactly what we are going to do.'

There was another swell of noise. From the back of the room someone swore loudly, and charged her with glory hunting, trying to write her name into the history books. 'You're not fucking Mao, Jackie!' She did not answer to this, but she stared down her accuser with formidable patience.

'Oh come on! Rally who?' Chloe persisted, running her hands through her hair. 'Those idiots down there who have been walked all over for the last ten years? And because a bunch of women from the hills tell them to? I don't think so.' Lillian backed her up. 'Chloe's right. People are too afraid now. They won't put themselves at risk. Why would they break the only system keeping them alive? If we start attacking the town we'll just come across as bloody bandits. It's too late, Jackie, it's all too late! That's why we're up here, isn't it! Because everything else is a mess. And we don't want to be part of it.'

There were murmurs of agreement. It was remarked with bitterness that the idea was impossible; that life below in the towns was not Carhullan's problem, not Carhullan's responsibility. Jackie looked around the room, her eyes tracking over the faces. For a second or two she stared at me, then she came over, reached down, took hold of my arm and lifted me onto my feet. 'Stand up, Sister. Stand up. Tell them. Tell them why you came here. Tell them you have it in you, and that you're not so different from women down there. Tell them you're willing to fight.'

All eyes in the room turned on me. She had taken me by surprise. My guard was down. My face flamed red and I was speechless, mortified to have been singled out by her at such a time. Then I felt a cold trickle of horror in my gut as I realised what she intended, what she was asking of me, the choice I had to make. Of all the women, I would be the first to make it, publicly and under pressure. She was affording me no luxury in the decision. But she knew exactly what she was doing. As ever, her timing was perfect. Jackie knew I was a guaranteed recruit. She knew what I wanted. It was why she had turned me down when I offered to train, why she had kept me waiting in the wings during the past few months. I was a sleeper agent.

I almost hated her for it, hated her for marking me out, and using me, as if I were a piece in a game she was playing. But I could not hate her. And this was not a game. There was some deep part of me she had reached, some purpose to me she had foreseen. Her words had always clarified my thoughts. And her voice was the one I had always been listening for inside my own head. Whatever her methods, whatever her strategy, I knew that I was on her side. 'Tell them, Sister', she urged me.

From the corner of my eye I could see Shruti, sitting cross-legged and calm, as she had done on the wall of the croft; as she always did. She was waiting for me to speak, giving me the benefit of the doubt. I wanted the room to empty, or to be able to whisper to her, and tell her what she meant to me, that I was sorry. I wanted to say I loved the goodness of her, the mild pepper of her skin in my mouth, the way she could forgive all those who had injured her, including herself. I knew that I would have to give her up.

I don't remember what I said. The words were lost to me even as I spoke them. I felt Jackie's arm on my shoulder, acknowledging my allegiance, binding me to her. I felt the flow of energy leaving her frame and filling mine, circulating with my own blood through the vessels of my body. She had always understood what my potential was, the apparatus she could work with. She had known from the beginning, when the old photograph taken of her and Veronique standing at the door of Carhullan was handed to her from my tin box. After I had spoken she thanked me. It was the first and last time that she would.

In the kitchen the women became sedated, and I knew their anger had diffused. Standing before them, I had become their conscience, their empathy, a walk-in who had arrived long after anyone else was expected, long after Carhullan had locked itself down and disconnected from the collapsing world. They could no more send me away than they could their old selves. They were not so far apart from the ones left behind and they knew it. I was the best argument Jackie Nixon could make for solidarity, for intervention, and for hope among the people. She had made a soldier out of me without even giving me back my father's gun.

She took hold of my face and kissed me, like the others had done when I first came down the stairs, and I sat back down. I was glowing, and the heat in me radiated outwards. I felt as if bellows had been placed between the bars of my ribcage and the coals of me blown into full flame. Nobody touched me or said anything. Not even Shruti.

Ruthie busied herself with the meal. A group went out to the dairy and half an hour later brought in a quantity of fresh strained milk. After the sago was ladled, and the women were all fed, the distress in the room seemed lessened. Jackie talked more of her plan, and the women listened. Perhaps it had begun to dawn on them that she was their best chance of survival now. Once they might have thought her grandiose and eccentric, pessimistic in her visions. Once they might have believed her to be malfunctioning. In the dormitories and within my work group I had heard talk of her aggression and paranoia, her obsessions, the chronic symptoms of military damage. And I had seen for myself her blue flinty eyes glinting with too much intensity when she spoke about combat.

But now she did not seem so touched by mania. I could tell those listening were less dismissive of her ideas than they might usually have been. She had revealed herself to be the realist, and the sceptics had been proved wrong. If the rest of us felt weary and wrung-out, the night's events had served only to invigorate and embolden her. It was not that she was wired from lack of sleep and exhaustive discussion, from the adrenalin of emergency. She was simply confident. There was now something commensurate to her capabilities, something which she was truly qualified to tackle.

I will not forget that morning. It was the morning of her annunciation, her arrival. In the squalor of the terrace quarters, missionaries had often gone from door to door, preaching, and some people had turned once again to religion for escape. If they could not be lifted from the ruins by those in charge, then they would be rescued by God, by his rapture. There were faith cards tacked to every lamppost and pushed through every letterbox; American-sponsored leaflets were distributed at the factory and the clinic, and every shipment of food was bound with prayers. Others went to the dealers, slipped God into their veins, cracked open ampoules of bliss, and left the world behind for a time. People wanted to believe. People wanted to be exalted.

And perhaps I too had been looking for a messenger, looking for a path to take. I don't know. But there was the cut of a prophet about Jackie Nixon that morning. The light altered about her as she spoke, she drew it to her, and her eyes stole from it. I knew that what she was saying was right, that she was leading the way, and for the second time in my life I put my faith in her.

'I see you all looking around, counting how many of us there are,' she said, 'wondering if there are enough, wondering if it's even possible and how far we could see it through. I can't give you any comfort. I can't make any promises. And I can't tell you we'll see it through to the end. What I can tell you is this. History has always turned on the actions of a few individuals. History is on our side. You can do this.'

She was armed with examples from which we could take heart. If we thought a campaign was hopeless we should think again, she said. Afghan guerrillas had not only defeated the strongest military force on the planet, they had contributed to the USSR's disintegration. The British had lost more people to the IRA than they had during the Suez campaign, the Falkland conflict and the first Gulf war combined. Coalition forces were still suffering heavy losses in South America and China. They could not quash the rebels; their forces were too cumbersome, too conventional. And in the second wave of extremist attacks, ten men with detonation devices and a moderate amount of explosive had paralysed London's infrastructure for over a month. They had blown up two Southern dams, and two stadiums. They had never been caught.

She was qualified. The others knew it as well as I did. All personal histories eventually revealed themselves at Carhullan, even hers. We knew she had been in the Elites. She had been trained and counter-trained. If there was one thing she understood it was operational strategy and the logic of local land war. She knew the potential of irregular armies, non-state actors, because she had been charged with their elimination. She had spent the first part of her adult life at war. She bore the scars. After ten years she had retired, but like others of her ilk, she had only ever been dormant, never extinct. Sitting among the many books on her shelves by Lawrence, Osgood, Fuller, and Douhet, we had all seen the thick volume, bearing her own name, worked on during her Cambridge years. This was her speciality, her pedigree.

'I can't make any of you join me, and I won't try to,' she went on. 'I'll respect your position if you choose not to. I'll arrange for you to be placed back in the towns. Don't worry; you'll be safe. You are free, Sisters. You've been free for a long time. You've succeeded where others have failed. We've succeeded here. We've created true liberty. This place may be the last that's left of it. And we've always stood our ground when challenged. But I want you to think about what we stand for now.' She paused and licked her lips. 'Freedom comes with responsibility; it comes with privilege and a conscience. It comes with difficult choices. We cannot stand by and allow the Authority to do what it is doing any more. We cannot wait for them to come and take apart what we've made. I will not allow it. You know me. I will not allow it.'

A few heads nodded in agreement. The atmosphere was turning. She knew she had hold of them. She had always had them in her grip. They had come with her this far, and they would go further. She could have driven home her rhetoric, but she did not. The ire drained out of her. She smiled kindly at the women in the room, in their old worn clothing, with their braided and cut-away hair. 'It's been a good life here,' she said. 'I love this place. God, you know I love it. It's always been home to my family. My mother had this phrase. You've heard me say it in the spring whenever it's too warm. These are borrowed days. And they'll have to be paid back later in the year. I think that's what we've had up here.'

She talked about the end of Carhullan and her voice was husked and raw, not because she had been speaking through the night, but because it pained her. Her eyes were so blue I had to look away. The farm would continue to run as it had before, for the rest of following year. Then it would be wound down. The animals would be slaughtered, the ponies turned loose. She and Veronique had wanted it to serve as an example of environmental possibility, of true domestic renewal, but the world had changed too much, and the role of Carhullan had changed with it. One day in the future, the land would be used again, she was sure of that. One day, the fields would be sown and cropped. People would learn to use the earth well. But for now, it had to be given up for another cause.

She looked about the room once more, then turned to face the fire, leaving the women to draw breath, and giving them the only chance they would have to move towards her and slip a blade into her spine.

FILE SIX

COMPLETE RECOVERY

The men arrived later that day, accompanied by Megan and Corky. By then two inches of snow had fallen. There was a slight hesitation when they reached the courtyard, as if they were still unsure of the permission now granted them to cross the threshold. No man had been inside the farm since it had passed into Jackie Nixon's hands. They must have realised that this entry was a breach of some kind, that something was wrong.

They had rucksacks on their backs, and as many possessions as they could carry. The patrol dispatched to get them had obviously indicated that they would need to clear out of their settlement. They did not seem happy. Nor were the Sisters. Within the space of forty-eight hours it was yet another shock for them to endure. Those who had not yet gone out to work crowded round the windows and seethed about the violation of Carhullan's first rule. Then they gathered at the fireplace and took down the yellow banner.

From the kitchen, Chloe caught sight of her husband and ran to the farmhouse door, and I watched her take hold of Martyn. The two embraced hard and awkwardly, as if they had been separated for years. Then he held her chin and examined her bruised face. The mothers of the boys ran out too, and took hold of their sons. They had finally been granted their wish. But the circumstances were bleak.

Jackie followed them out into the courtyard. She extended her hand to each of the men in turn. She spoke too quietly for those of us inside to hear, but she must have presented them with a briefer version of what we had listened to, because after a time the men became animated, and their voices were raised. Martyn had his arm tightly round Chloe's shoulders. I watched his mouth working hard over the words he said. I stepped towards the door and from there I could hear his indignation. 'We're not going to be your hostages, Jackie. This is off the deep end. Who the fuck do you think you are to do this now?' His wife was looking at the ground. To the side, the rest of the men stood in an uncomfortable group, waiting to see where this challenge would lead, their breath puffing white in the air. Only Calum appeared to be at ease, gazing around the buildings and up at the carved date-stone above Carhullan's doorway, his long thin frame buckled slightly under the weight of his bag.

As Martyn continued, I could see Jackie's temper beginning to fray. Her hands curled inward, forming loose fists. She was almost a foot shorter than the men in the yard but she was visibly fitter; she was squarely on her own turf, she knew it, and had been queen for too long to put up with any visiting unrest. There was a shoulder holster with a leather pouch slung across her torso – I had seen her wear it before on occasions, its outline showing under her clothes – and in it I could see the square edge of a pistol grip. Suddenly I felt nervous. I knew now that she had used it before.

Then I heard Veronique's name spoken, and Jackie snapped. She made a sharp gesture with her hand, a slicing motion that cut Martyn off. I had never heard her shout, not in all the weeks at Carhullan, not even during a training session, when the heavy breathing of those on drill was brought to us on the back of the wind across the fell. The women lingering in the kitchen caught her dire volley of curses. They looked up and moved to the window again in time to see her step towards Martyn. His arm fell from Chloe's shoulders as if he might be about to defend himself. She did not strike him but her ultimatum was clearly and coldly articulated. 'I don't have time for your shit. You'll not be here in this place and come back at me. You're a kept man. Remember that, Martyn. If you want to go, get out now. But all arrangements are finished, and that's my fucking prerogative. You're living on my land. If you leave, you're on your own. Both of you.'

Chloe looked up then. Her face was twisted. She glanced at her husband and back to Jackie. Then she walked into the farmhouse, knocked past me and slammed the front door. It boomed against its frame, reverberating around the house. I heard her go into the parlour. There was a heavy thumping sound. I moved back to the window. Martyn was staring after her. He began saying something to Jackie, but she walked away before he could finish.

The men were shown into one of the outbuildings by the patrol. Then they were given breakfast at the long table inside Carhullan. As if foxes had come upon a group of moorhens on a lake, the kitchen emptied rapidly around them. When I passed Calum he was smiling inwardly, his hollow sunken eyes turned only to the food in front of him.

The basic chores continued that morning, and in the afternoon the sleeping quarters were rearranged. More of Jackie's unit were moved into the main house; there were now three women to a room, and the others were divided equally among the dormitories, like sentinels. Pallet beds were fashioned in the stables for the men. There was no heating system in there and no piped water, but they were given extra blankets and told they could wash in the bothy next door. Lorry checked them over individually, found them fit, more or less, though they were emaciated and lacking nutrients. The older man had kidney trouble, and Sonnelle set about making him some fennel tea. The boys had fared better since being excluded from Carhullan. Their mothers had seen to it that they were looked after, often taking them supplies from their own rations.

A sense of urgency came over the farm. People finished their tasks quickly and then returned to the main house, as if there might be some new word given there, a declaration of what to do next, an instruction from Jackie. But she was no longer around. No one saw her for the rest of that day. I wanted to speak to her about joining the unit, but there was no sign of her, and when I asked Megan, she just shrugged.

Shruti barely spoke to me as we cut down the trees and

brought in the wood for the stoves. I knew she was upset, and that she thought me naive, too enamoured by Jackie. I tried a couple of times to begin a conversation, but her answers were short and evasive. Too much of the day had been wasted already, she said, and she didn't want to be messing about with timber in the half-dark. I had become used to the timely and direct way that the women at the farm resolved their problems, so they would not impact and fester. But Shruti was more hurt than I had anticipated.

I knew there was no hope of her joining the unit. Though the girls teased her about her past, she had left violence far behind her and there would be no return to it, not even in the name of Sisterhood, or under the flag of anti-oppression. Instead the axe in her hand gouged down into the willow bark, again and again, without cutting a single straight line. Her breathing was ragged. Not knowing what else to do, I walked over to her and held her in my arms until the tension dissolved, the axe fell from her grip onto the crisp white ground, and I heard her crying softly.

That night Jackie returned to the farm and enlisted ten new volunteers for her unit. I was among them. More would follow in the next month, when any hope that she might not be serious about dismantling the farm and going out into the occupied towns was given up. I was surprised to see Lillian standing at the back of the group. I smiled at her and she shrugged. Jackie informed us that we would begin training the next day, and not to worry about the usual work patterns. Our Sisters would cover for us. She needed us for three straight weeks, she said, and then half a day every day until the campaign became active. There was an appalling formality to the language she used, leaving little room for us to speculate about her professionalism, and whether she would actually follow through. But she looked less tense, as if the return to her old occupation relaxed her.

There would be tests for stamina, endurance, physical and

mental strength, map reading, and navigation. 'We'll start
with the basics,' she said. 'Don't worry about the rest yet.
You'll be split into smaller groups for the first few hikes.
Then I'm going to expect you to train alone. You've seen how
things run in the unit. When you're up to speed you'll be
organised into patrols, like the others. When I'm not around
you're to follow the orders of those on the council. You
know who they are.' She did not thank us for stepping up or
commend our example. And she did not single me out again.
But there was a sense of pride in the way she looked us over,
and that was enough.

For those three weeks we were pushed to our limits. We
were woken each day in the black inhospitable dawn by mem-
bers of the unit shouting at us to get up. We dressed, sleep
drugged and assaulted by torchlight, took an early breakfast,
and gathered in the courtyard. By then the weather was sav-
age. The rain seemed too cold not to freeze but it remained sol-
uble, fat and icy, soaking us to the skin almost every day as we
walked. Jackie had instructed us to wear light-order dress, and
any dry shirt or woollen jumper we were caught trying to put
on over the layer of cold sweat would be taken from us. It
robbed too much vital salt from the body, we were told.
Movement would keep us warm.

The wind sheared off the fells around Carhullan. Above us,
the sky was charcoal-coloured and disturbed, the clouds
swirling in vortexes, ripping along their edges. Each new route
saw us travelling further across the hills, from five miles, to
ten, to fifteen, and the loads in the bergens that we carried got
heavier as more equipment was loaded into them. Always the
ridge would come first in the ascent, as if to stoke fire into our
thigh muscles, and we would descend it at the end of the hike,
shaking with exhaustion, often sliding on our backsides when
our legs buckled.

Though I knew it was going to be hard, I was not prepared
for the extremity of it all. I had become fitter from working
outside with Shruti, Chloe, and the others. But I was still slow,

173

weaker than those who had lived for years in the harsh environment, and mostly I was towards the rear of the group. It was only sheer determination, the desire not to fail, that kept me on my feet. The times I sat down I felt so dizzy that I thought I might pass out, and I imagined I would be found days later by the unit, lying on the Northern tundra, stiffer than rock, my eyes plucked out by the crows. As on the day I had left Rith, I did not look back when we started out. It was better not to see the warm lamps of Carhullan, better not to think of the women on the farm, moving like insects below us in the fields. And Shruti, asleep in her bunk, asleep against her damp pillow, her body pulsing gently as she dreamt.

We were given rations to take with us: dried meat, salt, and water. There was little time to rest and eat, and wherever possible we were supposed to jog the courses. I pushed myself on, and only when I thought my heart would swell too much as it powered the blood through its chambers, that it would rupture against the bone, did I fall back into a walk. There was little talk between the recruits. Space opened between us as we moved, and only when someone sank to their knees and retched, or began to stagger, did a colleague assist. Those in the unit stood over us when we fell or sought temporary shelter in a stony lee. 'Pick it up, Sister. Up on your feet. Show us who you are.' Some days, people turned back. I came home late but I never let myself succumb.

My whole life I had loved the upland terrain, deriving simple pleasure from it as a child – the views, the changing colours of the slopes, the brackish rivers – and though for years I had seen it at only a distance, I had often thought of the landscape as I stood beside the conveyor at the factory; it was a place of beauty and escape. Now I stumbled across its gills and over its marshland, bending to meet the wind when it roared against me, and dragging myself up the scars by handfuls of heather and thorn bushes, by any firm hold. And still, I could not say it wasn't beautiful. Despite its austerity, its vast and cowing expanse, and the agony of its traverse, it seemed more beautiful than ever. When we reached the walls of the farm and Jackie ordered us to turn round and climb the ridge one more time, and with sickening resolution we began back the way we had come, I did not fall to the earth and scream into the coarse brindle of the moor. If the mountains tested my limits, they also gave me satisfaction, they were the measure by which I gauged my resilience.

At night I would examine my feet, check that the bubbling mass of blisters was not infected, and each morning I would place the swabs of gauze we had been given between my toes. There were raw galls on my shoulders and lower back from the rubbing of the bergen straps. By the end of the three weeks I was carrying half my own weight, and I had begun to realise what a matchless device the human body was.

On the morning of the final march we gathered in the courtyard and waited for instruction as usual. I was barely awake and exhausted from the previous marches. Jackie came out, dressed in a military coat, and greeted us. 'Long drag today,' she said. 'It's an ordeal and it's meant to be, so make sure you pace yourselves. I don't want to have to bury any of you. Or feed you to the dogs.' There was nervous laughter. She jerked her head to the side. 'Now, don't thank me, ladies, but I've a special bonus for you. Come this way.'

We followed her to one of the stone bothies. I had not been into it before. It was always padlocked and bolted. She took a key from the pocket of her fatigues and turned it in the lock; the hasp sprang back slickly and she pulled open the latches. She turned on the light. Before us there were stacks of stencilled metal boxes. Jackie stepped forward, hefted one down, and opened it. Inside, as I had known there would be, were the rifles. She handed one to each woman, and with it an ammunition pouch filled with heavy brass fobs. When it came to my turn, she opened another case, lifted out my father's gun and smiled. I looked at the bad side of her face, the inert cleft running from her mouth to her ear. Then I took the rifle from her. It had been scoured of rust and repaired, and I knew it was still accurate enough to snipe deer.

There were no straps attached to any of the weapons. We were to carry them at all times, Jackie told us. Anyone seen putting their gun down en route would run the course again tomorrow. And again the day after if they dropped it. 'And be warned, I'll be coming along shortly to keep you company,' she said. 'Like the red light of morning.'

I set out, my bag full, the rifle in one hand, and the weighted pouch in the other. As the sun was rising Jackie cantered past on one of the fell ponies. 'Who's sticky now, Sister?' she called down to me, and laughed.

We had been given twenty-four hours to cover forty miles. We would make six circuits of the High Street range and we would walk through the night in darkness, tracking our way along the escarpment. It was the same distance as my journey from Rith to Carhullan. I had been told by the patrol then that it was impossible for me to have walked it all, and they had been right. This time I would prove them wrong.

There was no mutiny at Carhullan. If Jackie had anticipated there might be, and had moved her original unit into the house to protect herself, she need not have worried. There was no one to challenge her. And, under whatever law there was now, the place was hers. No one else could have held it together as she did. I was surprised so many of the women decided to go along with her plan. Deep down I had thought myself unusual, perhaps maligned with some kind of unnatural antagonism or need for leadership, for wanting to act in a way I had been programmed to think was wrong. But eighteen in all came forward. The older women in the colony were largely exempt. Jackie needed Ruth and Lorry and an experienced core of others in their original capacities. The farm had to keep ticking over, even if it was to be less a farm than a support system for the soldiers within.

A small group refused to train. Jackie respected their wishes as she had said she would, and she promised that when the time came she would escort them to one of the Pennine towns and see to it that they were set up, given a section number, and camouflaged from the Authority. Shruti was among them. We still spoke and often sat beside one another on the bench for meals, but we no longer met up alone, no longer sought each other out as we once had. Since the night of Jackie's announcement we had not slept together, and though I was still attracted to her I knew it was for the best. I did not tell her what I was doing with the unit, and she did not ask. Our company seemed defined by a gentle sadness now, as if we had never really had the opportunity to fall out of love, and everything begun had been curtailed instead of aborted.

I might have walked away completely, avoided her around the farm, to make it all easier, for myself at least, attempting to convert the relationship into a mistake in my head. But she made a point of maintaining a bond. She offered to wash my clothes with hers, left flowers on the crate next to my bunk. There was more grace in her than I could have managed, and without hers I would have found none. It brought a gentle ache to my chest to have her hug me at the end of a dinner shift and then walk away to her bed, or rest a hand on my shoulder and ask if I was faring OK when she saw my cuts and bruises, my newly shaved head.

We could have made passes at each other and it would have ended with our limbs tangled again, our bodies spilling outwards, wet and arching. And if she had come to me with that in mind I would not have stopped it or pushed her away, though I knew Jackie would disapprove. Shruti held back, as I did. Instead, she offered me a quiet, spiritual friendship.

I returned from training one morning to find a small velvet bag on the bed. My fingers were staved with the cold and filthy, two of the nails were black, and I struggled to draw back the slender cord pinching the bag closed. I tipped its contents into my palm. It was an Edwardian necklace with green, white, and violet stones. I knew it had been Veronique's, and it had come into Shruti's possession after her death, when all her belongings had been shared out. In the bag, on a tiny scrap of paper, she had written a note. *The day will come. Be strong.* I did not know what to say when I saw her that evening, and so I said nothing, just smiled at her across the kitchen, and then went into the parlour room where Corky, Megan, and the others were drinking.

I tried not to think about the times we had been together. But I know I felt more for her after we had separated than in the weeks of our fervour and discovery. She was a revelation to me. And if it had not been for the teachings of Jackie Nixon, hers would have been the most profound lessons of my time at the farm.

Carhullan was not perfect. If it had once been close to it, running to a high level of courtesy and enlightenment, a society that celebrated female strength and tolerance, the balance had now tipped back. There were arguments between those in the unit and those still running the farm, who thought they now carried an unfair burden of work, that they were at the bottom of the hierarchy. Some in the other group continued to try to talk Jackie down from her position during the evening meetings, and she began to tire of it.

Chloe remained outspoken on the subject. 'How do we know if what you say is true, Jackie?' she would ask. 'Where's the proof of it, other than your word? I've seen no Authority monitors here yet. Has anyone else? You're just hell-bent on this conflict. And you're dragging everyone else along with you.' Then she would turn on the room. 'Why don't you all wake up and see what she's doing! Do you really think she can sneak little Stella back into town without anyone noticing?' There was a zealousness to her when she talked, a desperation. Often she would work herself into a frenzy and storm out of the room, go looking for her husband in the stables. Jackie would close the door softly behind her.

The gatherings were finally suspended. I knew we were as guilty of failure and disunity as any other human society. I knew we were as defective.

The men did not belong. Though they had taken over some of the roles left open by those gone over to Jackie, they still ate their food separately and kept to themselves. They served their purpose, but their proximity seemed to engender discomfort in those who had never imagined they would have to share Carhullan with them. Dominic, Ian and the boys had offered to train with us, but Jackie turned them down, saying the dynamic of the group would be thrown out of whack. She did not want men in her army.

I began going to Calum. After joining the unit I went to him a few times, nights when I felt too tense to sleep in my bunk, or if I had drunk enough home brew not to care. I went after an exercise with the equipment, when the strange elation of accuracy, of lethality, lit me, made me want someone, and I went after the sickeners, to get rid of the images and echoes of what I'd seen and done in training; the forelegs of the dog we had killed splayed limp at its sides, the click of the knife slitting its windpipe and its ligaments.

He was obliging. He had chosen his own role and he fulfilled it whenever necessary. I knew he was essentially in Jackie's pay, that he was given tobacco by her, and a secure place within the community, on the understanding that he would let any of her women fuck him if they wanted to. That he would continue to offer them excitement and relief, as he had always done. I knew he was the father of at least two of the children at Carhullan, Stella included. But there were no pregnancies now. He controlled himself, and kept himself clean. Jackie wanted no disease to infect her women, rendering them unfit.

Calum's body was smooth and slim. His ribs jutted through his flesh and his hair reached past his shoulders. We did not kiss. He held my hips as I moved over him; he did what I told him. His grey eyes remained focused. He was an accomplished lover, compliant, and he knew what movements and words might kindle arousal in those seeking it. The pleasure from him was physical and limited. Those first few times on his pallet bed, I had closed my eyes and thought of Shruti. I saw her kneeling in front of me, circling her tongue until my nerve endings began to clench and spasm, or I thought of her eyes glazed over, her pupils dilated and staring into mine when she climaxed. And then, when I knew it was better not to keep her as a memento in such a way, when I knew I had to let her go, I blocked out those pictures of her dark body. I saw nothing but fragments.

The women new to the unit grew fitter. The marches continued. We were posted outside in holes overnight, told to keep still for days on end in bunkers dug below the heather banks. The women suffered hypothermia, sleep deprivation, strained tendons, boredom. We took on board whatever was instructed. The first rule of orienteering was to memorise all relevant coordinates. The second was never to fold the maps any other way but along their creases. Give nothing about the operation away, Jackie said. We were taught infantry skills, combat survival, basic medical knowledge. The hikes became longer, up over ice stacks on the summits, the bluffs along the ridge, and into the surrounding valleys.

In Ullswater there were groups of Unofficials living around the lake, and in the big empty houses. They looked ragged and poorly equipped. Breathing slowly, we tracked them through the iron sights of the rifles. We loaded the magazines in silence. Most of the guns were old; they had been used for army training before Jackie got hold of them, and there were only a handful of modern rifles with SUSATs that could be mounted for surveillance. This did not matter, she told us. We still had the upper hand – surprise. But we would need to prepare ourselves for strategic assassination.

In the locked storage room she had a twelve set of automatic pistols, three Barrett rifles, light mortars, grenades, and enough explosive to take out those constructions upon which the Authority depended and the people were held to. The butcher's bill would be kept to a minimum. No civilian would be intentionally hurt. In time she would teach us the handling of everything she had stowed away, all the armaments she had acquired, through whatever underground network, whatever solicitous means. She was careful not to waste live rounds, frugal with the reserves of diesel for the Land Rover and the decommissioned Bedford. To get close to Rith we used the ponies, and kept under the cover of darkness once the domestic grid went out, moving like raiders around the periphery.

I enjoyed riding the ponies. They were compliant and hardy creatures, and they tackled the rough ground, the steep gradients and swollen waterways, with stamina and surefootedness. I had never been nervous around horses. I had always been able to approach them in the fields around Rith, and I found that I was a comfortable rider. I fitted and felt right with the animals. It was apparent that Jackie had a genuine passion for the ponies. Once or twice she rode out along the range with me. When we got back to the farm she complimented my skill. 'You're good at this, Sister. They recognise confidence and loyalty: I trust those my ponies trust.' She told me that, years ago, her family had been breeders. 'The mountains made them naturally small,' she said to me, patting the dark glistening flanks of the mare she was unsaddling. 'The Romans broke them first, up at the Wall. They crossbred them. They were used as pack animals back then. But we made them fast. It was us who raced them. And now, they're going into battle.'

By the end of spring we had been taught which plants and roots were edible, which could keep us alive longer up on the fells, and which were purgative. The upland snows had thawed and the rivers were high and fast, full of meltwater and dirt. The unit was given a new test of fitness.

On the banks of Swinnel Beck, Jackie stripped out of her clothes and stood naked in front of us. Megan, Corky and the others who were familiar with the drill followed suit. I saw Jackie's body for the first time. It had been heavily employed over the years, put through exertions since she was seventeen years old, and it showed. She was full-breasted, and her nipples were damson red, but the rest of her seemed to be made of wire and tightly stretched bands. Spurs of bone pressed up against the skin at her joints. There were deep dimples in her shoulders, craters within the sinew, and across her back were a series of dark purple circles.

She picked up her rifle and an ammunition pouch, lifted them above her head, and strode into the brown racing water until it took her off her feet. Then she swam across, her head ducking under the current a few times, gasping as she surfaced. The thin dark hair lengthened around her shoulders and covered her face. She climbed out of the river, thirty feet downstream but safe on the opposite bank, and the sound that left her mouth was feral. One by one we went into the river after her. I felt the cold burn of the water as I stepped into the torrent, felt it pulling me along as I struggled into the depths.

On the crossing Benna went under and did not resurface. Her hand broke through the brackish wash once and then was lost from sight. Six of us ran a mile down over the bields, naked and barefoot, to a narrow culvert under a pack bridge. We found her lodged between two boulders, bloated with water, her face caved in where it had struck against the rocks. The river surged past her white body. At Jackie's command we carried her cousin's corpse back up the mountain and propped it against a dry-stone wall. She made us sit in a semi-circle, and we faced the body for an hour. 'This is what it looks like,' she said. 'This is what it looks like to be nothing. Don't fucking forget it.' I saw nothing in her expression that indicated the woman had been her relation. It was terrifying, and admirable.

Jackie handed Megan her service pistol and gave her instruction. The butt of the gun looked bulky in Megan's small hands, but she manoeuvred it lightly. The girl hesitated for a moment. Then I saw a reptilian dullness creep into her eyes. She cocked the hammer, aimed and fired. The muzzle jumped back and her arm absorbed the recoil as it had a hundred times. A watery slip of blood emerged from the hole in Benna's forehead. There was absolute silence in the group. Only the rushing of the beck could be heard as it sounded out rocks and hollows on its course. We buried her in the cemetery plot by the Five Pins. There was no ceremony.

For a few weeks training was suspended and an atmosphere of unity returned to the farm. The heat and humidity of the summer arrived, but it seemed less claustrophobic at this altitude, broken up by the wind. The grass grew tall on the moorland around us, and it was the exact colour of the fawns that grazed in its swathes. There were deer everywhere. Jackie told me that it was a temporary spike; their numbers would probably dwindle again in a few years, when disease and starvation knocked the population back. It seemed hard to believe. Everything was in abundance. Moss and lichen thrived, and the place was almost exotic with foliage. Buzzards circled the warrens, and hawks fell in long stoops towards their prey on the slopes. Without the human cultivation of the previous decades, I could see that true wildlife had returned to the Northern mountains. We were living in the wilderness.

Only the fields around the farm looked neat and tended, shorn one by one of their arables. The women worked hard to bring in the crops, as they had every year, as if this harvest was no different from the previous ones, though it was the last. We laboured together. The meadow grass was scythed and taken in carts to the barns. I was shown how to sharpen the leys, and how to tie haycocks. Across the fields, next to Shruti, I saw Helen, dressed in a long blue cassock with the baby in a sling across her back. She was bending over the rough, like everyone else. They called it booning, and no one in the community failed to pitch in during the high season. Even Chloe helped, though she stayed close to Martyn and the other men.

All day, and into the night, there was a strange rasping call from the moors. I had heard nothing like it before. Finally I abandoned the others in search of the noise. I crept round the buildings and out onto the moorland, trying to identify the creature that might be making it. In one of the outer pens Jackie had begun clipping the sheep. She was sitting on a stool and had a ewe braced between her legs.

Tufts of yellow and black fleece were caught on her vest. She looked up when she saw me stepping cautiously over the ground, cocking my head from side to side. She was smiling in her private, satisfied way. 'They're corncrakes,' she said. 'They've moved down from Scotland. I doubt you'll find one though.' She let go of the sheep. It scrambled to its feet and shook itself, bleating thinly. Jackie stood up and brushed herself off. 'You know what else I'd like to see back here? Wolves. We're still missing a big predator in the chain. But then I'd have the carcasses of these beauties all over my land. It's all give and take, isn't it? Don't worry. We'll be starting up again next week, Sister. Then you'll have something bigger than a bird to hunt.'

A year after I had arrived at Carhullan, I lay in the wet autumn bracken, camouflaged and motionless, so close to the stags that I could smell the skunk of their piss as they marked their rutting grounds, the musk in their ragged stolls. I heard the clack and ricochet of their antlers as they lowered their heads and charged towards one another. Lying in the bracken foss, I felt stings in my groin and my elbows as ticks buried their heads. I rolled onto my back, pinched off mounds of skin to cut off the blood supply until they emerged, gorged and sluggish.

I lost the ability to fear and panic. Instead I felt practical and causal. I had never known time to pass so acutely before. I sat out through the night with the patrol, watching the bitter glow of stars overhead, listening as the season exhaled and the layers of vegetation shrugged and compressed, like the ashes of burnt wood. On the hills I was aware of every corporeal moment, every cycle of light. I felt every fibre of myself conveying energy, and I understood that it was finite, that the chances I had in life would not come again.

As my resilience grew, so too did my understanding of what we would face. Jackie had said that occupation of the town was possible. If it failed, we could evade capture long enough to damage the vital organs, and perhaps even hold out for a while in the hills. But eventually, when the Authority's resources were consolidated, they would track us down and we would be caught. Then the payoff of our real training would begin. She pulled no punches about what she knew of the holding centres in the old industrial towns. She brought out a photograph and passed it round. It showed a firing squad. There was a wall in front of them with dark stains on, and at its base a slack, indistinct body. 'There is no Hague here,' she said. 'There are no human rights laws in this country. You won't get a trial. You won't even be charged. They will try and break you. They will find out whatever they can, any way they can. And they will be merciless, I assure you. If you end up here, in this place, you will be held as long as they think you are useful. Then you will be shot.' She nodded and her eyes moved across us.

If detained, there were only three things that we were permitted to say. Our names. Which militia we belonged to. And that we did not recognise the legality of the government. Nothing else could be given in response to interrogation or to incentives. Not yes, not no. 'All I ask is that you hold out as long as possible,' she told us. 'There will be a time to tell them about us. But not yet.'

Jackie had said she would not put me back in the dog box unless I agreed to it, and a year after the captivity, I did. She came for me in the night, with three others, and I was dragged from my bed across the floor of the dormitory and over the courtyard. I made an attempt to escape, twisting up and throwing a few punches with a free hand. It was a reflex action and it did little good. The women paused. I took a hard kick in the belly that knocked the wind out of me. I was turned onto my stomach and my hands were bound behind my back. A bag was put over my head and tied at the neck. Someone pressed a thumb into the plastic, tearing a hole for my mouth.

Within minutes I found myself back inside the iron enclosure, scratching at the knots of rope securing my wrists, trying to move oxygen smoothly into my chest, trying to calm myself. The ground was pliant and warm under my bare feet. A smell of fresh shit rose from the floor, as if it had been spread there for my arrival.

The first time it happened I had lasted four days. I took hold of myself and focused on what I had been told to do. I found the canister of water left at my feet, lifted it up between my soles and took the top off with my teeth. Its base was lathered with shit and I gagged as I brought it closer. I could not tip it on my knees to take a drink, so I manoeuvred it back down onto the ripe floor and worked to free my hands. The knots remained tight. In the small space around the stool I managed to slip my body through the loop of my arms, so my hands were now in front of me and I could remove the bag and reach down for the canister. I shook it. It was almost empty.

Despair rose up in me, sick as bile, but I swallowed it back down. I concentrated, repeating the instructions I had been given. Talk to yourself. Sleep, even shallowly. Sing. Find patterns on the walls: flowers, birds, faces.

For three days it worked. I saw letters drawn in the darkness in front of me. The words floated like red flares on the black. Then the water ran out and dehydration started to make me unstable. The same terrible images came walking back towards me, like prodigal ghosts, as if they had been waiting in the darkness of the corrugated coffin for me to reanimate them.

The second time they came for me I made it to seven days in the dog box. I drank urine caught in the container when the water ran out. I ate the food thrown in on the filthy floor. I did not call out. It was nearing winter, and the air in the metal enclosure was freezing.

On the seventh day I was dragged back across the courtyard to one of the small stone pens. The women from the unit interrogating me were dressed in dark clothing, masked. I thought I recognised Corky but I was weak and disoriented and could not be sure of anything. There were no apologies given. I was stripped, hit in the kidneys, and burned. One of them pushed a pipe a little way into me and told me I was a whore. They left me locked inside the pen, curled up and moaning on the floor, and another four women entered. Jackie was with them.

She smiled down at me, a gentle, sympathetic smile, and I saw in her blue eyes that the love she had for me was that of a mother. In her hand was a plate of cooked breakfast: bacon, eggs and bread. The yolks bloomed. She crouched down, set the meal on the floor at her feet and sniffed loudly. 'That smells so good,' she said. Then she took a rasher of bacon and waved it in front of my face. I lurched for it but the others pulled me back. She put the crisp sliver back on the plate and licked the grease from her fingers. 'Mmm.' Her voice was soft and compassionate. 'What's my name, Sister?' I looked up at her, pleading with her to stop. 'If you tell me my name you can eat this. If you tell me the names of all of us here, you are free to go, right now.'

It was no better and no worse than the treatment I gave the others, when the roles were reversed. It was no better and no worse than the treatment soldiers had always undergone in preparation for deployment. And Jackie saw to it that we were no different from them.

She did not make monsters of us. She simply gave us the power to remake ourselves into those inviolable creatures the God of Equality had intended us to be. We knew she was deconstructing the old disabled versions of our sex, and that her ruthlessness was adopted because those constructs were built to endure. She broke down the walls that had kept us contained. There was a fresh red field on the other side, and in its rich soil were growing all the flowers of war that history had never let us gather. It was beautiful to walk in. As beautiful as the fells that autumn.

FILE SEVEN

PARTIAL CORRUPTION

It was not clear whose idea the gorse cuttings had been. One evening, at the back of that second winter in Carhullan, Jackie gathered us all together and told us it was time to begin. Some kind of preliminary, neutral marker was necessary before things kicked off, she said, as a way to make a link with the civilian population. But it was not her that issued the instruction to shear sections of whin from the moorland reefs surrounding the farm. It was decided quietly among some of the Sisters that this should be the signal, and a group went out the next day and brought back the first batch.

That evening, after work on the farm was complete, the women who were not part of the unit busied themselves at the kitchen table tying the stems with rags of material torn from the tunics. All over the fell, every month of the year, the plant flowered with vivid buds, and there were plenty of blooms for the clippings. They kept on for two weeks, until the yellow fabric was used up.

On the first night I went into the kitchen and watched them work. The tunics lay in a pile near the iron range. I had laid mine down with them. When more material was needed someone cut a lip in the cloth and tore a long thin bolster out of the weave. They all wore gloves but their hands were continually being scratched as the spines cut through, and every so often I would hear somebody suck in their breath. I'd see them remove a glove and squeeze at the flesh beneath. Then blood would come scrambling out of the puncture.

I could not have said why exactly, but I liked watching the women work. The routine of their hands, the craft of what they were doing, was hypnotic, and the kitchen was filled with the heady scent of the blossom. I had always liked the plant; its sweet fragrance that intensified tropically in the heat of summer, the gouts of colour on the fellside. Its petals seemed inconceivably soft and bright against the dark static spines. I felt a calm anticipation too, as their hands moved, winding the bandages around the stalks. I knew that this industry heralded our actions; everything we had planned was about to start, and everything seemed right.

When the brobbs had been securely fastened they were placed in loose hessian sacks and stored in the stables. In the morning those of us who had volunteered to ride down into Rith strapped them onto our saddles and slung them over the hot flanks of the ponies. We set out as the sun was rising. Across the higher ground the ponies left hoofprints in the thick crust of frost, and I watched the ice dapple and melt away as we dropped down into the valley. We forded the streams and picked our way through the old settlements, past the abandoned cars, and over troughs cut out by flash floods. We encountered no one else along the way, and as we tracked through the old county it felt as if we were travelling in a hinterland, a place of lesser and greater being. There was thunder, but the rain held off. By dusk we were at the periphery of the safety zone.

We were careful not to be seen. We crossed the swollen brown water of the Eden after the electrical grid had powered down and darkness was spreading over the town. The flooding was worse around the bridge. We were miles from the estuary but sand had somehow found its way back upstream and it lay in swathes along the waterline. Lumber and tree trunks were stacked up against the buttresses, and those trees which had not been felled lay waterlogged and dying, with detritus snagged in their branches

I and the others dismounted, and we hid the ponies in the ruined river cottages, took off the sacks, and rested them on our own shoulders. Then we made our way on foot along the broken road, retracing the route I had used to get away. At the edge of town we divided into patrols and went about our business.

The settlement was the same as it had been when I left. Everything looked familiar, run-down and debilitated, still caught up in the failed mechanism of the recovery plan. Nothing seemed to have improved. The cyst-like meters hummed on the facades of buildings. Fetid rubbish was piled in open plots – electronics, prams, moulded plastics – and hundreds of vehicles lined the concrete aprons of the old supermarket. I saw a litter of feral puppies curled underneath a bus. They looked up with hungry solicitous eyes as we walked by, and growled. The lower-lying streets were under water and on the doors of the houses a red X had been dashed. We passed by the turbine factory. The gates were locked, and a heavy chain sat between their bars. There was a notice secured to the post. *Closed until further notice.*

It was disquieting to be back there, at night, under the browned sky, creeping as silently as I had done when I escaped. The echo of blood pumping hard was loud inside my head. I felt as if something in me might burst. I wanted to hammer on the doors and drag the residents from their beds, I wanted to shake them out of their stupor and have them follow us to the castle in an angry mob, tear those within it limb from limb. But I did not. I moved like a spirit, divorced from the dimension I found myself in, unable to manifest, unable to reach out and touch the solid world.

The others kept watch while I ghosted through the streets, leaving the wrappings at the doors of the occupied terrace quarters, in letterboxes, the cracks between bricks, and tied to the railings of the clinic; wherever people lived, wherever they suffered.

It was hard to know how well they would be received by the inhabitants of the combined residences; what, if anything, they would discern from a spray of ribboned foliage left at the foot of their homes. It was a strange rustic token that made little sense in the dark cobbled streets of the town, but its texture was like a warning, and its yellow bloom was somehow hopeful. There was no way to convey our true intent, no printed matter that we could distribute among the people. The gorse gave nothing away. It was simply a coded gift, a curious blossoming of colour in the wet unlit corridors.

I did not think of him often now, but when we passed through the street in which I had once been sectioned, I imagined Andrew sleeping upstairs in that room of huddled boxes, salvaged possessions, and consolidated existence. I did not know whether he would be alone or with someone else. I had been gone for a year and a half and it was doubtful that anything of mine would be left in the quarter. He was not a sentimental man. Most likely I had been reported and struck off, my remaining things examined by monitors and anything deemed useful removed. No one had come looking for me. For all I knew, I had disappeared utterly; perhaps I was even thought to be dead. Whatever my fate, Andrew no longer had a wife.

I pictured him picking up the corsage on the way to the refinery that morning, feeling the sharpness of it in his palm, and wondering about it, wondering what it meant. He would no doubt toss it back down on the step, leaving it for the other family to bring inside, or he would throw it onto one of the refuse piles at the end of the street. But he would hear that identical bundles had been found throughout the quarters. And he would realise, as many others would, that no gorse grew within the periphery of Rith, not even on the slopes of the Beacon Hill. It was a plant that flourished only in the uplands now, that had been brought in from the old Lakeland district. It was a message from without.

For two weeks we made night runs into town. We were not caught. We did not remain there long enough to witness the cuttings' discovery, or reveal ourselves in the process of delivering them. Instead we went quickly to where the fell ponies were tethered and rode back along the mountain tracks to Carhullan. We never went to the same street twice. And we never gave any other indication of what was coming. As I worked, I knew that Jackie was not far away, making her count, timing the movements of the Authority.

The castle loomed above the town on the small hill opposite the Beacon, and within its barracks was the Authority's headquarters, and the records of all those living within the official zones. Since the flooding of the Solway City it had become the central command post of the region. In the smaller Pennine towns there was a moderate Authority presence, enough monitors to maintain order, to oversee work details and the distribution of rations, but here lay the region's main chamber of power. To strike it would be to sunder the chassis that held everything together. Jackie's plan was not to hit and run, or to create havoc. She was planning a coup. We were going to hold Rith for as long as possible. Once word got out, once more ammunition had been taken, vehicles and supplies, then the other settlements would fall, she said. There would be mass uprising, a groundswell. The tide would turn against those who had abused their power for the last ten years. We would be the first place to declare independence, but others would follow. It was not about defending Carhullan any more; she was now fighting for the whole of the Northern territory.

As I walked through my hometown, remapping it in the darkness, my blood would slow and I would think about her vision and her courage. I would think of her standing in silhouette by the kitchen fireplace. We were on the cusp of a great moment in history, she had said, turning from the flames to face us. 'We've become used to change always happening elsewhere, haven't we? We've become used to waiting, hoping to be saved, hoping those in charge will reform and reform us. It's the sickness of our breed. And it has become our national weakness. Sisters, no one is going to help us. There is only us. So why not here? Why not now?' She had held a fist at her side, and white spittle had gathered on her lip. 'Remember this as you go down there,' she had urged us. 'Revolutions always begin in mountain regions. It's the fate of such places. Look around you. Look where you are. These are the disputed lands. They have never been settled. And those of us who live in them have never surrendered to anyone's control. Nor will we ever.'

At night the heavy doors of the castle's entrance were closed, opening only to let blue cruisers crawl in and out. Near the fortified walls, on the other side of the road, was Rith's railway station. Once a week freight arrived, brought up from the ports to the South; shipments of food and medical supplies. The clinic lay half a mile away, in the shell of Rith's elegant old hospital. And at the head of the town were the vast grey cylinders of the Uncon oil refinery. Everything was surveyed and marked out. Nothing would be left to chance.

On the last night of reconnaissance I stood in the streets and the rain hissed down around me. Litter blew along the gutters, empty containers, foils, and the little broken ampoules with silvery deposits inside. Faith cards lay rotting on the side of the road and rats scuttered along the filthy viaducts. I saw a thin dog slinking past the end of the terrace with a ragged grey scrap in its mouth. From inside a building I could hear the cries of a woman, and they went on and on, as if she could not stop, as if she were complicit in her own despair.

I had no love for the place. There was no residue of affection for the town in which I had been raised, and where I had seen out the country's swift demise. I did not feel bad for its fate. I was not sorry for what would be my part in it. Everything had fallen too far. The people were oppressed, just as they had been hundreds of years before; they were the slaves of Megan's imagining. The government had long ago failed them, and it would go on failing them. It was a place of desperation and despotism. Like the rest of the country, Rith was already a scene of ruin; nothing worse could have befallen it than its current state.

Once I had barely believed what I was living through. Now I believed deeply that the wrongs committed were tantamount, that the lives of the people within were worth saving and taking, that we had a duty to liberate society, to recreate it.

*

I was not among those who escorted the non-combatants off the farm. The original unit was issued that task. Over the course of two weeks that March small groups climbed into the back of the Land Rover and were taken down the fell, then on over to the Pennine towns. Jackie's network was slim, but she seemed to trust those she had contact with inside the zones. Though they would not fight, the women had agreed to spread word of what she was doing, and attempt to raise local support for any action that might occur there later, after the operation in Rith.

The separation was more painful than I had thought it would be. Though the unit had become hardened in its conviction, and a line had been drawn through the community, there were friendships over a decade old being severed as the other women left. Watching them embrace and draw apart I wondered briefly if what we were doing was the right course after all; whether it would have been better for us all to remain in Carhullan and pray that we would be left alone, just as some of them had wanted. It felt as if we were sending them towards absolute danger, towards the terrible internment camps of the last century, though I knew it was us who would face the worst of it.

Helen held Stella in her arms. She cried and struggled and tried to get down. Her mother attempted to comfort her, telling her they were only going for a ride, but the rumble of the Land Rover's engine had scared her, and she twisted about, looking at the vehicle with fear, then hiding her face away from it. One by one the women came forward and kissed the wet bloom of her cheek, and she knew something was wrong, and the pitch of her wailing increased. She was the youngest of them, the last daughter of Carhullan, and she was being given up for adoption, given over to a world which would not love her as she had been loved here. The women knew it, and some of them turned away, unable to stand witness to the casting out of an infant. Helen cradled her head tenderly as she climbed into the back seat. The door was shut, and the child's cries were muffled.

On the second evacuation I said goodbye to Shruti. She stood holding a small bag, looking in my direction, then she came to me, held me to her, and whispered in my ear. She spoke in her first language and I did not understand the words. I felt her warm hands on my scalp, supporting the flesh and bone above my neck, and it felt as if she were holding the full weight of me. I felt heavier than I ever had, full of lead and brass chattel, like the pouches we had carried on the long drag. I wanted to say something to her, but could not. I put my arms round her waist and carefully slipped the necklace back into her pocket. I could not keep it. We had not been intimate for long but she leant up and brushed my mouth softly with her own. I knew I would not see her again. Whatever the success of our campaign, it would not be of sufficient degree to give me the chance to be with her, even if we had desired it.

She climbed into the Land Rover with the others and Jackie took the driver's seat, started it up, and pulled away. I watched the vehicle tracking over the steep ground, its tyres biting in to the earth as it hauled across the bields. And then she was gone.

At the side of the remaining group, Chloe had her arms crossed tightly over her chest. She was crying. Her forehead was buckled and her cheeks sucked in and out. I knew she was upset about more than the departure of some of the colony. She had never been convinced by Jackie's interpretation of the events to come, nor her strategy, thinking her involved in a deception or conspiracy of some kind. She had never approved of the transformation of Carhullan, or the strong-arm tactics being employed. She felt bullied, and at Jackie's mercy. The panic showed in her. She was emaciated, her yellow hair was greying, and her once-brown skin looked pale. Even her eyes had been leached of their original hazel. Now they had the trapped, sallow glitter of citrines.

Since the gorse cutting she had been skittish and furtive, whispering with her husband whenever they were together and looking as if she might break down. Every day she walked out on the fell to look for monitors, and every day she came back and told whichever of us she came across first that there was no sigh of invaders. I was sorry for what had become of her. She was full of fear and paranoia. It made me uncomfortable to see her shouting at Jackie and being pulled back by Martyn, or pleading with the women to listen to her, making a fool of herself. Mostly people avoided her.

She saw me looking her way. I quickly dropped my eyes so as not to set her off, and tried to walk past, but it was enough of a connection for her to try again. She lunged and caught hold of my wrist as I passed by. 'Please, Sister, please listen to me,' she whispered. 'She's using you.' Her breath smelled sour, as if she had not eaten anything that day. Her hand was shaking but her grip was tight. 'You've been groomed by her,' she said, 'ever since you got here. Can't you see it? She's lying about everything. What you're doing isn't right. You're going to get killed. All of you. And she doesn't care. She's so bloody-minded. Please!'

She looked wildly about her at the women in the courtyard and raised her voice. 'Why won't any of you believe me?' I heard somebody close by snort and then murmur under her breath, 'Maybe because you're such a damn hysteric, you stupid bitch.'

I unfastened Chloe's grip and took her hand away. I couldn't bear to have her close to me when she behaved like this, and I could feel anger rising in me, the urge to lash out. I pushed her back and walked across the courtyard towards the house. 'You're a fool, Sister,' she shrieked after me. 'She's got into your head! She's pulling your strings. And you don't even know it, do you?'

That night Chloe and Martyn disappeared. Nobody heard them leaving, but in the morning they did not come into the farmhouse for breakfast. When Jackie found out they were missing she checked the storage sheds for a break-in, then gathered the unit in the courtyard. 'I would really appreciate seeing Sister Chloe and Brother Martyn back here,' she said, 'and if that means cutting their fucking feet off and carrying them back, then do it. If they've gone, they've gone. It doesn't change anything for us. We've worked too hard to have this jeopardised.' Her tone was even, controlled, but I could see her jaw was tense, and her face was bloodless. Her eyes were unblinking, stark and lashless as a jackdaw's.

She took a rifle from the store, saddled one of the fell ponies and took off in the direction of the croft settlement. The pony cantered away in the low cloud. About a hundred feet out on the moor she spurred it into a gallop and disappeared.

Lillian leant over to me. 'My God,' she said. 'Chloe must have snapped. She's well and truly asking for it now. What the hell was she thinking? And what are we supposed to do? Break her legs and haul her back here?' I shrugged. 'Yes, we are. If they're planning a tip-off, or if they get picked up and they let something slip, it'll be us paying the price. We can't afford to let her go.' Lillian arched her eyebrows. 'You're sounding a lot like Jacks these days,' she said, but she was nodding in agreement.

I set out with her, Nnenna, and the fourth in our patrol, Corinne, who had worked at the hives before joining Jackie. We had been together for the last eleven months, stationed on point at night, running mock fire raids and demolitions, or sniping at another patrol from the cover of the long blond grass. We could anticipate each other's timing and I was used to the musk of sweat buried in their clothing, seeing them undressed, showering, or defecating near the foxholes we had dug. I felt as unselfconscious around them as I ever had. I knew them intimately, elementally, almost as well as I knew myself. And I understood that my life would depend on them when we attacked Rith.

We walked towards the tarn, ran a circuit of its glinting granite edges, and then followed the dry-stone walls as they descended into the valley, keeping a distance from each other, communicating with hand gestures. Scouting with them had become second nature and I was used to this procedure, but it had not been vested with immediate purpose or consequence until that day. It felt different. It felt essential and important. The adrenalin made me tense and sharp, and I was glad to have something other than Shruti's absence to think about. I knew that after months of training, we were finally being mobilised and activated. It was sudden and it was a difficult prospect, not how we had expected to commence with the plan, but we were all keener and quicker over the rough ground because of it.

There was no sign of the couple anywhere. They had several hours' head start and were perhaps as far as the reservoir if they had been heading to Blackrigg in search of someone to contact, or were following the overgrown tarmac roads further into the district. We continued down into Vaughsteele. The village was almost submerged by bushes, creepers and rhododendron. Wild dog roses were out already, vying for space in the earth. After the barren expanses of the fells, the landscape of heathers and bracken, the valley's green interior looked overdressed. The birds flitting between the forked twigs were red-beaked and unrecognisable. I checked each abandoned cottage, forcing the doors and windows if they were locked, and moving rapidly through the damp musty rooms. In each of the houses I put my hand into the grate of the fireplace to feel for heat, smuts still alive from a fire the previous night. They were all cold.

Part of me could not blame them for trying to get away. Jackie had offered us few choices within her scheme, and Chloe did not have the stomach for conflict. Nor did she want to leave the fells. It was obvious that Martyn would have been happy to remain in the mountains, eking out an existence; catching fish, growing turnips and cutting firewood, living like a pauper, and remaining independent and Unofficial until that status too was revoked. I was not without sympathy. But in my gut I knew what they had done was small-minded, and inexcusable. I knew they had failed to see the importance of Jackie's operation.

We circled the village a final time and made our way back

to Carhullan via the long southern route. We found the two of them sitting behind a small hummock, leaning close together. One of Chloe's boots had been taken off. Martyn had his arm around her. She was weeping softly. He looked up as we approached. 'She's twisted her ankle,' he said. 'She can't walk any further.' His eyes were glassy and disconnected. I could see that any determination he had had was spent. Corinne and Nnenna left to find Jackie while I waited with Lillian. Martyn crooned to Chloe, soothing her, and after a few minutes she became quiet and seemed to be asleep on his shoulder. Nobody spoke. On the banks of the grassland all around us were small orange flowers. I stared down at Chloe's white foot, thrust out in front of her, until it looked like something other. Until it was abhorrent, and did not seem human.

An hour later I heard the dull thump of hooves. Jackie rode up behind us. The pony was lathered with sweat and looked exhausted. She wheeled it round on the spot and then dismounted. 'Go back to the farm,' she said to us. 'I need to speak to them alone. Go on now.' Chloe was crying again, and cowered against her husband. Lillian hung back but I walked off, and after a few moments she followed me.

As we were neared the ridge, I heard two gunshots. The sound echoed at a distance, the rip of its tail left long around the hills, but it was unmistakable. Lillian had stopped dead, and was rooted to the spot. Her hands were linked at the back of her head, her elbows almost touching in front of her face, and I could not make out the cast of her features. I walked on again. By the time we returned to the compound she was composed, but for the rest of that day there was a short lag between what was said to her and her responses. When Jackie got back the unit reconvened in the courtyard. She said nothing more about the episode, nor did anyone else. It was apparent that the matter was closed.

Before we were loaded into the back of the wagon, before we left Carhullan for the final time, I went to the spot where we had found Chloe and Martyn. I saw a mound of newly turned earth. It was a large grave, almost too big for two bodies. I knew I was complicit in their deaths. I knew it, and I did not feel any guilt. I did not feel remorse. I knew that it had needed doing. But in the nightmares I have had since then, the pit has been filled with the bodies of all those who left the farm, all those I have loved. My father, and Andrew. Shruti.

There was no other collateral damage at Carhullan. A small contingency stayed on to cater for those involved in the operation, Ruthie and Lorry among them. There was a dwindling store of food. The turkeys that had once roosted at night in the orchard trees, purring to each other and folding their beaks into their plumes, were now gone. There had been no breeding season for the livestock, and much of it had been slaughtered. Only the hefted sheep had been allowed to produce young, and they had been left up on the tops. We'd seen them as we hiked, ragged and virile on the summits, peering haughtily at us from the edge of the bluffs.

We still ate well, but there was a sense of rationing, of counting out the stocks and calculating how long they would sustain us. Every meal felt as if it might be our last, but every mouthful of mutton and venison tasted better, the early greenhouse currants were tart and exquisite on our tongues. The visits to the men occurred more often and were more thrilling. The bouts of wrestling were more spirited, and the fights continued on after the end of a round had been signalled. I could see it in everyone's eyes: the polished glitter, the ephedrine of anticipation.

And I felt it too. I could look at the gashes on my hands and see a grotesque attraction in them. I could put the tip of my tongue into the open red slit and taste the salt of myself there. When Calum and I fucked, it was without restraint, it was base and raw, and I left marks on him. We were living at the edge, and everything was amplified; it was beautiful, and it was rancid.

On my birthday, as I undressed beside the copper tub, I looked in the mirror and saw the change in my body, the metamorphosis that had occurred. My head was bald, newly shaved again, and a shadow of follicles ran the reverse globe of it. My skin had darkened almost to beech. I was leaner, had lost weight and gained muscle – there were lattices along my arms and back, docks around my shoulders and above my knees. Along my collarbone was a tattooed blue line. I had sat sweating in front of the dormitory stove while Megan scored my skin and rubbed the ink in.

It was the anatomy of a fanatic. It was the same body the rest of the unit had fashioned for themselves. They had seemed wild to me when I'd first seen them, Corky, Megan and the others, like creatures, both natural and rarefied, but now I was no different from them. If we had stood together on the shoreline two thousand years before, facing the invading ships with fire in our hands and screaming for them to come, they would have called us Furies, and they would have been afraid.

I liked what I saw in the clouded mirror and I was shocked by it. She was a stranger to me, this woman opposite, and yet I saw the truth of her. She moved when I moved, bent to turn off the taps as I did. Her face resembled the one I had sloughed off when I came to Carhullan, but it was newer, stronger. She was my anima.

Lorry knocked on the door while I lay soaking. She came in to the room, sat on the edge of the bath and looked down at me, smiling, her brow pinched in. I could see that she was in pain. She was sixty-three, and looked much older than she had. In the year and a half that I had known her she'd become more arthritic and less mobile. She crooked herself forward when she walked, favouring her bad hip. She continued to care for us as she always had. But we were stronger than we had been, fitter, hardy of constitution; we knew how to repair ourselves in the field, and in this respite she had allowed time to catch up.

'This is yours,' she said, and held out a small metal pin on her palm. I lifted my hand from the warm water and took the coil from her. 'You had it? I wasn't sure who did. I thought it was long gone.' She nodded. 'I borrowed it. I needed something to remind me of why I came here too, Sister, while all this was going on. I hope you don't mind. I thought it was about time I gave it back. But you haven't forgotten anything, have you?' I shook my head. The memory of its implanting was still vivid, as was my escape from Rith. I could remember the first days in the house, being given the oatmeal with butter, and the apple, the wonder of it as I bit down into its flesh. I remembered ghosting to the bathroom, the soiled sheets in my arms, and the strained concentrating face of Lorry as she took the regulator out. Holding it between my fingers, it was hard to believe that I had ever had it inside me.

Lorry was still smiling. 'Yeah, you're ready.'

I felt thankful. She'd been the first to accept me and I knew I would never forget it. I placed my hand on hers and asked her what she would do when we were gone. There had been no talk of taking her over to the Pennine settlements with Ruth. 'Oh, I've got my orders too,' she said. 'Don't you worry about me, Sister.' She patted my arm, stood stiffly, and left the bathroom.

It passed through my mind that she might have directions to fire the place, so that nothing was left of the original enterprise. And I could picture her doing it, coating the floors with paraffin and trailing it up the stairs. As if from above, I could see the orange glut of flame in the middle of the courtyard as the main house burned, and hear the crack and splinter of timber as the byres went up. And afterwards, only the smoking hull of Carhullan would be left, its masonry rimed with soot, its slate roof collapsed. And the fell wind; mournful, tugging at the granite fibres, unable to move a single blackened stone.

Megan and I carried her inside, away from the line of fire. Her midriff was soaked red, and though she had taken hold of the pale fletches of her own ribcage, she could not hold her flesh sufficiently closed. We could hear the summoning of bullets on the crenellations, the high-pitched tacking of them against the old sandstone guard. The Marines had laid charges at the walls, the soil leaping up behind the vallum as they were detonated, and though the fortified structure had held, the gate below the portcullis had been blown off its hinges. The women defending it were being cut apart, just as Jackie had been.

We took shelter for a few moments behind a barricade in the keep, and, looking around the cordon, I saw smoke blowing across the entrance, obscuring the bodies on either side of the gateway, and those firing through the breach. Above us hovered a military Lynx. The blades of its propeller bent the air around us. I had heard it coming above the noise of gunfire and shouting, and watched it rise up above the ramparts like a great prehistoric bird, horned and reptilian. It was so close I could make out the pilot's face. I had not seen anything put into the sky for almost ten years. But they had done it for her. In the end, they had been forced to.

I nodded to Megan and she knelt up above the barrier and let off a round. I dragged Jackie towards the barracks. Her hand unfastened from the bone and came away from her stomach. It was gloved in red. I folded the remnants of her jacket off the pulped flesh and examined the wound. It was massive and stippled with black fragments. I glanced up at Megan. She was crouched down behind the barricade again, reloading. Her expression was blank. She was fifteen years old.

Jackie looked up at me and gestured for me to lean down so that I could hear. Her dark hair leapt about her face in the shearing gusts. I could see the light going out of her eyes. The flame in them was guttering and their blue pigment was becoming dull and solid. She was cold, and pale. As she lay in the castle grounds, swallowing down her blood and fighting still, she gave me one final instruction. 'Lie down,' she said. 'Hands behind your head. And take off your vest. Lie down and wait. It's enough now. It's enough. Someone has to live through this, and tell them about us. Tell them everything about us, Sister. Make them understand what we did and who we were. Make them see.'

This is my statement. Let it serve as a confession if one is still required. I was a willing participant in the siege on Rith, and the occupation of Authority headquarters. I led the patrol that bombed the clinic and I gave armed support to attacks on three other targets, including the refinery and the railway station. I do not know how many men I have killed.

We regretted the civilian casualties and civilian deaths that occurred in the first few weeks of the conflict, when residents of the quarters attacked the remaining Authority cruisers and were shot. We were unable to provide adequate support. Their bravery will not be forgotten, and others will follow them. This is just the beginning.

We took the town and held it for fifty-three days before the air corps and a regiment of ground forces were called back from overseas and deployed. We executed those monitors that were captured, and three doctors from the hospital, and we destroyed all official records for the Northern territories. There are no remaining carbon prints, or medical files, and the census had been wiped. You will not find out who I am. I have no status. No one does.

My name is Sister. I am second in council to the Carhullan Army. I do not recognise the jurisdiction of this government.

I'd like to thank Cantrell Jones for help with military research, and Philip Robinson for his environmental predictions. Thanks to Jane Kotapish, Valecia McDowell and Joanna Härmä for their conversations over the years.

Thanks also to Jacob Polley for reading several drafts of this novel, and for coming up the fell in bad weather. Thanks to Clare Conville for all her support, and to Lee Brackstone and Trevor Horwood for their editorial advice.

The Carhullan Army is a work of fiction. Character, events and place names are either products of the author's imagination, or, if real, not portrayed with geographical and historical accuracy.

Also by Sarah Hall

ff

Haweswater

Winner of the Commonwealth Writers' First Book Award

It is 1936 in a remote village in the old, northern country of Westmorland. When a man from Manchester, Jack Liggett, arrives – spokesman for a vast industrial project to create a new reservoir to supply the growing city with water – the small community must come to terms with what this means for them. As the weeks pass and the works take shape, Jack begins a troubled and intense affair with one of the villagers, Janet Lightburn. Yet Janet, a woman of keen purpose and strength of mind, is intent on restoring the valley to its former state . . .

'A writer of show-stopping genius; everyone should buy this novel.' Helen Falconer, *Guardian*

'Immensely sensual. A remarkable debut.' *The Times*

'A strikingly original first novel, full not just of fury but also of the most sensitive compassion for the people and the place, and an understanding of both which is rare.' Margaret Forster

ff

The Electric Michelangelo

Shortlisted for the Man Booker Prize

On the windswept front of Morecambe Bay, Cy Parks works as an apprentice to alcoholic tattoo-artist Eliot Riley. Thirsty for new experiences, he departs for America and finds himself in the riotous world of the Coney Island boardwalk, where he sets up his own business as 'The Electric Michelangelo'. In this carnival environment of rollercoasters and freak shows, Cy falls in love with Grace, a mysterious circus performer who commissions him to tattoo her body. Hugely atmospheric, exotic and yet familiar, *The Electric Michelangelo* is a love story and an exquisitely rendered portrait of seaside resorts on opposite sides of the Atlantic.

'Hall is a writer to indulge, and her sensuous, poetic prose is every bit as evocative as sand poured from a pocket at the end of a holiday.' *Daily Mail*

'Wildly imagined and richly written . . . [it] has to be savoured.' *Independent*

'[Hall's] gorgeously embellished prose compels the narrative, along with the beguiling vignettes she conjures up . . . the effect is intoxicating.' *Financial Times*

ff

How to Paint a Dead Man

Longlisted for the Man Booker Prize

Italy in the 1960s: a dying painter considers the sacrifices and losses that have made him an enigma, both to strangers and to those closest to him. He begins his last painting, using the same objects he has painted obsessively for his entire career – a small group of bottles. Not long afterwards, a blind girl tends his grave, trying to understand the world she can no longer see. Years later in Cumbria, a landscape artist finds himself trapped in the extreme terrain that has made him famous. And in present-day London, his daughter, struggling with the sudden loss of her twin brother, finds herself drawn into a world of darkness and sexual abandon. Covering half a century, Sarah Hall's fourth novel is a fierce and brilliant study of art and its place in our lives.

'An intelligent page-turner which, perversely, you also want to read slowly to savour Hall's luscious way of looking at the world.' *Sunday Telegraph*

'A lyrical style so beautifully worked and savoursome that you can taste it.' *Daily Mail*

'Her writing is visceral and engaging, and the emotional lives of her characters are skilfully realised in this bright weave of disparate voices.' *The Times*

ff

The Beautiful Indifference

From the heathered fells and lowlands of Cumbria, to the speed and heat of a London summer, to an eerily still lake in the Finnish wilderness, Sarah Hall evokes landscapes with extraordinary precision and grace. Her characters, whether a frustrated housewife seeking an exhilarating encounter or a young woman contemplating the death of her lover, experience dark devices and desires – the human body providing a sensuous frame for each unfolding drama.

'Astonishing . . . A writer of rare vision and talent.' *Sunday Times*

'Fierce and sensuous.' *Guardian* Books of the Year

'Hall's voice is strong and distinctive – even, in single, elevated passages, exquisite.' Lionel Shriver, *Financial Times*

ff

The Wolf Border

For almost a decade Rachel Caine has turned her back on home and worked in Idaho at a reservation for wolves. As one of the few experts in her field she is summoned back to England by the eccentric Earl of Annerdale to help with his plan for re-wilding wolves on his estate in the Lake District. As Rachel attempts a gradual reconciliation with her estranged family, her work with the Earl begins to generate public outrage and the threat of sabotage. Set against a backdrop of Scottish independence and tumultuous power struggles both locally and nationally, *The Wolf Border* is a novel steeped in wilderness and wildness, both animal and human.

'One of the fiction highlights of this year.' *Observer*

'Stylish, intelligent and a cracking read . . . Wonderful.' *Sunday Times*

'A thrilling tale of politics and power . . . Compulsively absorbing and masterfully plotted, it confirms Hall as one of our finest fiction writers.' *Daily Mail*